GOODBYE
IS
FOREVER

GOODBYE IS FOREVER

A JACKSON GAMBLE NOVEL

GREGORY STOUT

First published by Level Best Books 2025

Author Photo Credit: Carol Stout

First edition

ISBN: 979-8-89820-065-7

Cover art by Level Best Designs

This book was professionally typeset on Reedsy.
Find out more at reedsy.com

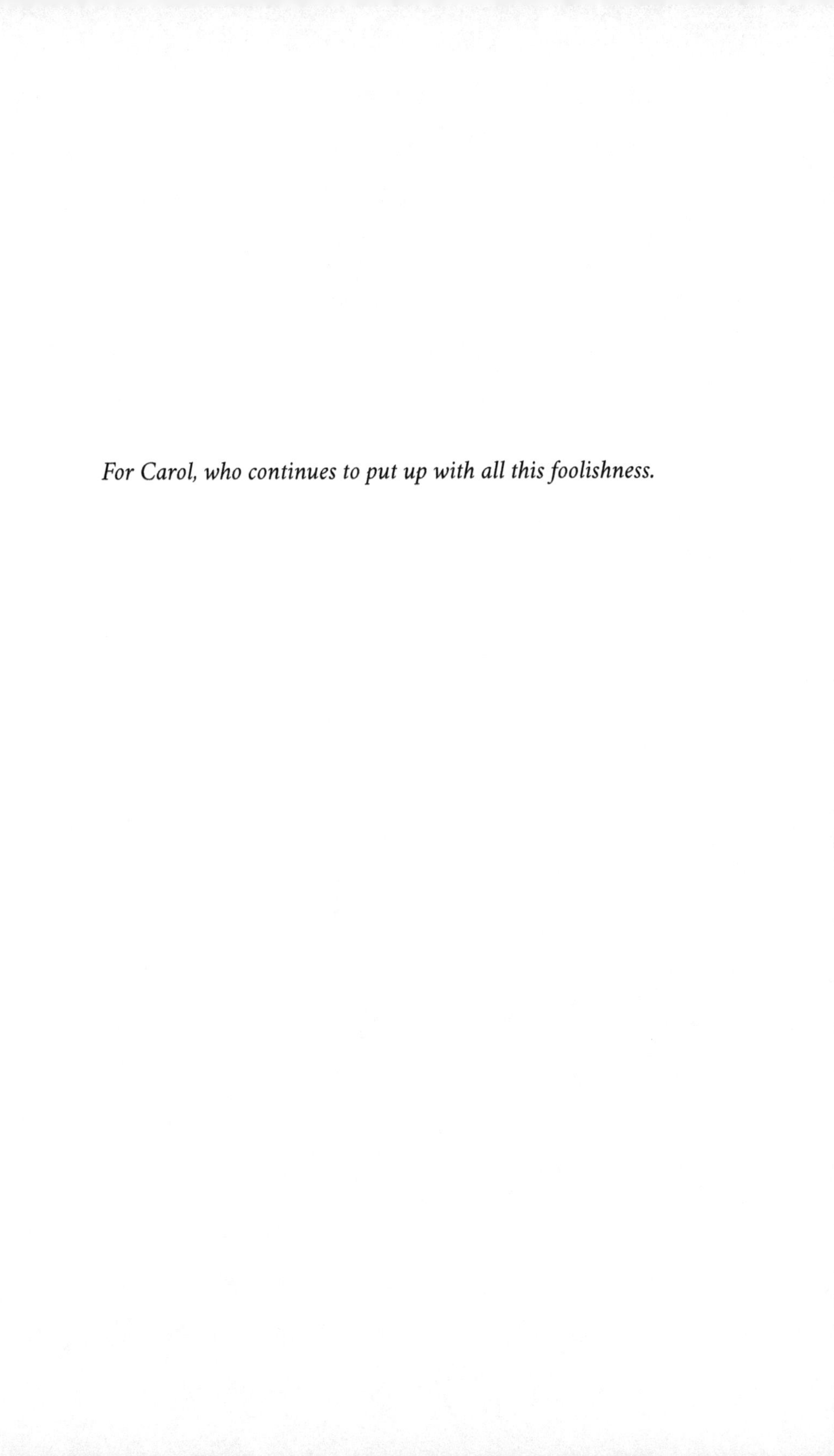

For Carol, who continues to put up with all this foolishness.

Praise for Goodbye is Forever

"Greg Stout's latest Jackson Gamble story, *Goodbye is Forever*, is an old-style page-turner, infused with the color of the Nashville music scene and characters engaging in rich, often humorous, banter. Best of all, Stout offers up multiple subplots that keep Gamble one step behind, until he's not. A great read with a satisfying ending that fans of Stout expect."—William Ade, writing as Nic Knuckles, *Big Scream in a Small Town* and *Big Scream in a Wee Village*

"Greg Stout's latest Jackson Gamble mystery, *Goodbye is Forever,* grabs you from the first page and takes you on a ride through the backstreets and music world of Nashville. When Gamble is asked to find the daughter of a dying man, his only clue is a ten-year-old poster for the Nashville band she was in. He locates one of the band members, only to arrive after the man has been murdered. The stakes are high, and the time is short to find the woman before her father dies. The book is a number one page-turner. And Gamble is the one to watch. Five stars!"—Linda Norlander, award-winning author of the Sheriff Red Mysteries, the Cabin by the Lake Mysteries, and the Liza and Mrs. Wilkens Mysteries

Chapter One

Whiteville, Tennessee, is located in Hardeman County, down near the Mississippi state line. The town itself sits about 60 miles east of Memphis and 175 miles southwest of Nashville. In the old days, back when people did things differently, the Louisville & Nashville Railroad ran a passenger train between Nashville and Memphis that stopped in Whiteville in the small hours of the morning. That train, however, came off more than sixty years ago. Nowadays, the quickest way to get to Whiteville from Nashville is to take Interstate 40 toward Jackson, get off at Exit 87, follow Route 18 down to Route 100, and then turn right. A four-hour trip end-to-end, about the same time as it used to take on the train, and you don't have to get there at four in the morning.

The town of Whiteville, whose motto, reasonably enough, is "The Gateway to Hardeman County," is home to around forty-six hundred souls, an astonishing ninety-plus percent of whom are male. That is because the two largest employers in the area are a pair of privately-operated, medium-security penitentiaries, the Hardeman County Correctional Facility and the Whiteville Correctional Facility. Together, the two prisons, which are located a short distance apart on Union Springs Road, house some thirty-four hundred male inmates. Perhaps for that reason, according to the website maintained by the city, Whiteville is the fifth-safest municipality in the entire state.

Today, the first Monday in June, I was in Whiteville to visit a convicted triple murderer at the Hardeman County Facility. The inmate's name was Harvey Harris. Harvey was serving a life sentence for holding up a convenience store ten years earlier in the Goodlettsville area of Nashville, killing a customer and the store clerk, a pregnant woman, in the process.

Unfortunately for Harvey, at the exact same time he was high-tailing it out of the parking lot, pedal-to-the-metal and balls-to-the-wall, another customer was pulling in for a fill-up, a Mountain Dew and a couple of Slim Jim beef sticks. Sensing something was amiss, since one of Harvey's shots had gone wildly off target and shattered the front window facing the pump islands out front, the customer hunkered down in the front seat of his car and waited until Harvey was well down the road before he went inside. He took one look at the carnage and then called the cops, who tracked Harvey down inside of forty-five minutes. Along with the two-hundred dollars and change he had grabbed from the cash register, Harvey had in his possession a .22 caliber autoloader, a stolen twelve-pack of PBR, a carton of smokes, and a handful of scratchers for the next day's Pick-Three drawing. Turned out, none of them was a winner.

Ordinarily, conviction of a crime like the one Harvey committed carries a death sentence. And indeed, he had been waiting on death row at Riverbend Max in Nashville for most of the time since his conviction, waiting for his appeals to peter out when a routine visit to the prison infirmary revealed that he was suffering from end-stage pancreatic cancer and had only a short time to live. At that point, the state decided that slogging its way through any more appeals and protests from anti-death penalty advocates and other assorted do-gooders wasn't worth the trouble. And so, the governor was persuaded to commute Harvey's sentence to life without parole, and he was transferred to Hardeman County to live out the rest of his few remaining days in relatively less secure surroundings. Shortly after he arrived, he asked his lawyer to get in touch with me.

As I soon found out, visiting an inmate in Tennessee is a fairly complicated process. First, I had to complete a visitation form accompanied by a recent photo, then mail it in and wait 30 days for approval. After that, Harvey was permitted to contact me to request a meeting. When he telephoned me, he was a little bit vague about what he wanted to discuss, and I almost decided I had better things to do that waste my time driving down to Whiteville to visit someone I assumed would be a hard case. But it was a warm, late spring day, and my calendar was clear. And anyway, his lawyer assured me that his firm, which was acting on Harvey's behalf, would pay me for the day, plus expenses, to make the trip.

From the highway, Hardeman County Correctional is nothing special to look at. There are no high stone walls and no parapets to make it look like a medieval castle. Instead, what you will see is a single-story structure that includes a reception and administrative building, and a series of inmate housing units, called "pods," all surrounded by high chain link fences.

I identified myself to a corrections officer who checked my name on a clipboard to verify that I had an appointment, then patted me down for weapons. After that, I had to sign a form affirming that I had read and understood the penalties for bringing anything on a very long list of prohibited contraband, including telephones, drugs, and weapons, into the prison. Then, satisfied that my business was on the up-and-up, he escorted me to a secure room with a table and two chairs. Harvey Harris was already seated at the table, waiting.

From across the room, Harvey looked more or less like any other sixty-odd-year-old man you might encounter anywhere. But when I got a closer look, I could see that his skin color was more bluish-gray than pink, and it was hanging loosely on his arms and under his chin, making the jailhouse tats on his forearms and neck sag misshapenly, so that they looked like caricatures of Salvador Dali paintings. His eyes were yellowish, as if he were also suffering from jaundice. His orange prison uniform fit him the way a worn-out topcoat fits a scarecrow, suggesting that he had lost a great deal of weight since the time it had been issued to him. I have had zero medical training other than basic CPR when I was with the cops, but even at that, I would have said Harvey Harris had no more than a couple of months before his clock ran out.

When he saw me, he tried to stand up, to shake hands, I supposed. But the effort was too much, and he sat back down heavily.

"Mister Gamble. Thank you for coming. I 'preciate it. I know it's a pain in the ass making the appointment."

"It wasn't a problem for me," I said. "Your attorney handled most of it. He emailed me a couple of forms, I printed them out, signed them, and emailed them back, and that was it, except for driving down here."

He nodded slowly, as if even that small movement took a considerable effort. "I suppose you're wantin' to know how come I asked to see you."

"In a minute. First, I'd like to know where you got my name."

"From a guy I met one time when I was at county back in Nashville. It was quite a few years ago. I don't remember his name no more. Tommy something, I think. He said you used to be a cop."

"I was," I said. "I was a uni for a few years before I made detective. Then I got loaned out to the district attorney's office as an investigator."

"And then what? You didn't like the job?"

"I didn't like the guy I was working for. Or rather, he didn't like me, so we agreed it was time for me to move on. I've been private for better than twelve years, now."

He nodded, as if what I had told him squared with what he already knew. "This guy I talked to, this Tommy. He said you were on the level. He said I could trust you. That you'd be straight with me."

I was pretty sure the Tommy he was talking about was a guy named Tommy Mack, a penny-ante thief and bottom-shelf grifter who had been in and out of stir for the better part of his adult life, and who had acquired a reputation as a repeated bail skip. The last time he legged it, about a year ago, he got away clean, but not before gunning down and nearly killing an organized crime boss named Red Cherry. There was bad blood between Red and Tommy, the result of a burglary Tommy had staged at Red's home. Red eventually recovered from his multiple gunshot wounds, and Tommy, who up to that point had never in his life been more than a hundred miles from the place he was born, disappeared into the wind. Smart, since his next encounter with Red would have certainly proved fatal.

"Okay," I said to Harvey. "Trust me to do what?"

"I need you to find somebody."

I waited. When he didn't say anything more, I said, "Anybody in particular, or are you under the impression I run some kind of a dating service?"

"It's my daughter. I haven't seen her in more than, let's see, it must be close to ten years. Which is to say, the whole time I've been inside."

"Then what you're saying, she didn't come to visit you at all during all the years you were whiling away the hours on death row at Riverbend Max?"

"No, she didn't. She came to the arraignment, but then, when they read the charges, she got up and walked out. That was the last time I seen her." He hesitated just for a moment. "I expect you know my situation. I haven't got much more time, and there are things I'd like to tell her before…you know."

"You mean before you die."

"Well, I expect that's one way to put it."

"Is there another way? Look, Mr. Harris, I drove down here today because your attorney paid me in advance to do it, and because I didn't have anything else on my calendar. So, forgive me for being blunt. But the fact is, you killed two people—three, if you count the baby that store clerk was carrying—for damn near nothing. I'm having trouble trying to think of a single reason why I should help you do anything."

"I'm dying, Mr. Gamble. Hell, you didn't need me to tell you that. You can see just by looking at me. I've done a lot of bad things in my life, and I know there ain't anything I can say to you or anybody else to make up for that. I for certain killed them people. I pleaded guilty, and that's that. I'm not asking you to get me a new trial, or hunt up some new evidence, or help me file another appeal. I just want to see my little girl one last time before, well, before it's all over. And I have to believe you'll help me, because I think you're a better man than I am."

When I didn't say anything, he said, "Is that a good enough reason for you?"

Chapter Two

"Okay, Harvey, let's assume I'm willing to look into this for you. What can you tell me about your daughter?"

"What do you need to know?"

"Oh, I don't know. Maybe her name would be a good place to start."

"Her name is Annamaria," and here he paused to spell it out for me. "Mostly, though, her friends just called her Annie."

"Annamaria, got it. You said it's been ten years since you last saw her. How old would that make her today?"

"Well, I'm sixty-three, so she'd be, let's see, thirty-five or six. It gets so I'm having a hard time remembering things. It's this cancer, you know."

I didn't, but I nodded anyway. "Okay. But I have to ask. After all this time, why do you want to see her?"

"Do I need a reason?"

"Yeah, I think you do. If she's been avoiding you for the last ten years, she must have a reason of her own. I don't know anything at all about your daughter, but I'm not interested in dragging her back into anything that's going to hurt her."

He paused for a moment, trying, perhaps, to think of a good answer. Finally, he said, "I want to apologize."

"For?"

"For being a shitty father. I mean, when Annie was young, her mom and I, we didn't always get along. Some nights, I'd come home drunk, and there'd be a fight, and the cops would have to come, lights flashin', bangin' on the door and wakin' up the neighbors. I know that must have scared Annie something terrible."

"And did you hurt her? Physically, I mean? Did you hit her? Or did you sexually molest her?"

He sat up a little straighter in his chair. I could see it took an effort. "Mister Gamble, I may be a bad man, but as God is my witness, I never harmed that girl. At least, not the way you're askin'."

"Okay. Let's say I take you up on this. Do you have a photo?"

"I got this." He reached into his pocket and took out a folded piece of paper that turned out to be a promotional poster for a band called "Midnite Oil" that was appearing at a Nashville bar called Sharps and Flats. The date on the poster was from twelve years ago, and showed a group of three young men and one young woman posing with pouty expressions in front of a setup of instruments that included a drum kit, an electric keyboard, several guitars, and some amplifiers. The woman was, to put it tactfully, generously proportioned, like Mama Cass Elliot, with a floppy hat, a knee-length flowered vest, and dark hair with a skunk stripe that hung straight down nearly to her waist. Black makeup that circled her eyes gave her a vibe that was somewhere between goth and zombie apocalypse.

"What am I looking at?"

"That's Annie, there on the far left, next to the guy in the leather jacket. I found the poster one night when I was out drinking with a few of my buddies. I was fixin' to go see 'em play that weekend, but then I got arrested for fuckin' with a few cars in the parking lot…."

I said, "Excuse me?"

"Aw, you know, it was just the same old same old. The night, I found that poster, I got drunk, and for some reason, I thought it might be a hoot to slash a bunch of tires. You know, just to see what happened when the people came out and seen their tires was flat. But 'fore I got too far, a couple big guys caught me in the parking lot and beat the hell out of me before they called the cops. By the time I made bail, the date had come and gone, and I never got to see Annie's band."

"So then, your daughter is a musician?"

He shook his head. "Not a musician, so much as she was a singer. For a big girl, she could shake her ass pretty good, and maybe a cowbell or a tambourine. Other than that, nothin', at least so far as playin' an instrument goes. But she has a voice like an angel. I shoulda done more, I know, but I never gave her much encouragement. Just one more reason why I expect I was a no-good father."

"Okay. And can I assume you don't know who any of the people in this band might be?'

"'Fraid not. I don't remember any names, if I ever knew 'em. But I heard she was shacked up with one of them guitar players for a while. But maybe there's a way to find out. I mean, musicians have to be in a union to play for money, don't they?"

"Depends on where they play, but generally, yes. This poster should help some, but I'll need to take it with me. Meantime, do you have any idea where she might be living now?"

"Not for sure. Last I knew, she was stayin' with her mother in Nashville, but that was right after she got out of high school and didn't have a place of her own yet. I have an address, but I don't know if it's any good. Everything I've tried to send her in the mail comes back 'Not at this address' written on the envelope."

"Any chance she's married and living someplace else under a different name?"

"Could be. Last time I actually seen her, she was still single. But I guess by now she could have a husband and six kids."

I made a note to run a check at the county clerk's office to see if a marriage license had ever been issued.

"What about gal pals? You know, BFFs, or besties, or whatever they call themselves? She must have had a few friends she was close with."

He shook his head. "Couldn't tell you. She didn't bring her friends around the house much. See, back then, before my wife threw me out for good, sometimes things could get a little crazy. You know, if I'd been drinkin' or smokin' some crack."

"How about this, then. Your wife. Annamaria's mother. What's her name?"

"Emmy Lou."

"Emmilou. Emmilou Harris? Like the singer?" I tried to think of an Emmilou Harris song, but the only ones I could come up off the top of my head were "Rose in the Snow" and "All I Left Behind," which was a duet she recorded with Linda Ronstadt in 1999. I did remember seeing her in a 1978 Martin Scorsese film called *The Last Waltz*, where she performed along with a number of other singers in what was the final performance by The Band. For all I knew, she could have won a dozen Grammys. Turned out, when I checked later, she'd actually won fourteen, plus a bunch of other awards. But then, I'm not a fan of country music.

"She don't spell it that way. It's two words. Emmy Lou."

I wrote that down. "And what's the last address you have for her?"

"I got it here." He handed me a slip of paper. It was an address in an older neighborhood on the north side of the city.

"So, either she's no longer living there, or else she is, and neither one of them wants to hear from you. I have to say, though, if Annie is in her mid-thirties, I doubt she's still living with her mother, unless…."

"You can go ahead and say it. Unless she's a good-for-nothin' who can't hold a job and support herself, or even hang onto a husband. Come to think about it, she just might be. It kinda seems to run in the family."

"Yeah, well, let's hope for her sake she's not, and it doesn't. Besides, I was more thinking she might be a caregiver. And also, while we're at it, let's hope the reason your letters keep bouncing back is that she just lives someplace else and didn't leave a forwarding address." I paused for a moment to consider how to phrase what I had to say next.

"Also, there is every possibility, and you might as well face it right now, that, even if I do find her, she won't want to see you. I mean, unless there's something you're not telling me, she hasn't made any effort to reconnect. And, after all, you weren't sitting on death row for the past ten years for knocking over a vending machine."

"You think that's possible?"

"That she won't want to see you? I wouldn't have mentioned it if it weren't. Plus, she is an adult, and I can't force her do anything she doesn't want to do."

"But you can try." It wasn't a question.

"I can try to persuade her, and I will when I find her. But like I said, it's also likely after this much time that she actually is married and living elsewhere, or possibly moved out of state. If she is out of the area, then I don't know what to tell you, except that it'll be a lot harder. Not out of the question, but it might take some time. And it'll get expensive."

He seemed to brighten a little at that. "I guess whatever you got to do." There was a pause. "Does this mean you'll help me?"

"Maybe. But first, I want you to understand that I don't work for free. Have you made arrangements to cover my fee and expenses?"

"My lawyer will take care of that. Give him a call when you get back to town."

"You can count on it. Also, I have a question."

"What?"

"I need you to tell me what you were thinking when you shot those two people during that holdup."

He looked at me. "What does that matter?"

"It matters because if I think you're feeding me a bunch of bullshit, like you were acting in self-defense or something like that, then I'll figure you're still a rotten person, and you've been lying about everything else you've said so far. And if that's the case, then I'll know that I don't want anything to do with you, or what you want me to do."

"You mean, you want to know if I've been telling you the truth."

"Yes."

"Well…I didn't go into that store meaning to shoot anybody, let alone kill them. I just needed money. Back then, I was doin' a lot of crack, and I was hooked pretty bad. I needed to score, and, you know, I figured the easiest place to get some cash was that store. I mean, Seven-Elevens do a cash business, right? And they get stuck up all the time, just like liquor stores.

"Anyhow, at that particular moment, it looked like there weren't nobody else inside except the checkout gal, and I figured it would be easy since she wasn't likely to give me any trouble. I went in, and I got a twelve-pack of beer out of the cooler, you know, like a regular customer, and I took it up to the register, where I asked for a carton of smokes."

"Okay."

"Well, the gal started ringin' it up, only instead of takin' out my wallet, I grabbed this little .22 popgun I used to carry and told her to hand over the money. And that was all fine, she was puttin' it in a paper bag, no problem, only then, some character, he come out of the back. I don't know, I guess he was in the bathroom takin' a piss or something. Anyway, he hollered, 'What the hell's goin' on here,' and I panicked and I shot him. He went down, but he wasn't dead, so then I had to shoot him in the head to finish him. By then, the girl was screamin' bloody murder, so I shot her too, 'til I ran outta bullets. Then I grabbed the money and a stack of them scratchers and beat feet out the door."

"And the smokes and the beer?"

"Yeah, I took those, too." He looked at me. "I mean, after all that, wouldn't you?"

Chapter Three

On the way back to Nashville, I had a chance to think seriously about the conversation I'd had with Harvey Harris. I could imagine all kinds of reasons why he might want to reconnect with his daughter, especially since his remaining time on earth was short. Maybe he wanted to apologize for being the crappiest dad in the world, or maybe there were some family secrets he wanted to pass along. I supposed it was even possible that, somewhere, he had squirreled away a substantial amount of money or other valuables that he had amassed during his years as a career lowlife. Now, he either wanted to pass it along to her or else have her arrange to make restitution. I quickly discarded that idea, however. Successful criminals, which Harvey certainly was not, run large illegal enterprises. They don't generally wind up on death row for shooting convenience store clerks. In the end, I decided it didn't really make any difference. He wanted to see his Annamaria one more time, and it looked like I was going to be paid to find her.

What I didn't discuss with him was that, assuming Annamaria had actually gone missing and wasn't just rattling around in some suburban Nashville tract house with a husband and three kids, she might not be easy to find. After so many years, she could be damn near anywhere, living in a different state, or a different country, or even under a different name. People go missing for all kinds of reasons. And although in my experience they usually turn up within a short period of time, that isn't always the case. Sometimes they're on the run from a bad marriage, or a business failure, or an intolerable home or work situation, or even, like Tommy Mack, a run-in with the law.

Of course, it was also possible that she was dead, a thought that I knew Harvey wouldn't want to entertain during the dark nights alone in his cell.

When I got to Jackson, before getting back on the Interstate toward Nashville, I pulled into a truck stop to fill up with gas and to grab a roller dog and a Diet Coke to keep me juiced for the rest of the trip. While the pump was running up a heart-stopping dollar amount, I telephoned Maggie to let her know what time I expected to be back. Not surprisingly, my call went to voicemail, which probably meant she was with a client. I left a message and asked her to call me back on my cell.

Maggie Totten and I have been seriously and monogamously together for the better part of five years. When we met, she was recently divorced and working as a guidance counselor at an inner-city Nashville high school. But the school district, in a cost-cutting move, decided to outsource their counseling services. She was offered the opportunity of staying with the district and going back to being a classroom teacher, but instead, she accepted a severance package and enrolled at Vanderbilt, where she earned a doctorate in sociology and went to work for the state as a crisis counselor.

A year or so ago, Maggie's ex-husband, a man named Michael Pomeroy, whom I had never met, came back to Nashville after his second marriage and the restaurant he managed in a suburb of Tallahassee, Florida, both failed. Upon returning to Tennessee, he decided he wanted to rekindle his relationship with his former wife. Over a short period of time, his misguided efforts to reconnect progressed from telephone calls to an invitation to meet over cocktails, to stalking her at her place of employment, and finally, breaking into her condo in the small hours of the morning. That mistake proved to be fatal, as Maggie put three nine-millimeter slugs into his chest as he approached her on a darkened stairway. She quite literally saved both of our lives, but there was a downside.

No matter how popular fiction portrays it, killing another person is not a casual thing. Unless the perp is a stone-cold killer for hire or a homicidal sociopath, taking a human life leaves a wound on the mind and in the heart that never fades away. In Maggie's case, even though she is as strong and tough-minded as any woman I have ever encountered, she sometimes slips into a funk, remembering that terrible occurrence. Occasionally, on nights when we are having one of our sleepovers, I will find her in another room in the early hours of the morning, crying and trembling at the memory of shooting her ex-husband, never mind that he was a home invader intent on doing who-knows-what. When that happens, I comfort her the best way I can, knowing that, no matter what I do, I will never be able to make the hurt go away. And I don't know whether it would have made a difference, but she has never told me whether she recognized him before she pulled the trigger. Either way, after that, Maggie no longer felt safe in her home. And so, right around the Christmas holidays, she sold her condo and moved into a high-rise apartment building on Church Street in downtown Nashville.

* * *

These days, when a gentleman caller—that would be me—or anybody else, for that matter, comes to visit, he or she enters a secure building and then takes a long elevator ride up to the second-from-the-top-floor level where Maggie and her cat, a gray, tiger-striped tabby named Stanley, now reside in a spacious, two-bedroom unit. Depending upon which way she's facing when she looks out her corner windows, she has a million-dollar view of the Cumberland River to the north, or the Tennessee state capitol building to the northwest. And to say her building is deluxe would be an understatement. Among its amenities, it numbers a saltwater swimming pool, an exercise room with a personal trainer on staff, valet parking, paid utilities, complimentary WiFi, and proximity to any nightspot worth visiting, all for an eye-popping rent that I have no idea how she affords on a state government salary. But it doesn't matter, because regardless of what it costs, I know she is safe. And if I had to, I'd pay for it myself.

* * *

When I got back to the city, instead of going to Maggie's apartment, I met her for dinner at a favorite restaurant a block away. I was late, mostly because

I had trouble finding a parking lot that didn't charge a sultan's ransom to stow my car for a few hours. By the time I found our table and got settled in, Maggie was already into her second appletini, her go-to drink when she was in a good mood. A green bottle of Stella cooling in a plastic bucket filled with ice was waiting next to my bread plate. It looked like this might be my lucky night.

"So," she said, after a quick kiss. "You've decided to help this guy, what's his name?"

"Harvey Harris. Yes."

"Sounds like somebody who should have an act with trained pigeons on the county fair circuit."

"It would have been better for everybody if he had been. He killed two people—three if you count a pregnant store clerk as two people—robbing a Seven-Eleven for drug money."

"Really." She took a small sip of her cocktail. "And his story moved you. Why?"

"Well, for one thing, he didn't claim he was innocent. That's something you don't generally hear from guys serving a life sentence."

"And?"

I shrugged. "He's a dying man. He sounded sincere, and maybe the prospect of seeing his daughter one more time gives him a thread he can hang onto while he waits to meet his maker. And, come on, admit it. You know I'm a sucker for a sob story."

"I know. It's one of those things that makes me crazy about you."

She excused herself and got up to go to the ladies' room.

Short skirt. Black stockings. Definitely not an outfit she would have worn to work. My chances were looking pretty good.

Chapter Four

After supper, Maggie and I went back to her apartment. We shared a dessert—part of a chocolate cheesecake she brought home from work earlier in the day, and a couple of nightcaps—another Stella for me and vodka and cranberry juice for Maggie, and then we turned off the lights and went to bed.

In the time we have been a couple, we have settled into a routine of regular sleepovers, sometimes at her apartment, other times at my house. I keep a modest inventory of clothes and toiletries in Maggie's second bedroom and guest bathroom. Maggie, on the other hand, has enough of her wardrobe stashed at my place to live there for a month without ever wearing the same thing twice. Her "sleepover kit" includes skirts, slacks, jeans, blouses, legwear, several pairs of shoes, underwear, nightgowns, cosmetics, hair care products, a raincoat, and even a spare pair of boots, "in case it snows." Which, in middle Tennessee, it almost never does.

* * *

After Maggie left for work, I showered, shaved, fed Stanley, who, for once, didn't try to bite, claw, or otherwise attack me, and fixed myself my usual breakfast-at-home—an English muffin with peanut butter and a Diet Coke— and then set out to meet with Harvey Harris's attorney, a man named Geoffrey Tate. Tate's office was located in what had once been a very large home in what was now a mixed-use residential area near Vanderbilt University. The building occupied by Tate no longer served as a private residence, but instead had been converted into a commercial establishment, with Tate's office on the first floor and an accounting firm upstairs.

I parked my car, a fifteen-year-old dark blue Crown Vic, which in its prior life had been a LAPD detective's sled with better than eighty thousand miles on the clock, at the curb in front of Tate's office. I bought the Vic after my previous ride was obliterated by a bomb planted under the hood by a "person of interest" in a case I was working on at the time. The blast also took out Maggie's car, a silver Volvo wagon parked in my driveway at the time, as well as the front door and windows of my house, plus the windows of several nearby neighbors' houses up and down my block. I locked the car—no sense making it easy in case somebody else wanted to blow me to kingdom come—straightened my tie, and climbed a set of brick-and-mortar steps up to the front door of the building. Next to the door, a postcard-sized brass plate polished to a high sheen announced that this was the office of Geoffrey Tate, Attorney at Law.

Very discreet, and very up-market, I thought.

I went inside and entered a waiting area that looked as if it might have been a sitting room in years past, but that now held several chairs and small settees, and a desk occupied by a receptionist wearing a blue blazer over a flowered-print dress. She had reddish-brown hair, hazel eyes, and a smile that could light up an auditorium. When I came in, she looked up from her keyboard. The engraved glass name plate on her desk said her name was Rita Adkins.

"May I help you?"

I handed her my business card. "Jackson Gamble to see Mr. Tate. I called earlier."

"Oh, yes. Mr. Tate is expecting you." She indicated a door on her right. "You can go right in." Then, "Can I bring you a cup of coffee, or perhaps a bottle of water? Mister Tate believes it's important to stay hydrated."

"Thank you, no," I said, and went through the door.

When I went in, Geoffrey Tate was already standing with his hand extended for me to shake. I would have guessed he was somewhere north of sixty, south of sixty-five. He was a little taller than me, very slender, with a full head of bushy gray hair, brown eyes, and a Boston Blackie mustache. He was wearing a blue pinstriped suit, a red-and-silver silk necktie, and a rose gold Patek Phillipe Nautilus wristwatch that probably cost more than my Crown Vic when it was new.

If I hadn't already guessed, his office furnishings and décor practically screamed that this was a high-dollar operation, upwards of $50K—in advance—for a criminal defense, and who-knows-what on a contingency. I couldn't imagine how a mope like Harvey Harris could have begun to swing that. The walls were plaster, not drywall, and covered with Alexander Calder and Pedro Friedeberg prints as well as a mix of framed awards, certificates, and diplomas, both earned and honorary, from several prestigious universities, as well as the Tennessee Bar Association. The furniture was upholstered in soft leather, the color of burgundy wine. The floor was dark oiled wood, oak, I guessed, with colorful oriental rugs strategically placed near the seating areas.

I was impressed.

Tate gave me a thin smile and waved me into a customer's chair.

After we both got settled, he said, "So, Mr. Gamble. What can I do for you? When you called, you said you had some questions for me."

"I do," I said. "Let's start with this. Why me?"

"What do you mean?"

"I mean, there are lots of investigators in this city, most of them with bigger staffs and more resources than I have. Why didn't you call one of them?"

He gave a small shrug. "I know a lot of people. I called around. The feedback I got said you were through, dependable, and completely honest."

"I'm not sure about that last part, but okay. Let me ask you this, then. What's your connection to Harvey Harris?"

"I would think that was obvious. I'm his legal representative."

"I understand that, but why? As far as I know, you're not associated with the public defender's office. I checked their website yesterday afternoon. Except for one or two of them, most of those guys and gals look like they're fresh out of law school."

"I took Mr. Harris's case *pro bono*."

"For what reason, can I ask? I mean, Harvey's case doesn't seem like one that would inspire a lot of sympathy, especially considering how he wound up on death row in the first place."

He looked at me blandly. "For reasons I don't feel a need to explain just now. That's all you need to know about that."

"Got it," I said, making a mental note to dig into the question a little bit deeper. "Then maybe you can tell me what this investigation is really about."

He made a small movement with his hands. "I'm not sure I understand. Didn't Harvey tell you what he wants you to do?"

"He did, but somehow it seems funny to me that, after all this time, now he suddenly wants to reconnect with his daughter. Why now?"

"Obviously because he's dying. I suppose you'd have to say that a man in his situation tends to focus more clearly on his priorities."

"Maybe. But in a way, he's been dying ever since he landed on death row at Riverbend."

"Well, as to that, all I can tell you is what you already know. He doesn't have long to live. He wants to see his daughter. I don't know, people in his circumstances often have a need to make amends before they...." He let the thought trail off.

"Okay, we'll let that go for now. When you first contacted me, I explained what it would cost whoever is paying me do this work. I just want to remind you, my rate is five hundred dollars a day, prorated, plus expenses. So far, I've been paid for the day I spent running down to Whiteville, so except for the mileage, we're all square as of this morning. But I have to ask you, Mr. Tate. Where's the money really coming from? How does a guy who's spent half his life committing petty crimes or parked behind bars in some lockup manage to afford what this is almost certainly going to cost?"

"Not your concern, Mr. Gamble. Just send me an itemized accounting at the end of each week, and I'll see to it you're paid promptly. And by the way, if you don't mind me saying so, you don't exactly work cheap."

I shrugged. "Do you?"

He gave me the barest hint of a smile. "Point taken. Now, if there's nothing else?"

"Just a couple more things. Have you ever met Annamaria Harris? Or should I say, Annie?"

"Never. I wouldn't know her if she was sitting in the waiting area right now."

"Or any idea where I should start looking for her?"

"None at all." He wasn't smiling any longer. "But that's your area of expertise, and we're wasting daylight here, Mr. Gamble. So, I suggest you get started."

And just like that, our discussion was over. And I was out the door, having learned absolutely nothing more than I already knew.

Chapter Five

After leaving Geoffrey Tate's office, I drove downtown to the Nashville *Times* building. I wanted to take a look through their archives to see what they had on the shooting, some ten years back, that had landed Harvey Harris on death row. I remembered the case had made headlines at the time, and I wondered, for no particular reason, whether there was more to the story than what Harvey had told me during our meeting the day before. As convicted murderers went, it seemed to me that Harvey had been unusually forthcoming. In my experience, killers more often than not offer up some specious rationale for their crime, such as, "…it was his own fault I shot him. If he'd just handed over the money, nothing would have happened." It was the same kind of thinking you get from a fourteen-year-old when he gets caught misbehaving in class or in the lunchroom at school. "It wasn't my fault. He made me do it."

As always, before heading down to the basement to begin my search, I rode the elevator up to the third-floor city room to check in with my friend, Dick Dohrn, these days the senior editor at the city's second-largest newspaper. Unfortunately, Dick was out of the office today. His PA, a perky young woman named Gillian, informed me that Mr. Dohrn had a dental appointment, being fitted for a crown. It seemed he broke an old filling in one of his molars biting down on a slice of overcooked bacon at a Sunday brunch.

"But you can go ahead on down to the morgue. I'll call ahead and let them know you're on your way." Then. "You do know everything is on computer now, don't you? I mean, we got rid of the microfilm a long time ago, so if you need somebody to help you look for whatever it is you're looking for, I'm sure I can get one of the staff to go with you."

I assured Gillian I was at least moderately familiar with twenty-first century technology, and I'd be just fine on my own. Then I got back on the elevator and rode down to the morgue, the commonly-used name for the place where newspapers store their archived materials. A generation ago, the *Times* morgue would have been crammed floor-to-ceiling with file cabinets, storage boxes, and microfiche readers and film. These days, you would find nothing more than a couple of outdated IBM computers, still with cathode-ray monitors rather than flat screens. I took that as an indication of how often somebody actually needed to root through the archives.

Compared to the brightly-lit, airy city room upstairs, the basement of the *Times* building, where the archives were housed, was a musty, somewhat cramped space that smelled of stale coffee, black mold, and tobacco smoke. Not the best place to be if nasal allergies or asthma were among your ailments.

I took a seat at one of the available work stations and typed in "Harvey Harris." Not surprisingly, since Harvey's is a relatively common name, I got three pages of matching entries, including obituaries, high school sports stories, and even the winner of an Elvis lookalike contest. I scrolled through two and a half pages before I found what I was looking for, an article headlined, "Killer Sentenced to Death in Convenience Store Holdup."

The article reported that Harvey Harris was convicted of first-degree murder after a trial that, including jury selection, lasted only two days. The victims were 28-year-old Charlene Williams, who was six months pregnant at the time of the shooting, and Thaddeus Bruckheimer, a customer in the store, who was also shot and killed. The jury deliberated for less than an hour before bringing back a verdict of guilty with special circumstances. In this instance, the special circumstances applied because Mrs. Williams's unborn child was also killed, and because the fatalities occurred during the course of an armed robbery. At his sentencing, Harvey Harris expressed remorse over what he had done, stating that he never meant for anybody to get hurt, let alone a pregnant woman expecting her first child. He simply acted out of panic brought on in part, he claimed, by the fact that he was high on crack cocaine at the time of the holdup. At the sentencing hearing, the jury, apparently unimpressed by Harvey's contrition, recommended death by lethal injection, and the judge was only too happy to go along.

I found another piece dated a few months earlier, with a headline that gushed, "Metro PD Apprehend Holdup Man Following High-Speed Chase." Harvey Harris again. This time, according to the piece, which ran a column and a half, police were alerted to a possible holdup after a witness, described as a customer stopping in for a fill-up at the Goodlettsville Seven-Eleven, called to report a shooting. Officers responding discovered two dead bodies and immediately requested an APB and a BOLO on what the witness described as a black or dark blue pickup truck, either a Chevrolet or a GMC, heading north on Dickerson Road. Almost immediately, the cops spotted the pickup tearing down the road at better than seventy miles an hour in a forty-five-mile zone and gave chase. Less than a mile later, the driver of the pickup lost control of his vehicle, went off the road in someone's front yard, and got bogged down in new sod that had been watered so thoroughly that the soil underneath was the consistency of cookie dough. And although Harvey attempted to escape on foot, he was tackled and taken into custody. And that was the last time Harvey breathed free air.

Chapter Six

After I wrapped things up at the *Times*, I drove back to the office to check my mail and voice messages. There was a letter from my insurance company, informing me that, as a result of the explosion that wiped out my car and damaged the front of my house, my premiums would be "subject to a review and possible increase," effective with my upcoming renewal. I tossed that into the wastebasket. There was nothing I could do about it until I actually got the renewal notice, and probably not even then. Insurance companies do not like paying off claims, especially when they involve out-of-the-ordinary situations like attempted murder by explosive devices.

There were also promotional flyers for an "invisible" hearing aid at a new, low price and a walk-in bathtub. No joy, the only other pieces of real mail were the bill for the rent on my office, due and payable upon receipt, and a reminder that it was time to renew my private investigator's license, good for two more years. I wrote a check for a hundred dollars and mailed it off to the Tennessee Department of Commerce and Insurance, satisfied that now I could continue to work ridiculous hours for embarrassingly little money and even less appreciation.

There was nothing in my voicemail that required my attention, so I decided I might as well start earning my keep with the search for Annamaria Harris. I put in a call to a guy named Devon Sharpe, who was the A&R man at Red Dot Records, a B-list recording house over on Seventeenth Street, in the heart of Music Row. His PA picked up on the second ring and then asked me to hold after I identified myself. I found myself wondering how many calls Devon must get every day from wannabe C&W or country rock stars looking to break into the business, if only. Probably enough to keep two PA's busy keeping them at arm's length.

"Your timing is good," he said, without preliminaries. "I might have a gig for you, if you're interested."

"Depends on what it is."

"This is one I think you'll like," Devon said. "Saturday night, we're throwing a launch party for the debut release by the Braxton Brothers. It's by-invitation only, and I was thinking we'd have you work security. No heavy lifting, just gobble up some finger food, have a couple of drinks, and keep an eye out for gate-crashers. It's three hours. Pays fifteen hundred, and you can bring a plus-one if you want."

"I'll have to check my calendar. How soon do you have to know?" I said, not really feeling the vibe. "Also…who the hell are the Braxton Brothers?"

"Believe it or not, quadruplets. Real ones. They're from down in Tullahoma. They've picked up a following over the last year or so playing roadhouses and redneck shitkicker bars on the weekends, so they're over twenty-one, if that makes any difference. One of the guys who works here was out slumming a couple months ago and heard them. We sent our A&R assistant to give a listen, and it turned out they were pretty good. After we auditioned them, we offered a three-record deal plus a six-state tour. They signed, so we're doing the regular kickoff to generate some buzz before they go out on the road." There was a pause.

"So, what do you think? You want the job? If you don't, I'll have to hurry up and find somebody else."

"I'll let you know by tomorrow. Meanwhile, I've got a question for you."

"Okay, but it'll have to wait. I'm already running behind for a meeting. Can you come by the office first thing tomorrow? I'll have some time then, and we can maybe catch up a bit."

* * *

I spent the rest of the afternoon scouring the Internet. First, I searched for any reference to Annamaria Harris, Annie Harris, Ann-Marie Harris, and even Mary Ann Harris. There were twenty-five women with one or the other of those names living between Jackson and Nashville, none of whom were within a decade of the right age. I even checked the two local newspapers for obituaries, and once again, came up empty. Wherever this woman was, she had either changed her name, gotten married, or moved out of the area.

My search for "Midnite Oil" was another goose egg, although I did turn up a couple of Wikipedia references, including one that mentioned that "burning the midnight oil" was a kind of shorthand descriptor for the practice of working late into the night, most often to meet a looming deadline. I also found a reference to an Australian band called Midnight Oil that formed in 1978 and broke up in 2002. Turned out, they had thirteen studio album releases and two EPs, as well as an international hit song called "Beds Are Burning." There was a link to a video of the band performing their smash, so I clicked on it and listened to the song. It was actually pretty good, and I had a hazy recollection of having heard it once or twice on our classic rock station. Idly, I wondered if Annie Harris's band had changed the spelling of "midnight" to "midnite" to avoid possible problems with copyright infringement. But then, I discarded the idea. It seemed unlikely that an internationally acclaimed group from Australia would care one way or the other about a garage band from middle Tennessee unless they managed to rattle off a string of hits on their own, which it appeared they most definitely had not. Maybe whoever came up with the name simply didn't know how to spell.

There was one other link, this time to a local pizza restaurant operating under the same name that got pretty good Yelp reviews. Looking over their online menu, they offered a wide variety of pizza toppings, plus a list of available beer brands as long as my arm. I made a note of the address in case Maggie wanted to try something different on one of our date nights.

My last shot was to put in a call to the bar where "Midnite Oil"—the local band, not the Aussies—was supposedly performing the night Harvey got pinched for slashing tires. I learned it was under new ownership, and these days was catering to the gay and trans crowd. Not surprisingly, the guy who answered had never heard of Midnite Oil or Annamaria Harris.

It was time to call it a day. For billing purposes, I made a record of the time I had spent working on the case and headed for home.

Chapter Seven

Wednesday morning, I was up and out early. I wanted to get ahead of traffic headed into the city, and, to be honest, driving a car that Maggie refers to as "the three-bedroom Ford" during the morning rush can be a challenge. Between Old Hickory Boulevard on the south side of the city and the I-65/Broadway interchange downtown, during the morning rush, I am almost never able to get much over 30 miles an hour before having to come to a complete stop at the I-440 interchange to wait for the tidal wave of traffic to get moving again.

Once I got off the expressway, since I was running early for my nine o'clock meeting, I stopped for breakfast at a McDonalds. I opted for a McGriddle, no egg, no cheese, a side of hash browns, and a large Diet Coke. Then I drove over to Eighteenth Avenue and parked in one of the visitors' slots in front of the Red Dot Music Corporation office and studio building.

My first, and so far, only business dealing with Red Dot was a complete fuckup bodyguarding an up-and-coming young singer named Kady Standley. That one didn't turn out at all well, as the last night she was in town, she gave me the slip and was found three days later in a cheap motel room, dead from a drug overdose. After that, I thought I'd never hear from them again, to say nothing of ever cashing another one of their checks. But Red Dot had already figured out that Kady was a horse they could only ride so far, given her self-destructive tendencies. And in fact, when she died, they were not in the least upset, since her latest and last release went platinum the day it hit the stores. And in the music business, you're only as good as your last number one with a bullet.

Devon Sharpe was late getting to work, and so the receptionist asked me to take a seat in the lobby. She said Devon had gotten stuck in traffic heading into the city and had called to say he'd be there in about fifteen minutes. That left me time to thumb through the current edition of *Billboard* magazine. Not surprisingly, the cover story was about Taylor Swift's current concert tour, including the eye-watering ticket prices that did not prevent every seat being filled at every venue well in advance of her actual performance. *Well, good for her*, I thought. Although I knew very little about her as a person and even less about her music, it seemed to me she had a once-in-a-generation talent that made her worth every dollar she earned.

Flipping through the pages, I also found a forty-year retrospective on the career of the late Marvin Gaye, a brilliant Motown singer and composer who was shot to death by his own father in 1984 when he stepped into the middle of a family altercation. Not so good for him.

I was partway through an article about some singer I had never heard of, but whom the rest of the world apparently had, since his new release had already reached the Top Ten on the Billboard Hot 100 and the Billboard Global 200, when Devon Sharpe finally showed up, looking sweaty and a bit unhappy.

"Sorry for being so late," he said, after we got settled in his office, a cup of coffee for him and a can of Diet Coke for me, "Turned out, there was a wreck in the high occupancy lane on the expressway. One of those mega-pickups tangled with a FedEx delivery truck and brought the entire inbound side to a screeching halt. And since I wasn't anywhere near an exit ramp, all I could do was sit and wait. Hope I didn't mess up your schedule for the rest of the morning."

"Not a problem. I'm not on the clock."

"Okay, well, then, since I already wasted all our shootin' the shit time sitting in traffic, what brings you by this morning? And can I count on you for the Braxton Brothers party on Saturday?"

I yawned. "That was twenty-five hundred, right? Isn't that what you said?"

"I said fifteen."

"Right. How about we call it a deuce, and you've got a deal."

"I see where this is going." He sighed wearily. "All right. Two thousand it is, and that's only because it's too late to get anybody else. But then, you come early, and you stay late. And you don't shoot anybody. Okay?"

"Deal," I said. "And there's something else."

"What?"

I showed him the promotional poster Harvey Harris had given me. "Take a look at this and tell me whether you recognize any of these people."

He shrugged. "Should I? And how old is this?"

"Guy who gave it to me said twelve years."

"People can change a lot in that much time. What's your interest in this?"

"I have a client. He wants to reconnect with his daughter. He says she's this girl here."

He picked up the poster and looked at it more closely. "Midnite Oil. Aren't they from Australia?"

"Different group. Different spelling. Different century. This bunch is local, or at least they were when they played Sharps and Flats. It's a gay bar now, by the way, in case you haven't been keeping up. The girl's name is Annamaria Harris, or maybe you might have heard of her as Annie Harris."

"Nope." He shook his head. "But I think I recognize this guy." He pointed to one of the band members. "If he's who I think he is, his name is Jason Mackey. He's a session man. A guitar player. Sometimes we use him here. He's not first-call, but if we don't need an overly complicated bridge, he's good enough, and he doesn't cost nearly as much as the bigger names."

"A bridge," I said.

"You know. The instrumental part of a song that goes between the second and third verses. Sometimes it's used to change the tempo, or to break up repetition, so the song doesn't end up sounding like some kind of a chant. Remember 'MacArthur Park,' from back in the sixties? Jimmy Webb had the Wrecking Crew doing the instrumental tracks on that one. For a bridge, it was very long and very complicated, and you don't want to waste a lot of studio time getting it right. The Wrecking Crew is top-notch and very expensive, like the Funk Brothers were at Motown, or Booker T and the MGs at Stax. All the A-list artists use guys like that because they get it right in one or two takes. Jason Mackey isn't in that league, but he's close, and he does get regular calls."

"I'll keep him in mind when I cut my first album. Meanwhile, you got contact information for this Jason Mackey?"

"You sure you're not planning to serve him with a subpoena or anything like that, are you? I mean, if that's what this is really about, I don't want to get involved."

"Just need to talk to him, that's all."

"Okay, then." He fiddled for a minute on his computer and then wrote down an address and a telephone number.

"So. See you Saturday? Be here by six. I'll have your check waiting."

"Can't wait," I said. "And by the way, these Braxton Brothers. Are they any good?"

"They sing in close harmony. Imagine the Beach Boys with southern accents and steel guitars."

I didn't even want to try.

Chapter Eight

The address I got for Jason Mackey was on Hillsboro Pike, in the Green Hills neighborhood on the southwest side of the city. From the upscale character of that area, I guessed that, even though Jason might not be a first-call session man, he must still be doing pretty well for himself. I tried the phone number that came with the address and got a voice message informing me that he was away from the phone, and that I should leave my number and he'd call me back. Odd, considering that most people these days either go around with their phone in their hand or else stuck in their back pocket. But then, since he was a session man in demand, I supposed that maybe he was in the studio working and couldn't interrupt what he was doing.

In my experience, people do not like getting telephone messages from private detectives. Most often, they immediately become evasive or defensive, figuring they're about to be on the receiving end of a summons, or else they're dodging an overdue child support or a monthly maintenance payment. However, since as far as I knew, Jason Mackey wasn't lying low for any reason, I decided to just leave a message and wait for a callback. I explained who I was and that I needed his help locating a missing person. Then I recited both my cell and my office number and hung up. That left me with only one other active lead to pursue, Emmy Lou Harris, Annamaria's mother. Rather than call, I took a chance that, like Harvey, Emmy Lou had reached retirement age and might be at home.

The address Harvey had given me was a house on a potholed street in a *déclassé* neighborhood on the north side of the Cumberland River. No money had ever lived there, and probably never would, unless the relentless construction boom that had transformed downtown beyond imagining finally surged across the river and flattened everything for blocks in every direction. I parked at the curb and mounted the front steps to a sagging porch that fronted a narrow frame house badly in need of a fresh coat of paint.

I rang the doorbell and waited. Nothing. Then I tried rapping on the screen door. Still nothing. Not quite ready to give up, I got down off the porch and walked around to the back of the house. When I approached the back door, I realized the problem. There was a what looked like a brand-new flat screen television set blaring loud enough to rattle the windows, and when I peeked inside, I saw a gray-haired woman seated at the kitchen table, peeling potatoes and carrots and wrapped up intently in the closing segment of *The Price is Right*. With the volume cranked up as loud as it was, I doubted whether she would have heard me if I had driven my car through the front door and honked the horn in the living room. I banged on the door, hard. That got her attention.

She lifted herself out of her chair slowly, as if the effort was a serious strain, then shuffled, more than walked, over and opened the back door. She left the screen door shut.

"If you're lookin' for a handout, I'm afraid I ain't got nothing to give. You might try next door. Sometimes, they're willing to help a poor man out."

I seriously doubted whether any poor men had come looking for a handout at people's back doors since the darkest days of the Great Depression. And then I wondered whether the jacket and slacks I'd picked out when I was getting dressed earlier created the impression that I was in need of charity.

I said, "Mrs. Harris? Mrs. Emmy Lou Harris?"

"Used to be. Maybe I still am." She brightened a bit at that. "You from the insurance company? Did Harvey finally kick the bucket?"

I scratched on the screen. "Could you open the door, please, Mrs. Harris? I feel like a moth out here."

She opened the screen door and moved to one side so I could come in. Hazarding a guess, I would have said Emmy Lou Harris was in her early sixties and looked an easy ten years older. She wore a faded blue, long-sleeved blouse over a well-worn pair of blue jeans and black high-top tennis shoes. Her hair was gray and straight and hung down past her shoulders—definitely not a good look for a woman her age.

I said, "Mrs. Harris, my name is Jackson Gamble. I'm a private investigator." I opened my wallet so she could see my license and identification, then took out a business card and handed it to her. "I'm hoping you can help me with a small matter I've been asked to look into. I just have a couple of questions, and then I'll be on my way."

She turned the volume down on the television set. "Go ahead and ask your questions, Mr. Gamble. 'Course, I guess first you better tell me what this is all about."

I pointed to one of the kitchen chairs and raised my eyebrows. She nodded. "Make yourself comfortable."

I took a quick glance around the kitchen. In addition to the television, there was a high-end microwave oven and what looked to me to be a restaurant-quality refrigerator and stove, both of which looked jarringly out of place in what otherwise appeared to be an indifferently-maintained house. I wondered where the money had come from to pay for all of it, but then, that wasn't the reason I was there.

"It's like this," I said, taking a seat on a vinyl-covered kitchen chair that was not at all comfortable. "Your husband, Harvey. Harvey asked me to try and find his daughter—your daughter, Annamaria. In case you didn't know, he's dying. He has a cancer, and he hasn't got long to live. He says he wants to talk to her before, well, before he goes."

"So, he's still alive."

I nodded. "I expect you know you already know about the cancer. From the look of him, I'd say he'll be leaving very soon."

"You mean leaving for hell."

"I guess that would be one way to put it."

"'Cause that's for sure where he's headed. Now. You say he wants to talk to Annie May? That's what we called her, Annie May. Did he say why?"

"He did not. I got the impression he wanted to apologize for not being a better father."

She made a noise that could have been a laugh. "He couldn't hardly have been a worse one. When he wasn't in jail, he was either drunk or high on some damn thing or other."

I didn't know what to say to that, so I waited.

"Well, I don't rightly know how I can help you find Annie May. I mean, I haven't seen her or heard from her in, let's see, it must be close on to ten years now. I couldn't say where she is, or if she's married, or got kids, or anything else. Last I knew, she was in some kinda band, but I don't recollect that ever came to anything."

"Now that's interesting. When I spoke with Harvey, he said he wrote to Annie May at this address, but that the letters always came back marked 'not at this address.'"

"That was me done that, but it didn't mean I knew where she was. I stopped doin' all that after a while, and just threw them letters in the trash."

"You never read any of them?"

"Harvey never had nothing to say I wanted to read."

"Okay," I said. "So, when Annamaria—I'm sorry—when Annie May moved out, did she say where she was going?"

"She said she was moving in with one of them fellas in that band. I think she might've said his name was Jake, or Jacob. Something like that."

I said, "Could his name have been Jason?"

"Might have been, I suppose. I never met him, though."

"And that was ten years ago? And you haven't been in touch since?"

"More or less, I guess." She shook her head. "We didn't exactly part ways on the best of terms. I thought she was wasting her time running with that bunch of so-called musicians. Guess I must've said so once too often."

Then I had an idea. "When Annie May moved out, did she leave any of her things here?"

"Her room is just the way it was the day she left." There was a distinct note of sadness in her voice. "I didn't want to change nothing just in case she decided to come back. I wanted her to feel like she was still welcome in her home."

"I understand. Mrs. Harris, would you mind if I took a quick look around Annie May's bedroom? She might have left something behind that could help me find her." When she didn't answer, I said, "You just got finished telling me she's been gone ten years now. Wouldn't you like to see her again, too?"

She gave me a look I couldn't quite read. "Annie May's bedroom is down the hall, all the way at the end. Look all you want, but please leave things just the way you find 'em."

At first glance, I could have saved the trouble of looking. There was a double bed, neatly made with a floral-print spread, and a black and white stuffed dog with sad eyes and long, floppy ears perched in the middle. There was also a desk and a dresser, neither of which had anything I could use in the drawers. The top drawer of the desk had a few pens and pencils, a yellow pad of Post-it notes, a box of paper clips, and a battery-powered calculator with a dead battery. No address book, no diary, and no photo album, any one of which might have pointed me in the right direction. The other drawer held a half-full package of lined notebook paper, a box of envelopes, a hairbrush, and a hand-held mirror. Just the thing, I supposed, for a girl to check her makeup before, well, before what? Balancing her checkbook? Making out a shopping list before a trip to the mall?

I moved on to the dresser. The bottom two drawers contained folded bed linens, plus an extra blanket for nights when it was cold enough that one wouldn't be enough. The next drawer was where an extra pillow was stashed. Just the thing to go with the spare blanket if Annie May had one of her girlfriends sleeping over on a Friday or a Saturday night.

I checked the closet. Nothing. No clothes, no shoes, and no skeletons, either. When Annie May left, she evidently took every stitch of clothing she owned with her. Either that, or her mother hauled it off to the local Goodwill. There was a bookshelf that didn't seem to offer much, either, except a few paperback novels, a couple of empty three-ring binders, and—lucky me—a yearbook, I guessed, from the high school where Annie May attended classes before she took off on her own. Interestingly, I did not find a framed diploma hanging on a wall, suggesting that perhaps Annie May had not graduated.

I sat down on the edge of the bed and opened the front cover, where there were a few pages left blank where kids could sign one another's book at a graduation party. Sure enough, Annie May had no shortage of friends, all of whom wrote farewell notes to her, wishing her all the best in the years to come. Typical of high school-age girls, a few of her gal pals dotted their "i's" with miniature hearts or smiley faces. I flipped past the autograph pages and searched the senior class headshot pictures, and there was a young Annamaria Harris, sandwiched alphabetically between Jennifer Louise Irwin and Jonathan Thomas Hatcher. In this photo, which was just a head-and-shoulders view, she was still chubby-looking, but her hair was shorter than it appeared in the Midnite Oil poster, and there was no heavy black makeup around her eyes. For all intents and purposes, she looked like a normal teenaged girl who probably fretted about her weight in her private moments. I decided to take the yearbook with me.

When I returned to the kitchen, I found Emmy Lou still seated at the table where I had left her a few minutes earlier. "The Price is Right" was over, somebody had gone home with whatever prizes were part of the Showcase Round, and now she was tuned in to a soap opera.

"Did you find what you were looking for?"

"I found this." I held up the yearbook for her to see. "I wonder if you could take a minute to look through it. Maybe you can tell me if there was anyone in her class Annie May was close with. It might give me a place to start."

She looked at me with sad eyes. "Mister Gamble, why do you want to help that awful man? He never brought nothing to anybody his whole life except misery. Why can't you just let him stay there in that prison and die? Couple more months, he won't be nothing but a bad memory."

"I could do that, Mrs. Harris. And, as it so happens, I came very close to just walking away five minutes after I met him. But I guess it comes down to the fact that, even if I do find your daughter, I have no control over what happens next. I certainly can't force her go down to Whiteville to visit Harvey. I'm just being paid to find her and deliver a message. What she does after that is none of my concern."

She sat quietly for a moment, thinking, I supposed. When she spoke again, there was an angry edge in her voice.

"Well, then, you should understand this. I don't know where Annie May is right now, or where she has been since she walked out that very door you just now came through. I expect she's got her reasons, but I don't figure after all this time she wants to see me, neither."

"I understand that, believe me. But if by some chance you do hear from her, could you give me a call? There might be a few bucks in it for you." I got up to leave.

"Mister Gamble, before you go, can I ask you something?" Her voice dropped an octave, and her tone got softer. "This might seem funny to you, but when you talked to Harvey, did he say anything about me?"

"He did," I lied. "He said if I saw you, to tell you he was sorry for how things turned out, and if he had it to do over again, he'd be a better man."

"I wonder. Maybe he's just tryin' to get right with Jesus before his time comes."

"Maybe. Or maybe he meant what he said," I told her, and for just a moment, she looked like she might have actually believed it.

Days like this, I hate my job.

Chapter Nine

Another day went by, and then another, and I still had not heard back from Jason Mackey, despite having called his number several times during those two days. Maybe, I thought, he was performing on the road somewhere and wasn't picking up, or had his phone turned off, or maybe he had moved and not updated Red Dot regarding his current whereabouts. Frustrated, I went online to see whether I could get any additional information from the Nashville Musicians Association, which was, in fact, the local 257 affiliate of the American Federation of Musicians. It was a fairly interesting website, and I spent several minutes browsing around, including a "Do Not Work For" link which listed a number of organizations that had gotten themselves onto the union's shit list for such offenses as not paying into the union pension fund, hiring non-union musicians, bouncing checks, and treating musicians disrespectfully, whatever that meant. It also included a listing of the Association's membership that showed their area of specialization, such as engineer, arranger, vocalist, keyboardist, percussionist, and so on. There was even a link to contact the individual, although that turned out to be a mailbox routed through the union. Finally, since none of those avenues seemed likely to produce a favorable result, I called the local telephone number to see if I could plead my case to a real person.

I ended up speaking first to a receptionist named Valerie, and then to somebody named Ronald Parker, who wanted to know why did I wish to get in touch with Jason Mackey. Was I planning an event such as a wedding reception or a corporate function where I might need musicians? I thought momentarily about making up a story about how I was looking for music lessons, then decided it would be simpler to just identify myself and lay my cards on the table.

"I'm a private investigator. I need to speak to Mr. Mackey in connection with a search for a missing person I've been hired to undertake. Mister Mackey is not in any sort of trouble, nor do I intend to make any trouble for him. I'm simply looking for some information."

There was a humming noise on the line, as if whatever he was thinking about was accompanied by a soundtrack. "Is the person you're looking for also a member of the NMA?"

"I wouldn't know. I didn't see her name on the list of your members."

"Oh, wait. So, you're looking for a woman." It wasn't a question.

"Yes," I said. "Is that a bad thing?"

"You'd be surprised. People claiming they met some gal singing in a bar lounge or at a company event, she gave the guy her phone number, and now he can't find it, things like that. We try to protect our members."

"Sounds like you're in an exciting business, Mr. Parker."

He let that pass. "What's the name of the woman you're looking for. Maybe I can help."

"Her name is Annamaria Harris. She also goes by Annie May or just plain Annie."

"Annie Harris. I seem to remember that name." There was a pause. "Wasn't she in some band or other back about ten years ago? Something like Midnight Oil?"

"Yeah, that's it, but with a different spelling in case you're going to look it up. Jason Mackey was in that same band. I was just hoping the two of them might have stayed in touch."

"Well, let me check something." I heard what sounded like typing on a computer keyboard. "Okay, I don't have anything here on anyone named Annie Harris. And, as far as Jason Mackey is concerned, I can't give you any personal information because, as you might imagine, that would be a violation of the confidentiality agreements we have with our membership. But I can tell you he's scheduled to be performing at a reception for the

Braxton Brothers tomorrow night."

"The Braxton Brothers. Really." That, at least, was good news. Now I knew where I could find Jason Mackey.

"Yeah, Ronnie, Donnie, Johnny, and Lonnie. Don't tell me you've heard of them."

"I have, but this is the first time I've heard their individual names. Tell me, do they have sisters named Bonnie and Connie?"

"I wouldn't know. Personally, I've never heard their music, but supposedly they're all primed and ready to be the next big thing. Unfortunately for you, the reception is a by-invitation-only event, but maybe you can hang around the parking lot or something and catch your man on his way in or out."

* * *

Since I was working the Braxton Brothers' gig, I didn't need to worry about having an invitation. I scooped Maggie up at her apartment a little before six, plenty of time to get to the Red Dot studio where Donnie, Ronnie, Johnny, and whoever were set to make their *entree* into Music City royalty. I tried to dress in such a way that I wouldn't stand out in the crowd, which meant gray slacks, a pale blue shirt, blue-and-gray necktie, and a navy-blue blazer, which also served to conceal the Colt .380 I wear in a shoulder rig.

As she generally did for upscale social events, Maggie was dressed to kill in a form-fitting black-and-red dress, with red shoes and evening bag. She had pinned her hair up and applied just enough makeup to bring the average middle-aged man to his knees, drooling with primal lust. Despite the fact that the liquor would be flowing freely throughout the evening, I wasn't worried about anybody hitting on her, since I was aware that in her professional capacity as a state-employed crisis counselor, she knew how to handle all sorts of questionable behaviors. I also knew she carried a pocket-sized Ruger .380 in her purse.

I checked in at the front entrance with Devon Sharpe, who handed me an envelope containing my check for the evening's work. Then I introduced Maggie and left her to visit with Devon while I went to work, checking out the venue for possible security problems.

Given the way the room was set up, I estimated it could comfortably accommodate somewhere in the neighborhood of a hundred and fifty people. At the end, farthest from the door was a medium-sized stage with an assortment of musical instruments and four microphones already in place. That meant Johnny, Ronnie, Lonnie, and Donnie were vocalists. Whether they played any of the instruments remained to be seen, but I supposed that if Jason Mackey had been hired to play guitar, perhaps all the brothers actually did was sing.

On one side of the stage was a door that I knew from past experience led to a second, smaller room. Devon had told me that, for tonight, at least, it would serve as a green room, where the headliners could hang out until it was time for the introduction. On the other side was a fire exit that I would have to keep an eye on, just in case one of the guests got an idea about trying to sneak somebody in who did not have an invitation. I was thinking maybe a *paparazzo*, or somebody hoping to grab a pirate recording, but the way things are nowadays, it could just as likely be a mass shooter.

The largest part of the room was set up with tables for four and six, although they could easily be moved in case a larger group wanted to sit together. I hadn't seen the guest list, but I imagined most of the invitees were print and broadcast media types, plus producers, musicians, and assorted other movers and shakers from various segments of the business community.

At around quarter to seven, people started drifting in. The early arrivals, I suspected, were Red Dot staffers, who had no excuse for being late, fashionably or otherwise, plus the band that would be providing the entertainment before the Braxton Brothers were introduced. The musicians, all dressed identically in black shoes and slacks and white shirts with banded collars, began getting themselves placed on the stage. There was a keyboardist with an electric piano, two guitarists, one with a steel guitar, one with a Fender Stratocaster—I guessed that would be Jason Mackey—a saxophonist, who also had a clarinet, and a percussionist with a fairly simple drum kit, including a bass, tom, snare, and cymbal. I knew tonight was not going to be a concert, just background atmosphere while the high-rollers scarfed down free liquor and *hors d'oeuvres*, killing time until the headline event.

As the room began to fill up, I took a position near the entry, so I could get a look at who was coming through the door. I recognized a few of the invited guests as current performers who had recently occupied some of the top spots on the C&W charts. I also took note of more than a few has-beens, relegated these days to the county fair and local TV talk show circuit, and who were doubtless banking on tonight's event as a chance to schmooze with music industry big shots and maybe get some much-needed exposure. Maybe even a jump-start on a comeback. There were many more I didn't recognize, but then, I'm not in the music business.

Most of the men were dressed in what I understood to be country-club casual—sport jackets, linen slacks, high-end loafers—with and without socks—and open-collared shirts. A few, though, opted for the full cowboy crooner rig, with big hats, expensive jeans and boots, and jackets with lots of fringe. One individual, whom I did not recognize, showed up wearing a ten-gallon hat and what I guessed were prop six-guns with pearl grips. I caught Devon's eye and tossed my head in the direction of Hopalong Cassidy, who was drifting over toward the bar. He read my meaning and shook his head, no, which I took to mean the guy wasn't likely to start picking off the stage lights in the middle of the festivities.

There were also lots of pretty women, most of them dressed at least as upscale as Maggie, only with a lot more jewelry and makeup, not always applied with restraint or in good taste. All in all, quite a cross-section of Nashville music industry royalty. Rounding out the roster were media-types, including a recording crew from one of our local television stations. If it was a big coming out *soiree* Lonnie, Donnie, Ronnie, and Johnny were looking for, tonight was their night.

At seven, the band began to play, softly, so as not to make conversation difficult, but loud enough to be heard by those who might be looking for entertainment at their next *soiree*. Their repertoire was mixed and included a blend of soft pop and country hits, all rendered instrumentally and without vocals, as well as a few show tunes, including "Send in the Clowns," which I thought was appropriate for the way some of the invitees were dressed.

After a while, the influx of guests subsided to a trickle. Looking over the room, I decided this was not a crowd that was going to cause any problems. So, as the band spun up a smooth instrumental rendition of a Willie Nelson hit, "You Were Always on My Mind," I wandered over to the buffet table and filled a small plate with bacon-wrapped scallops, deep-fried alligator tidbits, boiled shrimp, and a spoonful of cocktail sauce. Then I grabbed a bottle of Stella and found a seat at an empty table for four near the back, where I could keep an eye on the goings-on. Guests mixed and mingled and posed for photos, or spoke enthusiastically into microphones held by entertainment reporters. Nobody started a fistfight. Nobody tried to crash the entrance. Nobody whipped out a gun and started shooting. And nobody paid the slightest attention to me, which was fine. Once, I spotted Maggie, on the other side of the room, chatting amiably with a couple of well-attired older men who had probably mistaken her for a pro.

I was on my third shrimp when a woman I had spotted earlier wandered over and sat down next to me. She was a little taller than Maggie with shoulder-length blonde hair and penetrating blue eyes. Hazarding a guess, I would have put her age somewhere between thirty-five and forty. She wore a simple sleeveless black dress that might have been just a bit too short and maybe showed just a little too much cleavage, at least for the Gospel-music cohort. Her outfit was accented with a black velvet belt fastened with a faux diamond-studded buckle. To go along with that, there was a heart-shaped Angara diamond pendant around her neck, a pair of Elsa Peretti diamond drop earrings, dove gray open-toed pumps, and a matching gray clutch purse capacious enough to hold her phone, compact, and, since this was Tennessee, maybe a small autoloading pistol. Her makeup looked to have been professionally applied—definitely airbrushed, not troweled on.

"So, what time do you figure the first gate crasher is going to show up?"

"Excuse me?"

"Well, you are working security for Red Dot, aren't you? I mean, I know just about everyone else in the room. Near as I can tell, you're the only one who's packing, although I'm not completely sure about that Roy Rogers lookalike."

"I'm pretty sure they're props." I put down my fork. "You have a good eye, Miss…."

"Miles. Mrs. Sonny Miles." She tilted her head in the direction of a smallish man of late middle age holding court with a number of listeners who seemed enthralled by whatever it was he was saying. "But you can call me Madelaine, or, if you prefer, Maddie." When I looked, the man had momentarily interrupted his conversation and seemed to be glaring at me, or possibly at Maddie.

"Maddie, okay. What can I do for you, Maddie?"

"Well, for starters, are you on the job?"

"No. Why would you think that?"

"Because the company sometimes hires off-duty cops for security."

I shook my head. "Used to be. Not anymore. I'm a private investigator. Just picking up a little money on the side. So, again, what can I do for you?"

"Well, I was wondering…." But before she could finish, Devon Sharpe hopped up onto the stage and grabbed one of the stand-up mikes.

"Ladies and gentlemen, good evening and welcome to what I believe will be the most exciting event of the year for Nashville and country music. But before we begin, I'd like to take just a minute to introduce the wonderful musicians…"

"Give me your hand," said Maddie Miles. She grabbed my right wrist, pulled it toward her, and wrote a telephone number on the back of my hand. "Call me. I may have a job for you." And with that, she got up from her chair and hurried off to mingle with the crowd.

"…on keyboards, give a big hand to…" Devon went on, introducing each of the musicians, but curiously, none of them were named Jason Mackey. Instead, the guy with the Strat was named Billy Watkins. A damn good musician from what I could tell, but definitely not the person I was hoping to connect with.

Another minute went by, and then the overhead lights in the room dimmed, bright spotlights illuminated the stage, and one by one, Johnny, Donnie, Ronnie, and Lonnie, the Braxton Brothers, dressed in a similar style to that of the backing quintet except for red shirts instead of white, entered from a side door and stepped up onto the stage. There was loud applause as Devon Sharpe made the introductions. After that, the brothers sang four songs. Two were country standards, including "Elvira," originally recorded by the Oak Ridge Boys, and, appropriately, I thought, "New Kid in Town," by the Eagles. After that, one of the brothers, Johnny, I think, or it could have been Lonnie or Ronnie—I was having trouble keeping them straight—said something about how people thought they sounded a little like the Beach Boys. And to prove it, they launched into a show-stopping version of "Help Me, Rhonda," which earned them a round of wild applause from the audience. Then they wrapped things up with another song, one I had not heard before, but which they said was on their first CD album, an autographed copy of which was included in each of the gift bags that would be available at the conclusion of the evening.

I had to admit, Devon had gotten one thing absolutely right. The brothers were very good, and their harmonies did sound like a gently countrified version of the Beach Boys.

After the Braxton Brothers' performance, the evening wound down fairly quickly. The brothers each took a seat at the front of the stage to pose for selfies with the guests, smile for photos and short interviews with the working media, sign autographs, and generally press the flesh with industry high-rollers. By nine-thirty, the brothers and most of the invited guests had departed, leaving just the Red Dot staffers and a handful of die-hards to knock back a last cocktail or two and congratulate themselves on a most successful evening.

Before Maggie and I took off, I went over to check in with Devon to ask whether there was anything else he needed me to do. There wasn't, so I said goodnight, he said thanks, I grabbed a couple of goodie bags, and Maggie and I went back to her apartment, where, much later, we fell asleep looking out her bedroom window at the lights of the city.

Chapter Ten

The next morning, I was up early and, while Maggie was still in bed, I headed for the guest shower to get cleaned up so I could start my day. On my way to the bathroom, I stopped to wish a good morning to Stanley, who was headed in the opposite direction, no doubt to rouse his mistress so she could fill his bowls with fresh food and water. When I bent down to scratch him behind his ears, something I'd figured out he would tolerate me doing, I felt a stabbing pain in my chest, something much more intense than I had ever experienced before. And just like that, I lost consciousness and plopped unceremoniously over, landing on top of Stanley.

* * *

When I woke up, I was flat on my back on an uncomfortable bed in what I learned was a triage room at St. Thomas Hospital. There was an oxygen mask strapped to my face, a blood pressure cuff on my arm, and a pulse oximeter clipped to my left index finger to measure my heart rate and oxygen saturation. My first instinct was to try to get up, but Maggie, who had apparently been sitting there with me since I arrived, pushed me back down with a firm hand.

"Just stay right where you are, Bucko. I'll let the doctor know you're back among the living."

I used my free hand to lift the oxygen mask away from my face. "Where am I? And what happened?"

"You're in the hospital. Saint Thomas, since you claim you used to be a Catholic. And what happened is, you took a header, right on top of the cat. She gave me a sweet smile. "Stanley is just fine, thanks for asking. At first, I thought you'd somehow tripped over him, but since you were unconscious, I called nine-one-one. You've been out like a light for the past two hours. I have to say, you caused quite a stir when they wheeled you out through the lobby."

"Well, I'm fine now, so let me get my clothes and let's get the hell out of here."

"Nope, not until we find out why you keeled over like that. Until we do, you need to just sit tight."

"Not a chance," I said. "We're leaving." I tried sitting up again, and immediately the room started to spin crazily, and my vision got a little bit blurry.

Okay, so maybe I'm not as tough as I'd like to believe.

Again, Maggie gave me a firm push back onto the bed. "No. We. Are. Not. Or, at least, you're not." She gave me a look that I read as something like, *just try to get past me.*

"What you are going to do right now is listen to me. I signed on with you, what's it been now, five years ago? And regardless of what you think about this situation, I'm not about to stand by while you walk out of this hospital without either of us knowing what got you here in the first place. So, until a doctor says you can go home, you just sit back, relax, and enjoy the flight. Besides, I have it on good authority that St. Thomas's green jello is the best in the city."

When I didn't say anything, Maggie said, "Understood?"

I did. And that was that.

* * *

And so, I spent the rest of Sunday being poked, prodded, and otherwise examined, as doctors tried to figure out what had caused me to collapse on top of Maggie's cat. There were a lot of questions:

"Do you smoke?"

"No."

"Drugs?"

"No."

"Do you drink?"

"Some."

"How much is 'some.'"

"Some is not a lot."

"Okay, we can come back to that. What were you doing when you lost consciousness?"

"Petting the cat."

"Good thing you weren't at the top of an extension ladder. Is there a history of heart problems in your family?"

"Yes. My father died when I was in high school. My mother followed, a few years after that. However, both were smokers, and both were alcoholics."

Then there were tests, including multiple blood draws, to look for God-know-what disorders. And, of course, because I had complained of chest pain, there was a growing suspicion I had something wrong with my heart. That meant a cardiac MRI to look for an incipient aneurysm. Next, there was an electrocardiograph to examine heart function. And finally, they did a coronary angiogram, and, boom, there it was. They found what they were looking for.

The cardiologist, a compact black man with what I found out later was a Nigerian accent, dressed in sharply creased slacks, a white shirt with a rep tie, and a white lab coat, and whose name I had a hard time pronouncing, visited me late in the afternoon.

"Got your test results here, Mr. Gamble. The reason you felt chest pain and passed out is that you have nearly complete blockages in two of your coronary arteries. That needs to be fixed right away, so we're going to give you a couple of stents, first thing tomorrow. And, so you don't get all stressed out, the procedure is not at all complicated. We'll give you something to make you drowsy, then insert the stents through your femoral artery. You won't feel a thing, and if everything looks good, you'll be able to go home later that afternoon. We'll also give you a prescription for a blood thinner and something else to reduce your cholesterol. And I want to be clear about this. I get complaints about how much this medicine or that one costs, but if you skip the blood thinner, you run the risk of something called stent thrombosis. Basically, that means blood components start to accumulate in the stent, causing the artery to clog. That will kill you, and pretty quickly, so you'll probably have to take these meds for the rest of your life."

He paused to check something on the clipboard he was holding. "Also, your blood pressure is too high. One-seventy-five over one hundred. That will also take time off the back end of your life if we don't get that under control, so I'll give you a prescription you can take for that. And, since you'll be on blood thinners, it would help immensely if you didn't get shot again."

When I raised my eyebrows at that, he said, "I saw the scar on your arm, and then I looked to see whether you've been here before, and what do you know? You're kind of a frequent flyer around these parts. Gunshot wound, about two years ago, right? And then, last year, there was something about your car getting blown up and nearly taking you with it. It seems like a lot of people want to kill you. Are you with the police, or maybe some kind of a gangster that you attract that kind of attention?"

"Used to be. With the police, that is. I'm a PI, now," I said. "Most of the time, what I do is pretty tame. Not like on television. It doesn't usually involve any gunplay or high explosives."

"Well, it's a good thing. If you were still a police officer, I'd recommend asking for reassignment to desk duty, because if you take a bullet in a vital spot while you're on blood thinners, you'll likely bleed out pretty quickly. Also, you obviously have friends in the right places, because I didn't find any of the usual paperwork that accompanies admission for a gunshot wound. Maybe you should think about another line of work."

Maybe I should at that.

After a few more minutes, a nurse came in brandishing yet another clipboard.

"Got a few more questions for you, Mr. Gamble. We couldn't get quite everything when you checked in."

"Okay."

"Actually," and here she paused to look over the form, "there are just two more things. Are you on any medications right now?"

"No."

"Well, I see here that's gonna change right quick. Also, I need a name for medical consent, in case we need to treat you and you're unconscious or unable to communicate. Is there a family member we should contact?"

"The contact is Doctor Margaret Totten." I spelled it for her.

"You said 'doctor'. Is she your primary care doctor?"

"No. She's a PhD. And she's my partner."

"You mean, like a business partner? Does she work with you?"

I gave Maggie a long look. "No. She's my life partner."

* * *

That night, Maggie stuck around until visiting hours were over, keeping me company while we watched television and made small talk, both of us avoiding any discussion of my upcoming procedure and the prognosis thereafter. At about nine o'clock, another nurse came in, and for what seemed like the twentieth time that day, she took my blood pressure. Then she gave me some meds, Heparin as a blood thinner, and Amlodipine, which was what they decided I needed for my BP. She followed that up with a tranquilizer, which almost immediately made me drowsy. I dimly remembered Maggie giving me a kiss on the forehead before she left.

Early the next morning, I was wheeled into an OR, given a mild sedative, and had two stents inserted into my cardiac arteries. By nine o'clock, I was back in my room, and was informed by the doctor that everything had gone well. I could leave, he said, any time after lunch, but with a caution to take it easy for the next couple of days. Around four o'clock, after I'd had a shower, Maggie brought me a clean change of clothes, and we went back to her apartment. On the way, in the car, she asked, "So, what did the doctor tell you?"

"He said I should try not to get shot again."

"Always good advice. Anything else?"

"Not that I can remember, other than I should take it easy for a few days. Oh, and maybe I should try to find a different kind of job. Something less strenuous."

"I see. So, in other words, I'm going to have to stick to the basics with you in the future. You know, we can't have you conking out just when things are beginning to get exciting."

"I don't think he was talking about that. Of course, if you'd like to give it a try, I'm willing to give it a shot."

"Sorry, not tonight. Tonight, it's early to bed. And no strenuous activity."

After that, we had a light snack, and then I slept the rest of the afternoon and well into the evening. The next morning, I was feeling good, almost as if nothing had ever happened. I was ready to whip my weight in wildcats.

Chapter Eleven

T he morning after the hospital cut me loose, I was on the phone to Devon Sharpe. I wanted to find out if he knew why Jason Mackey hadn't performed with the other studio musicians at the showcase event for the Braxton Brothers.

"I couldn't tell you. He was supposed to be here. We'd already cut a check. He just didn't show up. At first, we weren't too concerned. We assumed he was working a recording session, and it's not unusual for them to run late. But then it got close to showtime, so we just grabbed one of the guys who was hanging around the studio and put him to work. His name is Billy Watkins. He was pretty good, didn't you think? We use him for a lot of our sessions."

"He was fine," I said. "It's just that I really needed to talk to Jason Mackey. For the moment, he's the only lead I have on that missing person case I'm working on."

"Well, we had him on this morning's schedule for one of our sessions, but he didn't show up, and he didn't answer when we called, so we snagged Billy Watkins again. I guess you could try giving him a call. I did give you his number, right?"

He had, and I tried it again right after I hung up. When I got no answer, I decided to drive over to the address I'd gotten from Devon when I had spoken to him last week. Of course, I didn't know whether the guy was married, or had a roommate, or if he was just somebody who mostly worked nights and slept during the day following, and kept his phone turned off to avoid being awakened by pesky telemarketers. But I still needed to talk to him.

The Hillsboro Pike complex wasn't a big one, and I had no trouble finding the unit number I was looking for. Unfortunately, neither had the police, who had already showed up in force. In addition to the sizeable crowd gathered on the sidewalk outside the apartment building, there were two radio cars, plus what I knew was an unmarked detectives' Dodge Charger. There was also a van from the medical examiner's office, and a "Television News 4" vehicle parked next to the curb. That meant somebody was dead, and I had a sinking feeling I knew who it was. I thought about turning around and going back to the office, but if I was right about who had gotten dead, I knew the cops would dump the guy's phone and come looking for me anyway, since it would show at least a half-dozen calls from me. And so, I parked my car and walked over to see what was going on. I got as far as the line of yellow crime scene tape before a very large uniformed Metro PD cop with an appropriately large right hand stopped me.

"I'm afraid this is as far as you go for right now, sir. This is a crime scene."

"As in 'crime scene,' you mean there's been a murder." He looked at me, hard, as if I had just jumped to the top of the list of possible suspects. I showed him my identification.

"I used to be on the job. I'm here to talk to an individual named Jason Mackey…or am I too late for that?"

"Wait here." He turned and went inside the building. It took maybe five minutes before he returned, this time with a detective following him. The detective's name was Lorraine Proctor. Proctor and I had crossed paths several times in the past, usually under less-than-optimal circumstances. She hadn't changed much since the last time we'd spoken, which was about a year earlier. She was WNBA-tall and slender, with close-cropped dark hair and eyes, and a coffee-with-cream complexion. She wore a tan, lightweight jacket over an off-white blouse, brown slacks, and Sketcher soft-soled shoes, for the moment covered with blue disposable crime-scene booties. And she wore a .40 caliber Glock on her hip.

"Mister Gamble," she said when she spotted me. "It's been a while. What brings you to our humble crime scene?"

"Maybe nothing. I didn't know there was a crime scene until just now."

She gave me a look of mild amusement. "Mister Gamble, one thing I've learned about you. Any time there's a body and you within the same zip code, there's a connection. And since you didn't answer my question, I'll ask you again. Why are you here?"

"There's a guy I need to talk to. It's got to do with a case I'm working on."

"I see. And that case would be?"

"Does it matter?"

"It might. Who is it you're looking for?"

"His name is Jason Mackey. I have a source says he lives in this building."

"And there you go."

"Wait a minute." I tried to look surprised. "Jason Mackey is your vic?"

"Quite a coincidence, don't you think? Someone got here ahead of you, and unless you're here to conduct a séance, Mr. Mackey won't be talking with you or anyone else ever again."

"How did it happen?"

"I don't know why I bother messing around with you." She dug into her jacket pocket and pulled out a spare pair of crime-scene booties. "C'mon in. You might as well see for yourself. And do not touch anything."

I followed her up the sidewalk, through the front door, and into a carpeted hallway. I slipped on the booties, and Proctor replaced the pair she'd worn when she came outside to meet me. Up and down the hallway, two MNPD uniforms were knocking on doors, looking for possible witnesses. Meanwhile, another uniformed officer stood outside an apartment numbered 4A. He asked to see my identification, and then logged me in.

Mackey's apartment was a two-bedroom unit, sparsely decorated, if that's the right word, with single-guy-type furnishings. There was a dark brown, leather-covered couch and a matching recliner that faced a massive, flat-screen television mounted on one wall. Hanging on the opposite wall was an acoustic guitar autographed by Stevie Ray Vaughn, and a handful of framed photos with Jason Mackey, I supposed, since I'd never actually met him, mugging it up with various celebrities. There was also a distinct odor which,

I knew from experience, meant that the body, whose ever it was, had been there for some time.

In the kitchen, I saw the usual array of appliances—toaster, microwave, coffeemaker—plus a table and chairs and a small desk piled high with what looked like unopened mail and magazines, including *Music Inc.*, *Music Week*, *Rolling Stone,* and *Billboard*. Jason Mackey was evidently a guy who liked to keep up with industry trends.

"In here." Proctor pointed toward the smaller of the two bedrooms. "You may want to use some of this." She handed me a small jar of Vicks. I used my finger to smear a dab of it under my nose. It wasn't perfect, but it would help mask the smell of decomposing flesh.

In the bedroom were two more uniformed cops, plus a tech with a video camera recording the scene, and a guy from the ME's office dressed in Tyvek coveralls. At the moment, he was bending over the body of a late thirtyish man. He was lying face down in a dried pool of his own blood. What I could see of his face was swollen and discolored past the point of recognition, the result of being shot in the head, probably with a small-caliber bullet. There was no apparent exit wound. He was dressed in gray sweat pants, white socks, no shoes, and a white, long-sleeved t-shirt with a large red circle on the back that read "Red Dot Records."

I looked around for another detective. Ordinarily, Proctor partnered with an older homicide cop named John Spillner, who had been around, it seemed, since the dinosaurs roamed the earth. Today, he was nowhere in sight.

"You flying solo these days, Detective Proctor?"

"Just for a few days. I'll have Detective Spillner back as soon as he gets out of the hospital. He's got a kidney stone, he says hurts like hell." She gave a small shrug. "I wouldn't know about those. I guess they're more of a guy thing."

"Well, when you see him, give him my best." I walked over to take a look at the body. "You got a TOD yet?"

"He's out of rigor, and that plus lividity and the state of decomposition suggests three days at least, maybe four. So, until we get a full workup, that puts it sometime late Friday or early Saturday. Of course, that's just a guess until we get the examiner's complete report."

I nodded. That, at least, explained why Mackey had missed his gig at the Braxton Brothers' coming-out party.

I had seen dead bodies before, both during the time I was with the cops, and later during the dozen or so years I've spent as a private investigator. Sometimes, they look relatively peaceful, as if whatever they'd left behind during their lives was less preferable than wherever they'd gone in death. Usually, these were deaths from natural causes, such as a prolonged illness. As a uniformed, first-on-the-scene cop, I had been summoned to my share, and more of scenes like that.

Other times, the deaths were violent, the result of a traffic accident, or a fall from a height, or, in a few instances, suicide or intentional murder. Sometimes their deaths were fairly recent, other times their bodies had not been discovered until much after their lives had been lost. Those people rarely looked at peace. Whomever I was looking at now—presumably Jason Mackey—fit into that category.

"This the individual you were you coming to see? According to the apartment manager, this is Jason Mackey. There's some mail on the kitchen table addressed to him, and what we can see of him matches the description on his driver's license."

"Then it probably is him, but if you're asking for a formal identification, I can't help you. I've never actually met the guy. All I ever saw was his picture, and that was taken a dozen years ago. You'd have better luck talking to somebody at one of the record companies. He's a session man, and from what I hear, he's very well-regarded on the Row, so you shouldn't have any trouble finding someone who knew him."

"Then you've never been in this apartment before? We aren't going to find your fingerprints on any of the surfaces?"

"No, and no."

"And you definitely don't know for sure who this is."

"Like I said, I've never met him. But I do have a question for you. Or is this where you say, 'We're asking the questions here?'"

"We'll see. What have you got?"

"For starters, is this how you found him?"

"Yes. And as you can see, he took a single bullet to the back of the head. He's facing away from the door, so that means whoever killed him first marched him in here at gunpoint. Either that, or else he knew his killer and wasn't worried about turning his back. No matter which, he was shot at close range, so whoever pulled the trigger couldn't have been more than a step or two behind him." She paused, waiting, perhaps, to see if there was a reaction from me.

"We're just getting ready to roll him, if you want to take a look."

"Wouldn't do any good. In the shape he's in, he could be anybody. Did you find the murder weapon?"

"I'd say the shooter took it along. And no shell casing, either, so either a revolver or else the shooter was paying attention and cleaned up his brass. Anything else?"

"Yes. Did you find his phone?"

"We did, but it was turned off. Plus, it's password-protected, so we don't know for how long. Why? Do you think his killer made an appointment to drop by and then shoot him?"

The phone had been turned off. That was at least a partial explanation why my calls weren't getting through.

"Possible, I guess. Another thing. Why do you suppose he's in this room? I mean, it isn't the master. You think maybe he was in here with the killer, looking for something?"

"Could be, I guess." She made a show of looking at her watch. "That it?"

"Couple more things. First, can I ask how is it that you're here in the first place? I mean, somebody must have called you, unless nowadays you're just driving around knocking on doors looking for dead bodies."

"Across-the-hall neighbor called us. It seems when he came home late last night—he was in Atlanta visiting friends since last Tuesday. When he got home, he noticed an odor in the hallway. He didn't think anything of it, but then, when he went out this morning, it smelled even worse, so he went over to Mackey's apartment to ask if he knew what it was. He thought maybe a toilet had backed up, something like that. He knocked, and got no answer, but the door wasn't locked, so he went in, you know, to find out if anything was wrong."

"And obviously, there was."

"No putting one past you, is there? So, he called, and we came running."

"And you checked him out?"

"You mean the neighbor? We're working on it. If his story about being in Atlanta is on the level, and if the ME is right about Mackey being killed four days ago, that eliminates him as a suspect. And besides, he said he and Mackey barely knew one another, so it's not like they had some kind of a feud going on. We'll dig into it a little more, but I don't think he's our guy."

I couldn't argue with that. "Okay, last question. I imagine your people have had a chance to look around a little bit, and I was wondering. Is there any indication that the late Mr. Mackey might have had a wife, or maybe a live-in girlfriend? You know, photos, or anything like that?"

"We haven't completely tossed the place yet. But as far as I can tell, this is strictly a bachelor pad, if people still use that term. Why? Does this have something to do with the case you're working on?"

"Maybe, maybe not. I'm just trying to get a clearer picture of his situation." When I didn't offer any more information, she gave me a look that said she absolutely wasn't buying everything I was telling her, but that, for the time being at least, further discussion would have to wait."

"Then I guess we're done here. Or at least you are, unless you want to confess to the murder. If not, I'd appreciate it if you could come by the station tomorrow morning to make a formal statement. And while we're about it, I think I'd like to know a little bit more about this case you're working on."

I wanted to ask if it would be okay to take a minute to look around the apartment, but I was pretty sure she wouldn't go for it. And then I had a thought. I squirmed a little and tried to put an uncomfortable look on my face.

"Okay if I use the washroom before I go?"

She handed me a pair of surgical gloves before pointing at a spot behind me. "It's through the other bedroom. And put these on before you flush.

Fingerprints, you know."

I slipped on the gloves and went down the hall into the other bedroom. I figured I had no more than a minute or two before she started wondering what was taking me so long, so I had to move quickly. In addition to a nightstand on either side of a king-sized bed, Jason Mackey kept a desk and a computer in his bedroom. There were also a couple of guitars, one electric and one acoustic, leaning in a corner. I wasn't interested in any of that, though. I wanted to get a look in the desk drawers.

I hit paydirt on the first try, as the middle drawer held a number of items, including a monthly date book, a notepad, a box of paperclips, some business cards, a pair of scissors, a checkbook, a small flashlight, a roll of postage stamps, and, wouldn't you know it, a pocket-sized address book. I scooped that up and put it in my jacket pocket. Then I went into the bathroom and flushed the toilet.

After that, I wanted to get out of there as quickly as possible. I was hoping there might have been something more in the closet, like maybe a box of old demo tapes, that might help me connect Mackey to any of the other members of Midnite Oil. But I'd have to figure out a way to come back later and check on that. Besides, I knew that anything I found, including the address book, would be off-limits to me as far as the cops were concerned. And either way, I was already out of time. As it was, if Proctor found out I had grabbed the address book, she could very easily charge me with tampering with evidence. So instead of spending any more time looking, I walked back out to the living room, where a couple of the ME's people were getting ready to place Jason Mackey's remains into a body bag.

I gave Proctor a wave and promised I would come by her office the next morning. And then I got the hell out of there and drove back to the office, where I put my crappy copier/printer/scanner to work copying every page in Jason's address book. I knew that the cops likely would not notice right away there should have been one in Mackey's desk, since these days, most people keep their contact list on their telephone. But eventually, they'd start to wonder, and then it would occur to them that maybe the person they should be talking to was me.

Chapter Twelve

The first thing I checked in Jason Mackey's address book was whether there was an entry of any kind that might connect me with Annie Harris. That was a dead end. There was no one named Harris listed on the "H" page, and no one on any page with the name Annie, or Annamaria, or anything even close. That meant I would have to continue my search the long way around.

And so, over the next three hours, I went through all the names on all the pages. I spoke to receptionists, producers, HR staff members, and sometimes I just left messages on voicemail. Regardless, after more than two dozen telephone calls to recording studios, independent producers, and publicists in and around Nashville, I got no useful information regarding the fate of Midnite Oil or a vocalist named Annie Harris. That made me think that neither the group nor their singer had ever progressed much past the stage of being just another bar band, one that had never gotten so much as a sniff from any of the major, or even mid-level labels.

On the other hand, there were lots of other companies in other cities I could have tried, including Memphis, Muscle Shoals, Miami, Austin, and even Los Angeles. However, I doubted whether Midnite Oil would have had the wherewithal to travel to any of those places, except maybe Memphis or Muscle Shoals, without the backing of somebody with deep pockets. I remembered that, back in the early days of punk rock, Hilly Kristal, the proprietor of the famed CBGB nightclub in New York City, nearly went broke backing a punk band from Cleveland called The Dead Boys, whose career pancaked off the end of the runway after two unmemorable albums,

Young Loud and Snotty and *We Have Come for Your Children*. At that, compared to Midnite Oil, the Dead Boys were shoo-ins for the Rock and Roll Hall of Fame. At least they had cut a couple of records and toured around for a while.

By four-thirty, I was tired and frustrated, and my ear was starting to hurt from having a telephone receiver pressed up against it. That, plus the fact that going-home traffic was starting to pick up in a big way, meant it was time to call it a day. And then I remembered the telephone number that Madelaine Miles had written on the back of my hand the night before, and that I had transferred onto a slip of paper and then tossed into my top desk drawer. I was rummaging around looking for it when my telephone rang.

"Mister Gamble, this is Geoffrey Tate." He pronounced it "Joffrey." I hadn't noticed that earlier. "How are you coming with your search for Annamaria Harris? I was hoping you could give me a favorable progress report. After all, as I'm sure I don't have to remind you, the meter is running."

"Yes, sir, I'm aware of that. But I'm afraid that so far, I can't give you or Mr. Harris any encouraging news. I did have a lead. I was able to identify an individual named Jason Mackey, who was one of Annamaria's bandmates. My plan was to speak with him earlier today. Unfortunately, when I arrived at his apartment, the police had gotten there ahead of me."

"You mean they arrested him?" The tone of his question made it sound very much as if he smelled a possible client coming his way. "What is he accused of?"

"Nothing. They didn't arrest him. They took him to the morgue with a bullet in his head, so I guess you could say he was accused of being dead. He was shot and killed sometime late last week. He was supposed to be performing at a recording company event on Saturday night, but he didn't make it. I had planned to talk to him at that time, but since he didn't show, I decided to pay him a visit."

"Please tell me you haven't mentioned any of this to Harvey Harris."

"No, I haven't. I was waiting until I had some better news."

"Then leave it that way. We didn't discuss this earlier, but I would prefer you leave any communication with Mr. Harris to me. Please do not contact him directly."

"I'm not sure I can do that, Mr. Tate. After all, Harvey Harris is the client."

"That may be, but I'm the one paying your fees, and you would do well to keep that in mind. Unless, of course, you have another well-paying assignment you can begin to work on." And with that, he hung up.

* * *

Later, after I'd gone home to shower and change clothes, so that I didn't bring the odor of death along on our date, I met Maggie at a downtown restaurant. After we ordered drinks, I got around to telling her about my day. However, I left out the part about swiping Jason Mackey's address book out from under the noses of the cops. In case they ended up talking to her later, I thought it would be better if she didn't have to lie about me telling her I'd taken it. Even at that, though, my story wasn't going over very well.

"Why don't we take this from the top," she said, sounding neither impressed nor entertained. "We already know you got hired by a triple-murderer who is now on death row and who wants you to find his daughter—Annamaria, right? And his lawyer is paying your fees?"

"Yes, except from what I was told, his daughter goes by Annie."

"All right, Annie. Thanks for clearing that up. And then the very first lead you turn up is found a few days later, shot to death in his own apartment. Do I have that part right?"

"More or less, except the client isn't on death row any longer. His sentence was commuted to life without parole."

"Because he has terminal cancer, and the state figured he'd die faster on his own than if he lived long enough to be executed. That makes all the difference in the world. And why is this attorney paying your fee? Does this guy—what's his name again?"

"The lawyer or the client?"

"The client. I don't care about the lawyer."

"Harvey Harris."

"Right, okay. As you can tell, I'm having trouble keeping all this straight.

So, unless this guy Harvey Harris has some kind of a trust fund, where is the money coming from to pay you for the work you're doing? And if he does have his own money, what was he doing holding up a convenience for a few bucks and a twelve-pack of beer?"

"Don't forget the scratchers," I said.

"Oh, well then, you're right. I guess that explains it. Forget I asked."

I made a what-can-you-do movement with my hands. "Look, I don't pretend to understand this any better than you do. As far as I know, Harvey's lawyer—his name is Geoffrey Tate, in case I didn't already mention it—Harvey's lawyer is paying the bill out of his own pocket, although I don't have the first idea why."

"Well, don't you think you ought to find out?"

"Working on it." I caught the waiter's eye and signaled for another round of drinks—an appletini for Maggie and, since they didn't have Stella, a Rolling Rock for me. "Also, if you're interested in cashing in on my client's apparently bottomless financial resources, there's something you can help me with."

She raised her right eyebrow a fraction of an inch. "And that would be?"

"I spoke with Annamaria's mother the other day. She wasn't any help, although I got the impression she knew more than she was telling me, which was nothing. However, she did let me take a quick look in Annamaria's old bedroom."

"And did you paw through her underwear drawer?"

"I thought about it, but it seemed tacky. I did manage to snag her senior class high school yearbook. You know, the one that has the blank pages for your BFFs to sign and leave cutesy farewell messages on the last day of school."

"Okay."

"And I thought, if you have some time and you're willing, you could maybe look through all the messages and pick out the ones that sounded like they might have been written by friends who Annamaria would have been especially close with."

"What makes you think I could do that any better than you can?"

"Why else? Because you're better at girl talk than I am."

When she didn't say anything, I went on. "Look, this lawyer is paying me my regular rate to work this case. I'm sure I could add whatever time you put into the bill."

"I don't need a PI license to do that?"

"Did Effie Perrine need a license to help Sam Spade?"

"Who?"

Not a fan.

"You can name your price."

"Who knew detective work could be so lucrative?" We waited while our second round of drinks arrived and the waiter took our dinner order.

"So, what happens next?"

"Next, I've been invited to show up tomorrow morning at police headquarters to give a statement regarding the dead guy's connection to the case I'm working on. There isn't very much I can tell them, other than Annamaria and this Jason Mackey—that's the dead guy, in case you forgot—the two of them used to be in a band together, and they might have been an item for a while. I had hoped that maybe they'd stayed in touch, and he might know where I could find her."

"Maybe he did know. And maybe that's why somebody killed him." She took a sip of her appletini. "In case you haven't figured it out already, you should know from experience that there is something very wrong with this case. I'm not sure what is, but from what you've been telling me, something seems off." She took another sip and gave me a look over the rim of the glass.

"You do know that, don't you? And when you finally get to the end of it, you must also know it's almost certainly going to turn out to be something very ugly."

"Well," I said, "don't they always?"

Chapter Thirteen

The next day started off badly and got worse as it went along. First, I got stuck in a three-mile-long traffic backup on Interstate 65 heading into downtown. I had planned to make an early start so I could pay a visit to Devon Sharpe at Red Dot before his day got too crazy. My hope was that he could match one or two of the names I'd copied from Jason Mackey's address book with former members of his old band. Unfortunately, the backup on 65 turned out to be the result of an overturned tractor-trailer rig that brought traffic to a complete standstill for better than two hours until a TDOT cleanup crew finally got things moving again. By the time I got to the Red Dot studio on Music Row, it was ten-thirty, and Devon wastied up in a meeting that his administrative assistant told me, since she had already ordered in lunch, would probably run into the afternoon. It must have been important, because no amount of cajoling on my part was able to persuade her to drag him out, even for just a few minutes.

Since it didn't appear there would be any use hanging around waiting for Devon's meeting to wind up, I got back in the car and drove over to police headquarters on Murfreesboro Pike. As usual, there was no place close where I could park, and so I ended up leaving my car half a block away on Polk Avenue. Fortunately, it was a pleasant day, and I didn't mind the walk.

I checked in with the desk sergeant and informed him that Detective Proctor was expecting me. He asked me to wait while he confirmed my appointment, then pointed to a doorway at the end of the reception area.

"She says to tell you you're late."

I found Lorraine Proctor seated at her desk in a bullpen area. At that moment, hers was the only occupied desk. The rest of the detective division was either on an early lunch break or else running down wrong-doers in a city that had become increasingly violent in the last several years. I had recently seen a statistic indicating that the murder rate in Nashville, including deaths by gunfire, knifings, vehicular homicides, arson, and "other"—whatever that meant—was up nearly nine percent over the previous year, with the most dangerous neighborhoods clustered in the north and northwest side of the city. That made the murder of Jason Mackey something of an outlier, as the area around Green Hills was considered relatively safe by comparison. I wondered if Detective Proctor had any thoughts about that.

"Mister Gamble," she said when she spotted me. "I expected you first thing this morning."

"You never said what time. I had a couple of errands to run."

She glanced at her watch and then motioned me into the visitor's chair next to her desk. "It's almost noon, and I've got things to do, so what do you say we get right to it? First thing. We now have a positive identification on the body we found yesterday. It's definitely Jason Mackey, and he was killed with a single shot to the back of the head with a .22 caliber bullet. A hollow-point. We didn't find a shell casing, so we don't know if it was a revolver or an autoloader, although let's face it. Who uses a revolver anymore?"

"Okay, so then, what do you need me for?"

She leaned back in the chair and crossed one leg over the other. "You mentioned you were looking for the late Mr. Mackey in connection with a case you were working on. I was thinking you could tell me a little bit about that."

I thought about giving her a line of bullshit, just in case there was more to Mackey's death than what she was telling me, but then I decided, why bother? As far as I knew, I wasn't involved in anything illegal. And even if I was, my fee was being paid by a highly-regarded attorney, so what was there to worry about?

I said, "I'm looking for a young woman. Well, maybe not so young anymore.

Her name is Annamaria Harris, although as I understand it, she mostly goes by Annie. Her father lost touch with her some years ago, and now he wants to reconnect with her."

"And her father is?" I have dealt with Lorraine Proctor on several occasions, and it never fails to impress me how she is able to keep her tone of voice even and non-accusatory, and still somehow manages to convey the impression that she not only knows the person she is speaking to is guilty of something, but that she also knows exactly what it is.

What the hell? Let's find out.

I said, "His name is Harvey Harris."

"Never heard of him. Who is he?"

"Before your time, most likely. He's a lifelong fuckup who was convicted of a triple homicide several years ago and wound up on death row at Riverbend. But now he's got pancreatic cancer, and he's dying." I shrugged. "From the way he looks, I'd say he's got a month or two at the most. He's at Whiteville now, in medium-security, waiting until his time runs out."

"And this has what to do with the late Jason Mackey?"

"The way I got it, Annie Harris and Jason Mackey were an item a dozen years ago, when they were together in a band called Midnite Oil. Since nobody else, including Annie's mother, seems to have stayed in touch with her, I thought Mackey might be able to point me in the right direction. But the band broke up about that same time, and for all I know, none of the members has seen each other since."

"Yeah, it does seem like kind of a stretch, unless…." She picked up a pencil and began tapping it on the top of her desk. "Any chance Mackey was killed because somebody doesn't want this Annie Harris found?"

"The thought had crossed my mind."

"Well, all right, then. Now, we're getting someplace. Care to speculate who this 'somebody' might be?"

"I wouldn't have the first idea. Oh, and by the way." I took Jason Mackey's address book out of my jacket pocket and laid it on her desk. "Funny thing. I found this next to one of your cruisers in the parking lot outside your victim's apartment. I didn't think anything of it at the time, but then I wondered if maybe it might be important to your investigation."

"You found it. In the parking lot. And you didn't turn it over right away." She threw me a look that could have made a dead man sit up in his coffin and pay attention. "How do you suppose it got lost in the parking lot?"

"No idea," I said. "Maybe the killer dropped it on his way out."

"That must be it," she said, in a tone that made it clear she wasn't buying a word of anything I'd said. "But if you happen to think of a better explanation, be sure to give us a call. And another thing. You're looking for this woman, not trying to grease your way into a homicide investigation, right? I mean, I don't have to remind you, you don't carry a badge. Because if you forget, and you get in our way, or worse yet, screw things up, well, we wouldn't take kindly to it."

"Understood."

"Good. Oh, and by the way, before I forget, how's your lady friend getting along? I know she was cleared, but that was a bad business with her and her ex-husband last year." She shook her head slowly. "You know, Mr. Gamble, all things considered, I'd say your Ms. Totten has had something of a bumpy ride since she hooked up with you. Two killings she was involved in, plus a half-dozen more bodies you've left in your wake, and that's just in the short time since you two have been together."

I said, "Your point?"

"Just this. I've been a cop for going on thirteen years. I worked patrol, I went undercover with narcotics, I worked vice, and now homicide, and I have never so much as pointed my weapon at a suspect. You, on the other hand, are like a cadaver dog. Wherever there's a body, sooner or later, you turn up, too."

"Maybe it's just bad timing."

"Maybe. But I hate to think that one of these days, some of that timing is going to spill over onto your lady even more than it already has. Because I don't think that would be something even you could live with."

Chapter Fourteen

I walked out of police headquarters feeling like I had come away with a draw. On the one hand, I was able to hand over the Mackey address book without getting arrested for withholding evidence or obstructing a homicide investigation. On the other, I didn't know anything more about the possible whereabouts of Annie Harris than I did when I got out of bed this morning. In addition, even though there might not have been a connection, I also didn't learn anything more about the Mackey killing. And although Detective Proctor hadn't come right out and said so, I got the distinct impression the cops didn't have any more of a clue than I did who might have killed him. Well, okay, that was their problem, not mine. I still had a missing woman to track down, and an impatient client to keep at arm's length until I was able to do so.

When I got back to the office, the message light on my desk phone was flashing. I pressed the "play" button.

"Mister Gamble, this is Todd Neely from Mix Masters. After you called yesterday, I got to thinking. So, I started looking through some old files we keep here. I found a reservation form for a session we were scheduled to do with that band you were asking about, that Midnite Oil. I don't know if it will help you, but if you want, you can come by, and I'll make you a copy. It's got a couple signatures on it, so maybe one of them is the person you're looking for."

I called the number Todd had left, and was informed he had already gone for the day, but that he would be back in the studio first thing tomorrow. I had no idea whether what he had would be of any use, but at least if I got another telephone call from Geoffrey Tate demanding a progress report, I could tell him truthfully that I had a lead. After that, I tried calling Red Dot to see if I could make an appointment with Devon Sharpe. Nothing doing there, either, as his PA informed me that, like Todd from Mix Masters, Mr. Sharpe had left for the day. I checked my watch. Quarter to three. It made me wonder what kind of hours these music industry types kept, and how they were able to get away with it.

Just for the hell of it, and because it was still too early to call it a day, I tried dialing the number that Madelaine Miles had given me on Saturday night, when we were briefly together at the Braxton Brothers's coming-out party. I wasn't really looking for another case, but I was curious about the job she said she wanted me to do.

"Mister Gamble," she said when she picked up. "Thank you for calling. I actually would have telephoned you before this, but my husband and I were away on a short business trip."

"And now you're back."

"I am. Wilton, that's my husband, although he likes it better when people in the business call him Sonny. I don't think you met him the other night. Wilton is still in Memphis. I drove the car back this morning. Wilton is flying back sometime tomorrow."

"Okay."

"My husband is an artists' agent. He represents musical talent, including now the Braxton Brothers, whom you met the other night. Yesterday, we got a call from a producer in Memphis, whom we've worked with before, who said he had a singer he thought might be a good fit for Wilton's agency. Generally, when it's a woman, I go along. You know, just so there are no, what? No misunderstandings, especially after that ugly business a while back with that Hollywood agent."

I hadn't realized there was a C&W version of the infamous motion picture casting couch, but then, I supposed even the possibility that there might be such a thing could be cause for concern. After all, the music business, like the movie business, is tough. And sometimes people let themselves get taken advantage of if it moves them one step closer to getting that big break.

And since that was the case, having another female in the room during an interview was probably a good idea.

I said, "How can I help you, Mrs. Miles?"

There was a pause. "It's, I don't know, it's kind of embarrassing. I'm not sure how to explain this to you."

"Well, if it's discretion you're worried about, whatever you tell me stays between us, unless you decide otherwise, or unless you're involved in some kind of illegal activity."

"Excuse me?"

"I'm not an attorney, Mrs. Miles. That means there are no legal protections, like attorney-client privilege, that apply to anything you tell me. So, if you're about to confess to a crime, or if you're planning to commit one…."

"Oh," she said. "No. It's nothing like that. It's just that…Mr. Gamble, my husband thinks I'm cheating on him."

"I see. And are you?"

"No, of course not. But Wilton is nearly twenty years older than me, and he's away on business a great deal of the time. He's in Los Angeles, or New York, or Austin, or someplace else, sometimes two weeks out of every month. He has clients all over the country, and when he can, he likes to get together with them. Once in a while, he takes me along, like the other day when we were in Memphis. But most of the time, when he's gone, I'm here in town by myself, and I don't know. He gets these crazy ideas."

"Okay. Why do you think that is? I mean, are you doing anything— anything at all—that would make him suspicious?"

"Like what?"

"Well, for instance, do you go out at night by yourself and get home late? Or if he calls you or texts you, do you not answer? Or do you have people coming to the house when your husband is at work?"

"No, nothing like that. I just need…I need you to help me."

"Help you how, Mrs. Miles? I don't know who you've been talking to, or what you were told about what I do, but you should understand, first of all, I don't do matrimonial work. So, if you're thinking about asking your husband for a divorce and you need help digging up proof that he's in some way abusive, the best I can do is recommend another investigator."

"I can see I'm not making myself clear." A harder edge crept into her voice. "I love my husband, Mr. Gamble. I don't want a divorce. I just want to reassure Wilton that he can trust me."

"Well, then, it sounds like what you want me to do is prove a negative. Short of following you around twenty-four-seven every time your husband is out of town, I don't know how I could do that."

"But that's just it, you see. Wilton already has somebody doing that. What I want is for you to get rid of him."

"Okay," I said, confused. "I'm going to need some clarification here. Who is it you want me to get rid of? Your husband, or whoever it is, he's got following you around?"

"My stalker," of course, she said in a tone that conveyed her feeling that I might be more than a little dense. "I have never broken faith with my husband, and I resent the idea that I have to have somebody following me around every time I leave the house to prove it."

"Isn't that a conversation that you should be having with your husband? Or am I missing something here?"

"What you're missing is, I want this man, whoever he is, to stop following me around. I want him to tell my husband he has nothing to worry about, and that he should stop wasting his money paying people to spy on me."

"Right. So then, what do you want me to do?"

"I want you to find this man and talk to him. Or, I don't know, get in his car and ride along with him. Convince him to stop following me everywhere I go. Do whatever it takes, but please, get rid of him. I'll pay you whatever you ask. I just need this to stop."

"Well, as to that, I want to be clear right up front, my standard rate is five hundred dollars per day, plus expenses."

"Fine. I'll mail you a retainer in the morning. I just want you to stop this man following me, whoever he is."

"Okay, I can talk to him, maybe, and I can try to convince him to give it up, but I have to tell you that probably isn't going to work. I mean, whoever he is, I imagine he's also getting paid to do a job, and unless he's either easily frightened or exceptionally lazy, me talking to him isn't going to do much good. Plus, what you're asking me to do is more likely than not to reinforce the idea that you have something to hide." And then I had a thought.

"Can you describe the man you think is following you? Or maybe the car he drives?"

"I've never actually seen his face. It's only at night that he follows me. And as far as the car, I don't know for sure. It's a dark color, black or maybe dark gray."

"How about a license plate number?"

"No."

I said, "Mrs. Miles, do you go out a lot at night without your husband?"

There was a pause. "What are you implying?"

"Nothing. I'm simply asking a question."

"Then, to answer your question, you already know my husband is an important person in the music business. That means he's often out of town, or scouting new talent that takes him out in the evening. Rather than stay at home by myself, sometimes I visit friends or go to a movie. I also belong to a bridge club, and I go to Bible study." Her voice took on an edge. "Is there anything wrong with that?"

"All right," I said. "Let's do this. When will your husband be out of town, or working late next?"

"I don't know, but tomorrow night I have Bible study, so I'll be going out about six-thirty. Bible study starts at seven and runs until nine. After that, most times we stay after for another hour or so, maybe have a glass of wine and some crackers and cheese or something. It's just girl talk."

"Okay. What kind of a car do you drive?"

"A Mercedes-Benz. A convertible. I guess that's kind of a cliché for a wealthy woman, isn't it?"

I let that pass. "Give me your address. If this individual, whoever he is, follows you tomorrow night, I'll follow him, and maybe we can have a conversation. Depending on what he tells me, it's possible we can threaten him with stalking or harassment, and maybe that'll get rid of him. At least it's worth a shot. If that doesn't work, or if he doesn't go for the bluff, then I don't know what to tell you."

* * *

The following evening, after making my excuses to Maggie, who had made other plans for us, I parked at the end of the Brentwood cul-de-sac where Madelaine Miles's home was located. I killed the engine, sat back in my seat, and waited. Sure enough, at six-thirty sharp, her car, a yellow Mercedes-Benz cabrio, backed out of the driveway and headed out of the subdivision. When she got to Concord Road, she turned right and drove a short distance to a large Baptist church. There, she pulled into the parking lot and went inside, carrying a large plate of cookies or brownies, or whatever a group of women snack on after their Bible studies. One other car, a Lexus, was already there. Since it was silver and not dark blue or gray, I figured it must belong to the pastor, or one of the other members of her study group. I parked at the far end of the lot and waited. After that, several other cars arrived, nearly all of them driven by sleek, well-coiffed women who also went inside the church. Like Madelaine, some were carrying what looked like plates of cookies and small cakes.

Just to be doing something, since I figured to be sitting for at least two hours, I got out of my car and walked around the church building to the back, where there was a separate, smaller parking lot. I thought it likely that whoever was following Madelaine Miles would already be familiar with her routine. And to avoid being needlessly conspicuous, he might have just driven to the church ahead of her and waited for her to show up. Of course, that would run the risk of losing track of her altogether if she didn't come to Bible study. On the other hand, if she went somewhere other than home afterward, he'd be in a perfect position to follow her. But that didn't happen.

At nine forty-five, Madelaine Miles came back out, this time with an empty plate. She spent a few minutes talking to a couple of other women before she got into her car and drove back home. She didn't stop on the way, and nobody except me followed her in either direction.

And that was that. Driving home, I wondered if maybe I'd been played.

Chapter Fifteen

The next morning, I was on the phone to Todd from Mix Masters recording studio. He was in the office when I called. He told me he had a recording session scheduled for two-thirty, but he could see me any time between noon and two. I said I would be there. He gave me the address and directions where to park, and we hung up.

Since I had some time to kill before my appointment, I decided to see what I could find out about Wilton "Sonny" Miles. It didn't take a lot of effort, since our local print media routinely produce features on high-profile individuals in the music business. In thirty minutes' time, I found several items of interest in online editions of *Nashville Lifestyle*, a "food, fitness, entertainment, fashion, and culture" magazine, and *Nashville Music Guide*, "the most widely read music magazine in Music City." In no particular order, I learned Sonny Miles was born in Pine Bluff, Arkansas, in 1959. He attended a small, faith-based high school, from which he graduated in 1975. That same year, he enlisted in the Army, served a three-year stateside hitch, and then returned to Arkansas, where he earned a degree in communications at a branch of the University of Arkansas. After receiving his diploma, he moved to Nashville and went to work for a public relations firm, the starting point for his eventual transition into the music business.

I found another article in a magazine I had never heard of, called *Nashville Christian Living*, which ran a feature on Sonny's active support, through his agency, for various charitable activities of a Williamson County Church of Christ, where he was apparently an industrial-strength churchgoer. Curiously, none of the articles I read made any mention of his wife,

Madelaine, beyond the fact the couple had met and married in 2016. It was a first marriage for both of them. Nothing I read in any of the articles I searched mentioned anything about his apparent paranoia concerning his wife's daily comings and goings.

* * *

Nothing special to look at, the Mix Masters studio was located in a small, cinderblock building on Hayes Street, down the way from a couple of Broadway automobile dealerships. In other words, nowhere near Music Square, where the top-of-the-line studios are located. The sign above the door showed an electric mixer and a mixing bowl, with musical notes, sharps and flats, and a couple of treble-clef symbols rising out of the bowl. Very clever, I thought.

I left my car in a small lot around the corner on Church Street and entered through the front door. I found myself in a small reception area that held two chairs, an intercom speaker, and a magazine stand piled high with back issues of *Billboard, People,* and *Nashville Scene.* All of them looked to be at least a year old. Next to a windowless inner door was a button that I supposed was the way visitors announced their arrival. I pressed the button and waited. When nothing happened, I pressed it again. After another minute or so, the speaker crackled to life.

"Help you?"

"Jackson Gamble, to see Todd." When that got no response, I added, "He's expecting me."

Another minute passed, and then the door was opened by a tall, mid-forties guy who looked as if he had just stepped out of the 1960s. Full beard, wire-rimmed glasses, tie-dyed, long-sleeved T-shirt, sandals, and, so help me, bell-bottomed jeans. All that was missing was a string of colored beads hanging around his neck, granny glasses, and maybe a doobie stuck in the corner of his mouth.

"Mister Gamble," he said. "Todd Neely. Welcome to Mix Master." He led me through the doorway and into a small studio that featured walls covered with sound diffusers and bass traps. There were also a couple of freestanding reflection filters. The carpeted floor space was crammed with recording equipment, including a digital workstation, pre-amps, standard amplifiers, a power supply, microphones and headphones, cables, a master clock, and a lot of other stuff I didn't recognize. There were also a couple of items I expected to see, but didn't, including some kind of a keyboard and a drum kit.

Todd caught me looking around. "I bet I know what you're thinking."

"Think so?"

"Well, if you're like everybody else who comes in here the first time, you're wondering where all the instruments are. Actually, they're here, they're just all virtual. Drums, strings, keyboards, brass, woodwinds, you name it, they're all digitized in software packages that run through a computer."

I must have looked puzzled. "Let me give you the short course. You go to many live performances?"

"Once in a while." I wondered if the Braxton Brothers intro counted. "Not as many as I used to."

"Then you probably know that a live performance doesn't usually sound exactly like the song you hear on the radio. Also, unless you're talking about the Eagles, or ELO, or Chicago, groups like that, who're trained musicians, most bands who come into the studio aren't that good. They're just getting started. They're wanting to make a demo to take around to the record companies to see if they can get a deal. And they don't have the money to spend an entire day in the studio doing one take after another until they get it right. They also can't afford top-drawer session people who can get it right the first time. In a bar or someplace like that, when a band is performing live, nobody cares if they're not pitch-perfect, because both the band and the audience are in the moment, and there's a lot of background noise. But on a recording, it has to sound just right. So, to save money, we provide the backing tracks electronically and just let the vocalist do his thing. It's much less expensive, and it sounds a hundred percent better. Of course, if the headliner is a real virtuoso on whatever instrument he plays, then that person plays his part on the record."

"So, if a Vince Gill or a Floyd Cramer wandered in here, you'd let him play his own instrument."

"Vince, yes, and if Floyd clawed his way back from the grave, absolutely. But guys like that don't come along very often. And even then, it's not that simple." He seemed disappointed I didn't ask why not, so he went on.

"Okay, on a recording, sometimes one of the members of the band—take the lead guitarist, for example—sometimes, that guy will put down a lead track and then go back and overdub an acoustic track or a rhythm track. That works great, because here in the studio, we can mix all those tracks together. But when the band is on tour performing live, unless they take along a couple other guys, which they then have to pay to tour with them, that one guitarist can't play three tracks at one time. In that case, he plays one of the tracks, and the other two are recordings that are fed through the stage speakers. Those are called click tracks. Same thing with backing vocals or harmony parts. When those overdubs are played during a performance, the guys on the stage hear a 'click' through their inner-ear phones, so they're able to stay in time with the recording. We can also add what are called sweeteners, which are extra sound effects like car horns or birds singing. Stuff like that." There was a pause. "But then, that's not why you're here, is it? You wanted to know about Midnite Oil. Don't tell me they're planning to make a comeback."

"Nothing like that, no. I'm looking for someone who used to be part of the band. She's been out of touch with her family for several years, and they want to reconnect."

He shook his head. "Man, that's a tough one. I don't see how I can help you with that."

"It's like this. The person I'm looking for is named Annamaria Harris, although she went by Annie Harris back when she was with Midnite Oil. So far, I haven't had any luck finding anybody who can point me in the right direction, and I'm hoping one of the people who signed that contract with you might have stayed in touch with her."

"Well, let's take a look." I followed him into his office. He handed me a piece of paper dated eleven years ago. I didn't bother to read whatever it was the contract spelled out. Instead, I scanned down to the bottom, where there were two signatures. One read "Jason Mackey," the other "Johnny Walker."

"Johnny Walker," I said. "Is that his real name, or a stage name? I mean, was there a Jim Beam, or a Jack Daniels, or maybe a George Dickel in the band, too?"

"Couldn't tell you. Best I can remember, those two guys came in and said they wanted to book some studio time. I quoted them a price and told them I'd need a deposit to reserve the time. They said they'd get back to me, but then, that was the last I saw of them. I called a couple times to see if they were still interested, but all I ended up doing was leaving messages. So, I thought maybe they got an out-of-town gig someplace, and I'd hear from them when they got back.

"But you didn't."

"No, but I did hang on to the contract, you know, just in case. That was, well, you can see the date for yourself. It was a long time ago."

So Midnite Oil stayed together in some form, for at least a year or so after their appearance at Sharps and Flats. After that, well, maybe Johnny Walker could tell me where everybody went. I knew where Jason Mackey was, but he wasn't talking. Now I had to find Johnny Walker, hopefully, someplace other than on a shelf in a liquor store. It wasn't much of a lead, but it was something.

* * *

After finishing up at Mix Masters, I stopped for a quick lunch and then headed back to the office. I wanted to call Madelaine Miles and let her know that, as far as I could tell, nobody had followed her to her Bible study the night before except me. When I got her on the phone, she sounded distraught.

"Somebody followed me. Did you get a look at him?"

"Mrs. Miles, if someone other than me was following you, then they're pretty good at what they do, because I didn't see anything, and I've been doing this kind of work for a very long time. I even camped out in the parking lot at your church while you were inside. Nothing."

"But I saw that same car as before. It was right behind me. I know you don't believe me, but I'm sure I did."

"If you saw someone following you, that was almost certainly me." But I wondered. I thought I'd done a pretty good job of shadowing her, particularly since I knew where she was going and had no trouble taking alternate routes so that I could stay out of sight. So, could she have picked up a tail along the way without my noticing? And then I thought, maybe it was me she saw in her rear-view mirror. The Ford is a dark color, and doesn't have a body shape that makes it stand out from a thousand other cars on the road.

I said, "Mrs. Miles, is your husband back from Memphis?"

"No. He called. Something came up with a contract he was negotiating. He's taking a private flight. He won't be back until after midnight."

"Okay, let's do this, then." And I laid out a plan.

* * *

At seven forty-five, Madelaine Miles backed out of her garage and, as I had instructed her, drove toward a popular and pricey restaurant located near the Cool Valley Mall. I waited until she was a couple of blocks ahead of me, and then I fell in behind, being careful not to get close enough to catch the attention of anyone who might have also been following. When she turned onto Interstate 65 heading south, I held back a bit further, keeping her in sight, but again, leaving several hundred yards between her car and mine.

When I saw her pull into the restaurant parking lot, I drove around for a few minutes before stashing my own car outside a sporting goods store at the mall, but close enough that I could keep an eye on the front door of the restaurant. Then I waited.

Fifteen minutes later, after I saw no other single customers enter the restaurant, I got out of my car, walked back over to the restaurant, and took a seat at the bar. From where I was sitting, I could see Madelaine Miles at a table on the other side of the room. She was dressed pretty much the same as she had been the night of the reception for the Braxton Brothers:

81

a low-cut black dress trimmed in white, with three-quarter length sleeves, black nylons, and four-inch heels. If her objective was to look like a working girl, albeit a one that could only be had for upwards of a thousand bucks a night, she had certainly succeeded. While I nursed a bottle of Stella, she looked over her menu and seemed to be chatting amiably with a young male server whom, I sensed, saw visions of a big tip dancing in his head. While that was going on, I ordered an appetizer of fried calamari and explained to the server I had an appointment later and didn't have time for a complete dinner.

An hour later, she finished her meal, and I finished my calamari—it was excellent—and another Stella. Madelaine paid her check, got up, and walked out. I followed. When we got outside, I took a look around, but couldn't see anything that would have suggested anyone was paying any attention to her at all. Nobody was sitting in a car with the engine running, nobody was pacing aimlessly around the parking lot, and nobody was seated on the bench by the valet park talking on a cell phone.

I followed Madelaine back to her home, just as I had the night before, and watched as she ran the garage door up, pulled inside, and then closed the door. After that, I drove to the end of her cul-de-sac and waited to see whether anyone else drove up. Nobody did, so, at ten-fifteen, I decided to call it a night and headed for home, having accomplished exactly nothing.

Chapter Sixteen

When I got to the office the next morning, I found a couple of individuals sitting in the waiting area I keep in the outer office. As waiting rooms go, mine isn't much to look at. Just a couple of vinyl-covered couches, a water cooler, and a magazine rack filled with copies of *Sports Illustrated*, *The Atlantic*, and *Smithsonian*, none of which have been updated for at least three months. One of these days, I'll have to throw the old ones out and bring some of the newer ones from home. But then, it's a comparative rarity when I ever actually find anyone sitting there.

My potential customers, if that's what they were, made as mismatched a pair as I'd seen for quite some time. There was an older man, who looked vaguely familiar, expensively dressed in tan slacks, a light blue broadcloth button-down shirt, and a dark green blazer, no tie. His alligator Lucchese Regis loafers, which I knew cost somewhere in the neighborhood of $1,500, were polished to a dazzling sheen.

Hazarding a guess, I would have said he was about 65, give or take a page on the calendar. His skin was nicely tanned, as if he was in the habit of spending his free time either on the deck of a boat or a golf course. His hair was salt-and-pepper, and he had a pair of black Tom Ford sunglasses propped up on top of his head.

His companion, by contrast, was somewhere in his early thirties. He wore a red-and-black patterned flannel shirt and faded, custom-fit blue jeans that were nicely offset by a pair of Cody James boots, available online for a thousand dollars, give or take—and that was for a cheap pair. He was a head taller than his companion, with close-cropped, sandy-colored hair, piercing blue eyes, a horseshoe mustache, and a nose that was slightly off-kilter, the result, I thought, from being flattened a few times in bar fights. He also had a noticeable scar on his chin.

"Mister Gamble," said the older man when I came in. He rose from his seat and extended his hand. "I'm Sonny Miles. I saw you the other night at the reception over at Red Dot. I'm sorry I didn't get a chance to visit with you just then, but it looked like you were working, and I was, well, I was a little bit busy myself, pressing the flesh. It kinda goes with the territory. I guess you might have heard I'm in the business of representing musical talent."

He tilted his head in the direction of the younger man, who had remained seated on the couch. "This fella here is my associate, James Figgins. He takes care of a few things for me when I'm out of town, which is a great deal of the time, as you might imagine. I wonder if we might come inside and have a word with you. I know you're a busy man, and you probably have lots of things to do today. So, if you don't mind, maybe we could just get to it. I don't reckon this will take too long."

"Not at all," I said, unlocking the door to the inner office. I stood to the side and waited until the two men settled into the visitors' chairs before taking a seat behind my desk.

"So, Mr. Miles, what can I do for you?"

"Mister Gamble, I'll come straight to the point. I believe you met my wife the other night at the Red Dot reception. Her name is Madelaine. She sorta wandered off for a minute while I was talking with a client. Sometimes she does that. She's not really involved very much in what I do for a living."

"Okay."

"She's a few years younger than me, so people sometimes wonder how we got together." I couldn't think of anything to say to that, so I let it drift.

"She's a pretty woman, wouldn't you say?"

I was beginning not to like the way he was steering the conversation.

"You don't really have to answer that, Mr. Gamble. It's just that, well, you know how it is. Sometimes, people can get the wrong idea about Maddie, especially when she's had a few cocktails, and she gets to talking. You mind telling me what she was talking to you about?"

"She's your wife. Why don't you just ask her? It would have saved you coming all the way downtown to ask me."

Miles turned to the big man seated next to him. "James?"

"What Mr. Miles is trying to say is that when he's away on business, he pays me to keep an eye on things. Two nights ago, I was doing just that, and I saw you follow Mrs. Miles from her home to her Bible study. I watched you wait in the parking lot at her church and then follow her back home again." When I didn't say anything to that, he went on.

"Last night, you followed her again, this time to a restaurant over by Cool Valley. She went in by herself, and then you went in a few minutes later. I don't know what went on while you were there, if you had dinner together or what. But you were both there for better than an hour." He shot a glance at the older man, who nodded slightly.

"That was you, wasn't it?" He took a slip of paper out of his shirt pocket and read off a license plate number. "That is your car, right?"

Sonny Miles said, "I don't particularly care what you think you were doing, Mr. Gamble, and I don't care what my wife told you the other night. But I'm telling you now, you are not to be following her around anymore. If you do, I can assure you, you will regret it."

"Regret it. Mister Miles, let me stop you right there. I don't respond very well to threats, so let's get a few things straight right here before we get too far off into the weeds. Your wife—Mrs. Miles—didn't say anything to me at the reception, other than to give me her telephone number. She said she might have a job I could do for her. She didn't say what it was, so I called. She told me she thought someone was keeping track of her movements when you were out of town, which I guess is correct, since your man here seems to be doing exactly that. She claimed it had been going on for some time. She wanted me to find out who it was and what his purpose was. So, I tried last night, and the night before. I didn't notice anyone following her, and that's what I was planning to call and tell her this morning."

"I see." He rubbed his hands together and leaned back in his chair. "Well then, Mr. Gamble, problem solved. My wife has a very vivid imagination. She often gets to thinking things are happening when they're not. This business about somebody followin' her around is a perfect example. I can assure you, nobody is followin' her when she goes out. She's free to come and go whenever and wherever she wants."

"But somebody is following her around." I nodded in the direction of James Figgins. "Your guy. Because if he isn't, how would he know where your wife went the last two nights?"

"As I said, she's a pretty woman. Lots of men seem to take a liking to her. I just want to make sure she's safe, so I like to know where she's goin' when she's out by herself."

I wasn't completely sure what he was telling me, but it didn't sound right. "I never heard it put quite that way. Are you saying your wife has to check with you every time she goes out? You make it sound very much like she's living in some kind of a halfway house."

"No, sir, I'm not saying that at all. But even if I were, it's none of your concern. Maddie is my wife, and what goes on between me and her is nobody's business but ours. Now, I'm done talking to you, and I think the best thing for all of us would be for you to just forget about followin' her around and call it a day. Better still, while you're at it, why don't you call her and let her know you won't be working for her any longer, 'cause she hasn't got anything to worry about. Naturally, I'll be happy to pay you for your efforts so far—double your usual rate, if it helps any—but then, I'm afraid that's going to have to be the end of it."

"Got it." I leaned back in my chair. "Mister Miles, I appreciate your concern, but I'm afraid it doesn't work like that. Your wife hired me, and unless she tells me otherwise, I'm still working for her. If she wants me to stop what I'm doing, she'll have to tell me herself. You're in business yourself. I'm sure you can understand that."

He stood up to leave. "Okay, then, I guess you and I are done here for now, but I'm sure we'll be able to figure out a solution. My offer still stands, and I'll leave it to James to work out the details with you."

He turned to the big man. "James, I'll wait for you in the lobby downstairs." And then he walked out of the office, leaving me, as he said, to sort out my problem with James the best way that I could.

James waited without saying or doing anything until we both heard the elevator bell at the end of the hallway ping. Then, as if it was the most natural thing in the world, he stood up, walked around the edge of my desk, and before I could react, punched me hard on the side of my face. It felt like somebody had hit me with a bowling ball. I toppled over backward in my chair, cracking my head on the windowsill behind me before I hit the floor, flat on my back. In another moment, he had his massive hands around my throat and began to squeeze.

Say this for the guy—he wasn't one to beat around the bush.

"So, as they say in the movies, what's it going to be? The money or your life?" The smile he showed me made it clear that he was enjoying himself.

I tried to say something, but with my windpipe partially constricted, nothing came out other than a ragged, croaking sound. My assailant, realizing perhaps that if I couldn't breathe, I couldn't talk, relaxed his grip just slightly. That, I figured, was the only opening I was likely to get. I clasped my hands together, forming a wedge with my forearms, and jerked violently upwards, breaking his hold on my throat. Then I went for his eyes, pressing my thumbs in as hard as I could. In that moment, I didn't care if his eyeballs came out stuck to my thumbs like martini olives on a skewer. He made a guttural noise, like a man choking on a piece of meat, and pulled away, breaking my hold on his face.

Before he could react further, I reached up with my right hand, grabbed a letter opener from the top of my desk, and drove the point into his shoulder, just below the collarbone. I knew it wasn't a serious wound, nor did I intend it to be, and I was fairly sure the blade hadn't hit anything but soft tissue. A few sutures, maybe a tetanus shot, and in a few days, he'd be good as new. But it would hurt like hell, and in the moment, would at least partially immobilize him. Sure enough, James howled in pain and tried to stand up. But before he could completely get his balance, he took a step backward, tripped over my wastebasket, and collapsed into the open doorway between my inner and outer offices.

A few years back, someone had broken into my office searching for material related to a case I was working on. They didn't find what they were looking for, but to keep it from happening again, the building super installed a new door to my inner office. The new door was steel, set in a steel frame, and was practically impenetrable for any intruder to get through, equipped with anything less than a sledgehammer. While James struggled to get back on his feet and to regain clear vision, I slammed the office door on his head as hard as I could, knocking him semi-unconscious. Then I sat him up, and while he was still limp, bound his wrists together with a zip tie I retrieved from a bundle I keep in my desk drawer. Once he was secured, I dragged him down the hallway to the elevator stop. I pressed the call button, and when the car arrived and the doors opened, I wrangled him inside and pressed "lobby." Just before the doors shut, he opened his eyes and looked at me.

"Tell your boss. If you come back here again, I will fuck you up."

After that, I went back to my office, closed the door, and locked it. After two hours, when the phone didn't ring and the cops didn't show up to arrest me on an assault charge, I figured I was home free, at least for the moment.

And I didn't bother mentioning the incident to Maggie. She never reacts well to me getting beat up, even when I win.

* * *

Later that night, I was home, seated on the couch, with a bag of frozen peas against the side of my face and several empty bottles of Stella on the coffee table in front of me. Next to those were half a dozen plastic cups of chocolate pudding, now also empty. As good a dinner as I could muster up with a sore jaw: a six-pack of pudding and a six-pack of beer. A song by Anita Baker, "Sweet Love," was playing on the radio. In the moment, it made me wish Maggie were here with me, but then I'd have to explain the bruise on my left cheek and eye, and that would definitely kill the mood. Plus, I would probably get a pep talk about overexerting myself, particularly in light of my recent health scare.

Madelaine Miles had telephoned me shortly before I left the office. "I spoke to Sonny when he got home this afternoon. He said he'd stopped by your office earlier, and that he had asked you not to pursue the investigation you'd taken on for me."

"And?"

"And, he said after you, and he spoke, you both agreed that probably I was imagining things, and that I was perfectly safe. He said you told him you had followed me to Bible study, and then again to the restaurant, and nobody was shadowing me."

"That's true." What I didn't say was that somebody was evidently following me.

"Anyway, I want to pay you for your time, and to thank you for trying to help. I guess there was nothing to worry about after all."

"Guess not," I said. I reminded her that, as we had discussed, my usual was five hundred dollars per day, plus expenses, but that under the circumstances, half a day would be acceptable. I expected an argument, but she just asked for my email address and said she would send the funds via PayPal. I told her that would be fine, and we hung up.

PayPal. I should have been ashamed. Sam Spade or Phillip Marlowe would have held out for cash.

Chapter Seventeen

On my way to the office on Monday, after a long weekend by myself cutting grass and watching old movies on television—Maggie was at some kind of a professional retreat in Pigeon Forge—I stopped at the Office of Vital Records, which is maintained by the Davidson County Department of Health. I wanted to check whether Jason Mackey and Annamaria Harris had ever applied for a marriage license. It took a little talking to find out what I wanted, because to obtain a copy of a license, you have to either be the person whose name appears on the license or else have written authorization from such a person. There is also a fifteen-dollar fee. I explained to the clerk that I was a private investigator hired to search for a missing person, and that I didn't want a copy; I just wanted to know if a license had ever been issued. After consulting with a supervisor, he agreed to take a look, but said it would still cost me fifteen bucks. A few keystrokes on his computer later, I was informed that no license had been issued to either party in Davidson County.

"What about a death certificate for Annamaria Harris? Or does that cost extra?"

"Nah. Long as I'm looking. Just a second." I waited. "Nope, not in this county, anyhow. 'Course, that doesn't mean she isn't dead someplace else."

"That's a comfort. How about somebody named Johnny Walker?"

"Married or dead?"

As it turned out, there were several Johnny Walkers, who were variously listed as John, Jonathan, Johann, and even Johnson. All had applied for marriage licenses during the previous ten years, but none with a woman named Harris as his blushing bride. The only recent death certificate was issued for a man who was well into his eighties at the time of his passing. That meant, once again, I was back to square one, which sent me back to the Nashville Musicians Association.

I called the number and this time asked for Valerie, hoping that she might remember me from our earlier discussion. She did, and was willing to look up Johnny Walker, who, as it turned out, was an actual person named Edward John Walker, who still lived in Nashville, and was a dues-paying member of the union. Valerie was good enough to provide me with contact information, including his cell number and email address. She was also able to inform me that Johnny Walker was currently a keyboardist in a band called Take Five, and that the band played regularly at a bar called the Jam Joint. According to Valerie, who seemed to know a great deal about Johnny Walker and his group, Take Five was a cover band, mostly reinterpreting rock, country, and pop hits from the late 1960s through the early 1980s.

I got on the phone to the Jam Joint and learned that Take Five was, indeed, performing that evening. However, the band didn't start playing until around nine o'clock, which gave me time to meet Maggie at a restaurant near her office. I got there just after six, and was informed by the hostess that my party had arrived a half hour or so earlier, and was waiting for me in the cocktail lounge. She was on her second appletini, which was both good news and bad. Bad news because she was already two drinks ahead of me. Good news, because an appletini usually means she's in a good mood. As an added plus, there was a bottle of Stella cooling in a plastic ice bucket sitting on the table.

"I thought I might have to send out a search party to find you."

"Parking. It's always a bitch downtown. I had to walk two blocks."

She tossed her head in the direction of the guy working behind the bar. "Michael, that's his name. Michael was nice enough to inform me that there's a good-looking fellow sitting at the bar who's been checking me out. I was just thinking, if you didn't get here before too much longer, I was going to invite him over."

I glanced toward the bar, which was already filled with the usual after-work crowd. "Point him out, and I will shoot him right between his beady eyes."

"That's why I fell for you, Gamble. You always know just what to say to make a gal feel special."

After dinner—a Caesar salad, a small filet, and garlic mashed potatoes for me, shrimp *fra diavolo* for Maggie—we split a slice of key lime pie for dessert. Maggie had one more cocktail, her third, while I switched to a Diet Coke.

"So, since you're not drinking, was all this just leading up to a roll in the hay, or do you have other plans for the evening?"

"Actually, I thought you might want to go and listen to some music."

"Tell me it's not the Braxton Brothers."

"Better than that. Take Five, at the Jam Joint."

"And after that?"

"After that, I was thinking, definitely a roll in the hay. That is, if you think my heart can stand it."

* * *

The Jam Joint was located on Elliston Place, about a block away from St. Thomas Hospital, and a short distance from Centennial Park. Perhaps because of its proximity to the Vanderbilt University campus, it was a popular hangout for college kids, some of whom did not appear to be of drinking age. But then, as I knew from my earlier days as an undergrad at a middling Missouri compass-point college, fake IDs are not hard to come by.

On the way from the restaurant, I explained that I had never been to the Jam Joint, never heard the band Take Five perform, and had only a very general idea of what kind of music they played. What I wanted was to talk to their keyboardist, Johnny Walker, to find out if he knew anything regarding the whereabouts of Annie Harris, or if she was still living in the area under a married name. The plain fact was, I didn't really have any other leads, and if Walker couldn't point me in a productive direction, I might have to tell Harvey Harris there was nothing I could do for him.

When we got there, the parking lot was only half-filled, but even so, there was a ten-dollar cover charge, which got us a grunt of acknowledgement from the guy at the door and a red ink stamp on the back of our hands.

"You know, in case you want to go outside and give your ears a rest. It can get kinda loud in there after a time."

Inside, the Jam Joint was nothing special. There was a bar with subdued lighting and a tattooed young woman with a nose ring and multiple piercings in her ears and lower lip, serving draft and bottled beer, wine, and mixed drinks. There was a dozen or so tables and a platform that served as a bandstand. The walls were painted in a dark shade of purple, or maybe black—it was impossible to tell in the low light—and hung with floor-to-ceiling, dark-tinted mirrors and reproductions of promotional posters for bands performing during the old days at the Fillmore West. Among others, I noticed the Grateful Dead, The Doors, Moby Grape, Big Brother and the Holding Company, Jimi Hendrix, Scott McKenzie, and the Jefferson Airplane. All in all, very Bill Graham, and very trippy.

Maggie and I got settled and waited for somebody to come and take our drink order. When nobody did, I figured out there was no table service and walked over to the bar to order a Stella and an appletini. When the bartender gave me a WTF look, I said, "Okay, how about a Bud Light and a vodka and cranberry juice?"

This time, she gave me a nod. "Got it."

While I waited for her to get our order together, a very large man wearing a leather vest with a green-and-black camo T-shirt underneath wandered over to the other end of the bar and said something I couldn't quite hear to the tattooed lady. She glared at him, but otherwise seemed to let it pass. He said something else which I didn't quite catch, except at the end, when I hear the word "bitch." That got a response. She drew a glass of beer from one of the taps, walked over, and threw it in his face. He let out a shout and started to climb over the bar. At that point, the guy working the door took three quick steps across the room, pulled what looked like a leather sap from his back pocket, and clipped the big guy behind the right ear. Then he and another bouncer, one whom I hadn't noticed earlier, dragged the unconscious guy behind the bar and into a back room. We didn't see him again that night. When the tattooed lady handed me our drink order, I raised my eyebrows a bit. She shook her head and said, "My ex." Then, before I could pay for the drinks, she said, "On the house. Sorry for the disturbance."

When I got back to our table, Maggie took a sip of her cocktail and gave me a sly look. "I'll say this for you, Gamble. You really know how to show a girl a good time."

I picked up my beer and clinked the neck of the bottle on her glass. "My specialty."

About quarter to nine, by which time the room was pretty well filled with customers, one of the musicians took the stage. He spent a few minutes fiddling with amplifiers, adjusting lights, and testing microphones. Eventually, four others wandered up, including two guitar players, a drummer, and the keyboardist, whom I assumed was Johnny Walker. One of the guitar players stepped up to a floor mike and said, "Let's get ready to kick out the jams," and with that, the band launched into a rough-and-tumble version of Bob Seger's "Hollywood Nights." They followed that—with apologies, the singer said, to Debbie Harry—a near spot-on rendition of Blondie's "Call Me," and in quick succession after that, "Kick Out the Jams," a 1969 hit originally recorded by the MC5, a Detroit-area garage-rock band that broke up in 1972. That one brought the crowd to its feet, whistling and foot-stomping. And it happened with such perfect timing that I understood it was not a spontaneous response, but an extension of the performance, something like the way audiences used to get into the act at a midnight showing of "The Rocky Horror Picture Show."

After another twenty minutes and a half-dozen more kick-ass songs, including "Boom, Boom, Out Go the Lights," and Led Zeppelin's "Heartbreaker/Livin' Lovin' Maid," the singer announced that the band would be taking a short break, as he said, "To let y'all take it easy for just a bit before we really get into it." That was my cue. I excused myself and left Maggie, who was clearly ready to go home, and went over to the bar where the keyboard player, a mid-fortyish guy wearing black pants and a black t-shirt, sat, sipping a tall glass of club soda with a wedge of lime.

I took a seat on an empty stool next to where he was sitting. After a moment, he felt my presence and looked over.

"Can I do something for you?"

"Johnny Walker, right?"

"Do I know you?"

"No, you don't. Not at all. I was just wondering whether this is a better gig than what you had when you were with Midnite Oil."

"You remember Midnite Oil?"

"Truthfully, no. I never heard your old band perform, or ever even heard of it before a week or so ago. But I have a couple of questions about one of your old band mates, and I was hoping you could answer them for me."

He turned and looked directly at me. "I might, if you tell me who you're looking for and why you're looking. Also, how you got my name."

"Fair enough." I showed him my identification. "I spoke to a guy named Todd at a recording studio here in town. He told me you and Jason Mackey spoke with him way back when about coming in for a recording session, but you never followed up. But that's not why I'm here. I'm looking for Annie Harris. Fact is, she's gone missing, or at least her parents have lost touch with her. They've asked me to find her, but so far, I haven't had much luck."

"I'm not sure how I can help you. I mean, I haven't seen her in a long time. Not since right after the band broke up. That was years ago." He stared into his glass, as if he thought she might be swimming around in the bubbly water. "Don't tell me she's back."

"Back from where?"

"I don't know. I heard she left town. But like I said, that was a long time ago."

"Okay. I imagine you heard about Jason."

He nodded. "Word gets around." There was a pause. "Did him getting killed have something to do with you trying to find Annie?"

"Why would you think that?"

"I don't know. No reason. It just seems like kind of a coincidence, Jason getting killed, and you asking about Annie."

"You think they were involved in something they shouldn't have?"

"Well, no. It's just, you know, back then, when we were all still together,

Jason and Annie had a thing for one another. They moved in together for a while, and we all thought—well, first we thought they might go off on their own, you know, just the two of them. Maybe try to be the next Sonny and Cher. But then I guess things didn't work out, and the next thing we knew, she was gone, and Jason started getting gigs over on the Row. Doing pretty well, too."

"Let me ask you something else. Is the band breaking up the reason why you never followed through on your recording date at Mix Masters?"

"Well, yeah, I guess. Plus, even back then, studio time was kind of expensive, and, I mean, let's face it. We weren't anywhere near good enough to get a recording contract. Jason played a damn good guitar, and I do okay on keyboards, but as a band, we sucked. And if we tried to make a record, we would've just been wasting our money."

"Do you think that was why Annie and Jason split up? Because the band wasn't going anywhere?"

"I don't know. Maybe. Musicians are like actors and athletes in a way. We all have big dreams, but for most of us, it doesn't work out the way we hope. We don't become headliners or hall of fame candidates, and so we do the best we can. Like playing somebody else's music in a place like this. But Annie, you know, she had big ideas and expensive tastes. And she wanted more than what she figured she was apt to get being married to a session musician, so it wasn't long before she moved out."

"But you don't know where."

"No." He took a last swallow of his club soda. "Not sure. I heard she drifted around a little. Made the rounds of some of the other recording companies. I guess she thought she was a pretty good singer, and she figured she could hit the big time on her own."

"Was she good?"

"Well, if you needed a singer to do a TV commercial, maybe you could say she was good enough for that. She just didn't have the range or the chops to be a headliner. I heard she got an audition from a recording company in Muscle Shoals or someplace like that. But far as I know, she wasn't offered a contract. I did find out she sang backup on a few recordings, but I think that was about it. That was pretty much the last I heard, and that's going on near ten years ago."

"So, you have no idea where she might be now."

"Not a clue. She could be anywhere."

"Okay, let me ask you this. In the promotional poster I saw for an appearance by Midnite Oil, besides Annie, there was you, Jason, and one other guy. Any idea where I might find him?

"You're probably talking about Lucas Pratt. He was our bass guitarist. I think he's still in town somewhere. I don't know where he lives, but the last I heard, he was doing this busker thing down on Lower Broad. You know, standing on the street corner playing his guitar and singing a little. People throw money into his guitar case if they like what he's playing."

"I'll be sure to look him up. So then, besides Jason, was there anybody else you can think of who was tight with Annie? Somebody who might have stayed in touch with her after you guys broke up?"

When he hesitated, I said, "Look, she's not in any trouble, and I can't force her to do anything. The plan is to tell her that her parents are worried and want to see her. After that, she can do whatever she wants."

"Well…you might try Robbie Porter. He wasn't part of the band, but he sat in with us sometimes, and I know he and Jason were pretty close, so he might have stayed in touch with them both."

"Okay. You know where I can find Robbie Porter?"

"No. And I'm not even sure Robbie's still in the music business. I haven't really stayed in touch with any of the Midnite Oil crew since we split up."

He got up from where he was sitting. "Listen, I got to get back to work here, but let me ask you right quick. You said her parents were trying to get reconnected. Were you talking about her mother, or her father, or both of 'em?"

"Her father, mostly. He didn't say why, except that he's got cancer. His time is short, and he wants to see her one more time while he still can."

"Well, I wouldn't know about that, but what I do know about that sorry bastard, if he's only got one more day left to live, that's one day too many."

Chapter Eighteen

My cell buzzing on Maggie's nightstand at seven-thirty roused me from a sound sleep. My first thought was, who the hell would be calling me at that time of the morning? My second was, did the noise wake Maggie, and if it did, would she be unhappy about it? No worries on that score, at least. As soon as I was able to gather my wits about me, I heard the shower running in the bathroom. I could also see Stanley, her cat, sitting on the bed next to me, staring expectantly, as if he were waiting for me to serve up a snack to get his day off to a proper start. Stanley could keep on waiting. I reached for my phone, and in the same motion, swept Stanley off the bed and onto the floor. His response was to give me a menacing hiss and bound out of the room.

I recognized Geoffrey Tate's voice even before he identified himself. And, of course, he had a question.

"I haven't heard from you in a couple of days, Mr. Gamble, but I did receive your latest account statement. You'll forgive me for saying so, but I rather hoped you might have included a progress report with your invoice."

My head was still a little foggy from sleep, alcohol, and certain extracurricular activities that commenced shortly after Maggie and I got back from the Jam Joint. "I wasn't aware that was part of our agreement, Mr. Tate. However, if you'd like some sort of written update, I'd be happy to provide you with one."

"Maybe you could save some time and just tell me what you've found out so far." His tone was chilly.

"Well, sir, to be honest, there isn't very much to report. I've spoken with

Annamaria's mother, as well as the owner of a recording studio where Midnite Oil—that's the name of her old band, in case you weren't aware—where Midnite Oil had booked studio time to make a demo recording. They never showed up, but I was able to get the name of one of her bandmates, who wasn't able to give me any information at all, other than she might have gone to Alabama, looking for a recording contract. Whether that was permanent or not, I don't know."

"And that's it?"

"Not quite, no." I barely was able to suppress a yawn. "I had another name, a guy named Jason Mackey. Reportedly, he and Miss Harris were an item at one time. It took me a little time to track him down, and when I finally did, it turned out he'd been murdered in his apartment. Shot in the head with a small-caliber handgun, so no help there, either."

He made a noise like he was clearing his throat. "What are you saying? That you believe this man Mackey—this boyfriend, or whatever he was—this man getting killed has something to do with your search for my client's daughter?"

"Couldn't tell you. It's possible, I guess. The police are looking into it, but as far as I know, they haven't turned up a connection. You have to admit, though, the timing seems more than coincidental."

"I wouldn't know about coincidences. And I would advise you to stick to the task at hand." There was a pause, and I heard him say something I couldn't make out to someone else in the room.

"I was also calling to bring you up to date on my client's situation. Yesterday, he was transferred to the prison infirmary, complaining of severe abdominal pain. And then he began spitting up blood. I'm in the process now of filing a petition to have him moved to the secure wing of West Tennessee Healthcare Hospital in Jackson for further evaluation. But I'm afraid his remaining time may be even shorter than we first anticipated."

"Is that a bad thing?"

"Comedy is not your strong suit, Mr. Gamble, and that is not why I hired you. I hired you to get results, so anything you can do to move things along would be greatly appreciated."

"I understand, Mr. Tate, and I will do my best, but this is not an easy case. As we discussed, Annie Harris has been off the reservation for a very long time."

"Yes. And as I pointed out in our earlier discussion, you do not work cheap. You've been at this for two weeks. I believe I'm entitled to some results, and I expect you to earn your fee." And with that, he hung up.

* * *

Maggie was still in the bathroom, getting ready for work, so I went down the hall to the kitchen to feed Stanley, who seemed to have gotten past his earlier irritation with me. Then I started the coffee maker for Maggie, and cobbled up some breakfast for myself. I was flipping through the news headlines on my phone when Maggie finally made an appearance. As always, she was impeccably made up and dressed for success in cream-colored slacks and a strawberry-red blouse with matching low-heeled pumps. And she was carrying the yearbook I had appropriated from Annie Harris's bedroom.

She dropped the book on the table, open to the inside front cover. "You owe me. Big time."

"Because?"

"Because I started looking through the autographs and little cutesy messages in the front, and I ran across a name I thought looked promising. The message was, well, here, let me read it to you. It says, 'For Annie, best friends forever. Let's hope we can make music together.' It was signed 'Rosie.' So, I paged through the pictures of the seniors, and I found a girl named Rosemary Althoff. Turns out, she's one of my clients."

"A client. Does that mean she's having some kind of a crisis? That is what you do, right?"

"Yes. Yes, she is, and yes, that's what I do."

"And what would her crisis be?"

She gave me a look. "You know I can't tell you that."

"Can you put me in touch with her?"

"No, absolutely not. The work I do for my clients is strictly confidential.

I can't just go handing out their information to anybody that asks. I'd be out of work in a heartbeat." She gave me a look. "Also, don't you think you should be starting your day with something more heart-healthy than peanut butter and carbonated beverages?"

"Well," I said, taking a last swallow of my Diet Coke, "peanut butter has lots of protein, and I could switch to bloody Mary's if you think that would be better."

* * *

By the time I was showered, dressed, and ready to go, Maggie had already left. I found a note on the kitchen table that read, "Early appointment and a full schedule this morning. Call you at lunchtime." I also found the high school yearbook I had asked her to look through next to her note. I gathered that up, petted the cat, who for once did not try to attack me, and headed out. By the time I got to the office, the phone was ringing.

The voice on the other end said, "Mister Gamble? You're a private investigator, right?"

I said I was. I should have answered with something other than hello.

"Mister Gamble, my name is Michael Nadler. I'm an associate producer with Encore Films. We're an independent, so not as big as Fox or Warner, but maybe you've heard of us?"

I had to admit, I hadn't.

"Well, maybe you've seen one or two of our more recent releases." He named a couple, neither of which rang any bells.

"No matter. The reason I'm calling is that, depending upon how our schedule works out, we'll be sending a crew to Nashville in the next month or so to shoot a few scenes for our current project."

"And?"

"And I was told you sometimes work security for film and music celebrities. You know, to keep them out of trouble when they're not in front of the camera. An individual I spoke with the other day said you looked after his man a few years back without a hitch, and we wondered if you'd be willing to do the same thing for us."

I remembered the last time I was hired to babysit a Hollywood personality. He was a second-shelf Welsh actor, widowed, and puddling his way through a moderately successful film career until he turned action hero in his early fifties. He caught lightning in a bottle, and after that, producers couldn't get enough of him. Before anyone knew it, he was A-list all the way, commanding eight figures to headline a film. He was in town just for a couple of days to shoot a few exteriors before heading back to California, or London, or wherever they were planning to go to use a sound stage before final edits, post-production, and then release. And perhaps because of his recent turnaround in fortunes, he had gained a reputation as something of a bad boy.

For my part, he turned out to be a charmer, easy to get along with, and more than willing to dish on more than a few of his co-stars—especially women, which I found fascinating—as long as I promised to keep the gossip to myself. He also had a prodigious appetite for Irish whiskey, American TV porn channels, and cocaine, in approximately equal measure, any of which could have been problematic. However, he was perfectly happy to indulge his predilections in the privacy of his hotel suite, meaning that I didn't have to worry about keeping groupies, pushers, or autograph seekers at arm's length. So, he finished his work on time, and to top it all off, when I took him to the airport, he spiffed me with a wad of cash big enough to choke a water buffalo.

"Mister Nadler, who are we talking about here, and how much trouble is he likely to be?"

He gave me a name, which I recognized instantly. And from his reputation, I knew with absolute certainty he was going to be a handful.

I said, "No offense, but I thought this guy was first call. If you don't mind my asking, what's he doing working with a company like yours?"

"Used to be. He's had some problems. He's trying for a comeback."

"Right. So, how long do you figure to be in town? And where will you be shooting?"

"Three days, four at most, unless the weather turns all Tornado Alley on us and we have to hang around longer. We'll be mostly downtown, mostly at night. Which in this case means, zero-dark-thirty, after the bars and the clubs are closed, but before the sun comes up. We'll turn the lights back on and fill the streets with extras. Plus, we've got other security to handle the sightseers, if there are any at that time of the morning. Your job will be to just keep close to our man, make sure he shows up sober and ready to work. You'll be sharing a two-bedroom suite at the Maxwell House, so we can be sure he's where he needs to be when he needs to be there. We're offering twenty-five hundred a day, four days guaranteed, plus expenses, no questions asked."

When I didn't say anything, he said, "Interested?"

"Maybe. When do you start shooting?"

"If we can stay on schedule, we're looking at six weeks from today. We'll let you know. Also, we'd like to fly you out to California a couple days ahead so you can meet our guy. I was thinking the two of you could get acquainted, maybe see some of the sights."

There was a pause. "So, what do you think? Can I count on you to help us out?"

It sounded like an easy ten grand, so, of course, I said yes.

Chapter Nineteen

I spent the rest of the afternoon and part of the next morning trying, without success, to track down Robbie Porter and Lucas Pratt, both of whose names had been given to me by Johnny Walker the evening before last. Calling around to the various studios in town yielded nothing, and the only information I could get from the union was that no one named Robbie Porter had ever joined, or even applied to join, the Nashville Musicians Association. That made me think that, whatever he was doing now, musically, Robbie Porter had never progressed professionally beyond being a part-time member of a garage band called Midnite Oil. As far as Lucas Pratt was concerned, yes, he had a union card, but the NMA didn't have any contact information they could give me. That meant tracking him down was likely to mean chatting up downtown street musicians in hopes one of them could point me in Lucas's direction. But that could wait.

In Robbie Porter's case, I had an idea. If he was no longer playing music professionally, maybe he was teaching music—that is, if he hadn't enrolled in the Vanderbilt School of Medicine and was these days a practicing neurosurgeon. So, I went online and looked up the website for the Metropolitan Nashville Education Association. I wasn't sure how to go about persuading someone at the union's office to give me information about a member, if, in fact, Porter was a member. But it turned out, it didn't really matter, since their website listed neither a street address nor a telephone number to call. And then I had an idea. And I knew just who I needed to talk to.

* * *

"First, tell me about this Hollywood deal." I watched while Maggie picked at her salad, not really eating much of it, while she was thinking.

"I don't really know much more than what I've already told you, except that it pays pretty well. Company is going to be in town for a few days, shooting exteriors down on Lower Broadway someplace. They'll be filming very late at night—or maybe I should say, very early in the morning, after the bars have closed. They'll bring in extras and pay the bar owners to turn their outdoor signs on, so it looks like a normal evening. Once they've got what they need, they'll pack up and head back to the studio or the next location to finish up. I just have to stay close to their guy until he's back on the plane and on his way to wherever they're going next."

"That doesn't sound too hard."

"Also, they want me to come out to California for a few days to do a meet and greet. Take some time to make nice with their guy so things go well. They didn't specifically say so, but if you want to come along and bum around SoCal for a few days, I'm sure it wouldn't be a problem. I can tell them you're my agent or something."

"I'll think about it. Did they offer you a cameo? You know, so you can get a screen credit?"

"And then do what? Advertise myself as 'Private Eye to the Stars?'"

"Well, when I was a girl, I used to daydream about being with a movie star."

"Not a country western singer?"

"Are you kidding? I'm from Ohio. And in this town, they're a dime a dozen."

Tell that to Midnite Oil, I thought.

After a dinner that was anything but heart-healthy—a large pizza with sausage, pepperoni, and green peppers that we were able to split, I explained that I needed a hook into the teachers' union to find out whether Robbie Porter was teaching music somewhere in the public school system.

"Gamble, I haven't been connected with the teachers' union for years. I'm employed by the state, not the city."

"Yes, but you used to be a teacher. Don't you know somebody at the union office you could call?"

"I wouldn't even know who to ask about this guy, what's his name again?"

"Robbie Porter. You still have teacher friends, don't you? I mean, these gal pals you go out with every now and again. There must be somebody you could ask for a favor."

"I don't know. I guess I could give it a shot," and here, she threw out a name I had never heard before. "I could try calling her tomorrow from work. Maybe I can make up a story."

* * *

The next morning, I was late getting to the office. I stopped on the way at a hardware store to pick up a bag of crabgrass killer for my lawn and batteries for the smoke detectors in the kitchen and hallway between the two bedrooms. After that, I bought gas for the car and then breakfast at a McDonald's about a mile down the road. By the time I got to the I-24 expressway heading into the city, most of the rush hour traffic had abated, and I made it downtown in less than twenty minutes.

The first thing I noticed when I got off the elevator was that the outer door to my office was standing partway open. That sometimes happens. I don't keep it locked because occasionally a potential client comes looking for me when I'm out of the office and decides to wait. Other times, the night cleanup crew forgets to close it. Even less frequently, I sometimes arrive to find the cops waiting for me to show up so we can have a chat. Once, I even found a homeless guy who had somehow gotten into the building after hours and then camped out overnight in my waiting area. I woke him up, gave him a few bucks to buy some breakfast, or, more likely, a pint of Jim Beam, and sent him on his way.

Today, there was somebody waiting. Unlike the last time I spoke with her in person, when she was dressed in a slinky black number and dove-gray high-heeled shoes, today she was wearing blue jeans, designer labeled to be sure, a loose-fitting tunic top, and white New Balance walking shoes.

I said, "Good morning, Mrs. Miles. Are you sure you're in the right place?"

"I came to apologize, Mr. Gamble. And to ask you for help. I need you to protect me. I don't know who else I can turn to."

Reflexively, I found myself on high alert, half expecting Sonny's muscle-for-hire, James, to pop up from behind the small couch I keep in the waiting area. "No apology necessary, Mrs. Miles. And from my experience with you so far, I'd say it's more likely me who needs protection from you."

"Really? Do you think I could do something like this to you?" She stood and lifted her tunic up to her armpits. The first thing I noticed was a particularly fetching ivory-colored bra that did almost nothing to conceal what was underneath. At the same time, I noticed that her upper body, from her waist to just below the bra, was a patchwork of blue and green bruises and red and purple abrasions. When she turned, I could see that her back had received the same violent treatment.

"Who did that to you? Was it your husband?"

A nod, and a tear.

I unlocked the door to the inner office and waited while she went inside. Then I closed and locked it again, in case Sonny or his henchman showed up while we were talking.

"He beat me with a strap. He's done it before. He's always careful not to hit me anywhere it might show. You know, in case I have to wear something sexy at one of his shitty social gatherings so he can use me as arm candy."

"But why? Why does he do it?"

"He likes to hurt women. I'm not the first."

"And he gets away with it." It wasn't a question.

"They think he can help them make it big in the music business. Or, they think he's got money, and he'll take care of them later." She made a small movement with her hands. "Can you help me? I need to get away from him."

"In a minute. Some of these marks aren't fresh. He's done this before."

"Yes."

"And he did again. Why? Because you asked me to find out who was following you?"

More tears. "He said I embarrassed him. I had to be punished."

"What about the other times?" I took out a box of tissues from my bottom drawer and placed it on top of my desk where she could reach it. Then I waited until she composed herself.

"In our house, we have what Sonny calls the game room."

"A game room?"

"It's more like a torture chamber. Sometimes, when he's in a mood, he tells me to go in there and get myself ready."

"Ready for what?"

"Do I really have to spell this out for you? He makes me go in there and take off my clothes and wait for him. Other times, he tells me to dress up in a certain way, and then when he comes in, I have to get undressed while he watches. The whole time, he records what's going on. It's all on video. Years of it. Late at night, he goes in there and watches the videos. He stays in there for hours. I'm sure you can figure out for yourself what that's about."

"How about when he does what he just did. Did he record that, too? Because if he did, you can go to the police. Tell them your story. They'll apply for a search warrant, and those recordings will be unshakable grounds for divorce. Not to mention criminal charges. You can get away from him, no problem, and with more money than you'll ever need. If you need time to contact an attorney, I know a place where you can stay for as long as you need to, where he can't get at you. You'll be safe there."

"No." She shook her head vigorously. "You don't understand. I don't mean I want to go someplace else. What I mean is, I want you to kill him. How much would you charge to do a job like that?" And before I could say anything, she went on, excitement rising in her voice. "Once he's dead, I'll have all the money in the world. I could pay you anything you ask."

I shook my head. "Mrs. Miles, you need to stop right there. The fact you're even asking me about killing your husband means you're committing a felony, and by rights, I should report you to the police. And if you somehow find somebody else to do it—and I know a few people who will—if the cops get around to asking me, I'll have to tell them. And they will ask me, because if Sonny turns up dead, the cops will dump your phone, and it will take about five seconds before they start to wonder why you were trying to get in touch with me."

She gave me a look. "Well, then, couldn't I stay with you? You know, just until I can find someplace else?"

"Mrs. Miles, that might be the worst idea I've heard all month. For one thing, once your husband figures out you're not just out shopping at the mall, or having lunch with your gal pals, he's going to come looking for me."

"Don't you think he'll do that anyway?"

"Probably he will. But even if he didn't, I don't have a big house, and I use my spare bedroom as an office, so there isn't anywhere to stash you."

Another look. "Why would we need a second bedroom? I could make it worth your while."

"Mrs. Miles...." I shook my head. "Absolutely not."

"So then, you won't help me."

"I will help you any way I can, but whatever other corners I might cut for a client, taking you home to bed with me is definitely off the table. And so is killing your husband. Now, if you want, I can direct you to a safe place where Sonny won't be able to get to you. Or would you rather I took you there myself?"

"Yes."

"Yes, what?"

"Yes, I want you to take me."

"Okay, I can do that. But first, I need to ask you a couple of things. To begin with, after this happened, I'm assuming you didn't go to the police? Did you seek medical attention?"

"No."

"Because?"

"Because it wouldn't make any difference. I know he'll get away with it. He's important, and he's got money. And because he knows things about people with connections who need their secrets kept secret."

I wondered what those things were, but it didn't seem like the time to ask.

"One more thing we need to do." I picked my mobile up from my desk. "Lift up your blouse, and then hold your arms away from your body."

"What for? Is this inspiration for some masturbatory fantasy of yours?

Isn't what Sonny makes me do enough?"

"Mrs. Miles, if that's what I wanted, I could find a lot racier stuff on the Internet. But since you don't want to go to the police or a hospital, we need to take some photos to document what happened. That way, when they fish your body out of the Harpeth River looking like the way you do now, only more bloated and decomposed, I'll have something to show them to see that you get justice."

She didn't move from her chair.

"On the other hand, if some morning you put cyanide in his coffee, at least you'll have a case for justifiable homicide."

Still nothing.

I said, "Mrs. Miles, we need to do this."

She waited another moment. Then she stood and lifted her top. I got photos of her back and her belly, plus a headshot.

"Good." I put the phone back on the desk and positioned it between us. "Now, also, I want to go back over what you told me, and we'll record it, again, for the same reason."

So, she went back over her story, this time at greater length. I asked her to identify herself on the record. I identified myself, noting the date and the time of day, and I asked a couple of questions to help clarify what happened and the sequence of events. I thought after that, we were finished. And then she said, "What you told me before about the police getting a search warrant. You know, to get a look at the videos Sonny's been making? They won't need to do that."

She reached into her purse, took out a computer flash drive, and placed it on my desk. "I've got it all right here."

"Okay." I plugged the flash drive into a USB port in my computer and, without watching what was contained on it, copied the contents onto my hard drive. Then I gave the flash drive back to Madelaine Miles.

* * *

The "safe place" I had in mind was a shelter run by a woman named Wanda

Beaudry. In what seems like a lifetime ago, Wanda and I were partners, newly-minted Metro detectives working on loan to the district attorney's office as investigators.

Wanda was a good woman with an uncanny ability to pair up with bad men. One winter night about fifteen years back, the long-out-of-work construction worker she was living with cooked off at the end of a night of drinking, and took out all his anger and frustration on Wanda, leaving her broken and bleeding on her living room floor. The result was an extended stay in the hospital, followed by a lengthy rehab. Though she could have had him arrested and convicted, she declined to press charges. That was when I knew what was going to happen next.

It took six months before Wanda settled up with her abuser. On a warmer-than-usual day in the spring, the partly decomposed body of her ex-boyfriend was found in a city park, shot in both kneecaps, both elbows, and then in the back of the head. Ballistics tests revealed that the murder weapon was a Walther P22 that had gone missing from the Metro PD evidence locker. After Wanda was arrested and charged with murder, a sympathetic female A.D.A. named Amanda Rosslyn, more or less tanked the case, and Wanda was acquitted for lack of evidence. However, her career in law enforcement was finished. Afterward, with a substantial amount of money she received from an off-the-books settlement from the police department in exchange for not pursuing a wrongful discharge suit, she opened a shelter for abused women. Now, years later, and thanks to a number of grants and endowments she's received from local businesses, charities, and religious organizations, the shelter, these days called Haven, is thriving.

But, Wanda herself, as I was about to discover, was not thriving. And there was nothing I could do to help.

Chapter Twenty

"Before we do anything else, I need to know. How did you get here today? Are you sure you weren't followed?"

"As sure as I can be. I drove to the mall at Cool Springs. I went in through Dillard's and called an Uber to pick me up in front of Macy's. That's on the opposite end of the mall, in case you don't get there much. Then I had the driver take me back into the city and drop me at Union Station. From there, I caught a cab to your office. I'm pretty sure nobody followed me."

"Okay, good. Then just sit tight, and we'll get you someplace safe."

* * *

There is a protocol that must be followed when contacting Wanda Beaudry at Haven. This is done for security reasons, as too often abusers call or show up at the door demanding to see or speak to the woman who has taken refuge to get away from that very same husband, boyfriend, or pimp. When that happens, apologies are offered, promises are made, victims relent, and within a short time, the promises are forgotten, and the abuse begins all over again. So, these days, with the exception of the terrified women who show up at the door panicked, bruised, swollen, and sometimes bloodied, no one gets inside without an appointment and without being met by Haven security. Telephone calls are screened. Call the number, leave a name and a message, and someone will call back, usually within half an hour. Wanda called me back in ten minutes.

Skipping past the usual pleasantries, I explained the situation with

Madelaine Miles, that her husband had beaten the hell out of her, she had proof on video, and, for the time being, regardless of what might happen next, she could use a respite. Wanda told me to bring her over.

I left Madelaine in the inner office with instructions to wait fifteen minutes. I told her after that, she should set the lock on the office door and take the elevator down to the parking garage in the basement of the building. I would scoop her up there, and we'd be on our way. When I was sure she was clear on what to do, I took the elevator down to the street level and walked around the corner to the public parking lot where I keep my car. After that, I drove around for about ten minutes, making several turns, and then doubling back to the office. I wanted to be sure I hadn't picked up a tail, and as far as I could tell, I hadn't. Satisfied nobody was following, I pulled into the underground parking area and eased up close to the elevator doors. Madelaine Miles appeared from around a corner and scrambled into the back seat.

"Keep your head down," I told her as we emerged from the parking area into bright sunlight. "I don't think anybody followed me, but just the same, there's no sense inviting trouble."

The shelter Wanda operates is on Hermitage Avenue, about ten city blocks from my office. It's a fifteen-minute drive in normal traffic, but today I took twenty-five, winding through downtown streets until, once again, I was sure we hadn't picked up a tail. Along the way, I got on the phone and alerted Wanda that we would be at Haven in five minutes. When we pulled into her parking lot, she was already outside, waiting. A very large man named Russell was standing next to her. In addition to CCTV cameras that covered every part of the exterior of the property, Russell was an integral part of Haven's security apparatus. Left to his own devices, Russell was as amiable and gentle as any man weighing north of 275 pounds—all rock-hard muscle—could be. Cross him by threatening Wanda, another member of the staff, or any of the women residing at Haven, and Russell would hammer you into the ground like a tent peg.

I took a moment to introduce Madelaine—first names only at Haven—and then got back into the car to take my leave. But before I could get away, Russell said, "Hang just a second, could you?" So, I waited. After a minute,

Wanda came back outside and climbed into the front seat next to me. She didn't look good.

Since the last time I'd seen Wanda, she seemed to have lost a considerable amount of weight. She is a couple years younger than me, but the lines around her eyes made her look ten years older. Her hair, which I remembered as thick and radiant, now hung limply, and her color was not good, as if she hadn't seen the sun for several months.

She noticed that I noticed. "It's okay. You can ask."

I didn't. "You look rundown," I said, sidestepping the question I actually wanted to ask. "Are you getting enough sleep?"

"You're sweet for saying that, but that's not it. It's ovarian cancer. And it's spread.

I didn't want to know. "And?"

"And, it's terminal. We're long past the point where there's a treatment. Now, I'm just running out the clock. Doctor says I might have three months. As it is, it feels like a dull knife stuck in my belly, so maybe three months can't come soon enough."

Shit.

"Are you taking anything for the pain?"

"Oxy. But it doesn't help much." She took a breath. "Gamble, I'm so scared."

I didn't know what to say. If there is a woman I care about as much as I do Maggie, it's Wanda. And although we were never an item, we have a lot of history together, including our time with the Metro police and later in our private lives. Sometimes, when she has a fundraiser for Haven, I pitch in, dealing cards or mixing drinks at a Las Vegas night. Other times, because she managed to hang onto her NCIC password when she left the cops, she has helped me run down information on suspects and victims that would otherwise be inaccessible for me. And every once in a while, I go along for the ride when she serves up a heaping helping of frontier justice to some shitbird who's sent a bruised and battered woman to Haven's door.

"There isn't anything the docs can do?"

"Palliative care. You know what that is?"

"I do, yes."

"Then you know there's nothing more to talk about." There was a pause. "So. Tell me about this woman you just dropped off. What's her story?"

"She's married to a music industry bigfoot named Sonny Miles, who apparently gets his kicks making video recordings of her performing various sex acts, and then going back later to watch the recordings and jerk his gherkin. She downloaded at least some of the recordings on a flash drive. She's got it with her, so you might want to take a look at it, just so you know what we're talking about.

"Have you seen it?"

"I haven't, but I did make a copy in case it needs to be introduced into evidence down the road."

"So, you just met her today?"

"No, a couple weeks ago at a recording industry event where I was working security. She approached me because she thought her husband was keeping tabs on her when he was out of town by having her followed when she went out. Turned out, she was right. I'm guessing now, but it looks like she and her husband got into some kind of a wrangle over it, and he beat the hell out of her. I did get a look at her injuries, and I'd say she's going to need medical attention. You might want to see she gets it."

"Okay. Anything else?"

"Yes. I'd say be careful with this one. Her husband is pretty well-connected. He's got money and friends in the right places, and from what I gather, he's very possessive. He could make trouble for you if he finds out she's here."

"It wouldn't be the first time," she said, and then there was nothing else to talk about. And since I didn't have a better plan, I went home and thought for a long time about my friend, and how much I would miss her. And then I got very, very drunk.

Chapter Twenty-One

Thursday morning, I got two calls in rapid succession. The first was from Maggie.

"Okay, I have some information for you. This individual you're looking for, this Robbie Porter. I checked with the teachers' union. He was never actually a full-time teacher, which is to say, he doesn't have a teaching certificate. But he did bounce around as a substitute for a while, which, now that I think about it, is something you could probably do as well. Your doctor said find something low-stress, and you have a degree. Maybe you could get into education."

"Because, what? You think managing a classroom full of unruly seventh-graders is somehow less stressful than what I'm doing now."

"Point taken." There was a pause. "Anyway, the person I spoke with said he hadn't done any subbing for better than three years. She thought he moved out of state. Someplace west. California or Oregon. She wasn't sure."

"Well, it's better than nothing, I guess."

"Also, and you need to keep this absolutely quiet, I contacted my client. You know, the one who signed Annie Harris's yearbook. I explained that Annie had gone missing and her parents had asked you to try to find her. She said she would be willing to speak with you, but she wants me to be there. I guess I must have told her you were irresistible."

"That must have been it," I said. "When?"

"She's a waitress at that new Brazilian steak restaurant downtown. She said she'd have time to talk with you when she goes on break."

"I see. That means dinner out, right?"

"On you, yes. And a big tip, too."

Well, what the hell. I was already planning to put it on my expenses. Geoffrey Tate could afford it.

The second call was from Sonny Miles. "I imagine you weren't expectin' to hear from me again, Mr. Gamble."

"That would be a fair statement, Mr. Miles. But now that you've called, you've got ten seconds before I hang up, so what do you want?"

"I think you already know, sir. And I don't have time to play games with you."

I was pretty sure I did know. And I thought, fuck him. He wasn't about to get anything from me. I hung up the phone.

Three-quarters of an hour later, Sonny Miles showed up in my office. Alone. I wondered if his sidekick, James Figgins, had taken to heart my warning from the last time we were together, or if he was waiting outside in the hall to shoot me if Sonny didn't get what he came for.

He sat down heavily in the visitor's chair. It was the same chair his wife had been sitting in the day before.

"Why don't we try this again, Mr. Gamble. And I'll try to mind my manners this time."

"Fair enough. But first, I have to ask. Where's your sidekick? I was looking forward to seeing him again."

"You must mean James. He is no longer in my employ. As they say in corporate America, he has left to pursue other opportunities."

"Other opportunities. You mean there's somebody else waiting to kick his ass?"

"Call it what you will. But the job is open if you're interested. I'm pretty sure it pays more than what you're making right now."

I had to smile at that. "As it so happens, business is pretty good these days, but I appreciate the offer. Meantime, my question still stands. What do you want?" I looked at my watch. "I haven't got all day."

"I need you to tell me where my wife is. I know you know the answer to that. I'll pay you, if that's what you want, and I'll pay you extra if you bring her back home. Whatever you want, you can have it. I mean, finding people.

That is what you do, isn't it?"

I had to be careful here. What I wanted to do was take out the .32 caliber revolver I keep in my bottom desk drawer and shoot him in the head for the way he treated his wife. But if I let on that I knew about that, he would know she'd talked to me fairly recently.

I gritted my teeth. "Mister Miles…."

"Call me Sonny."

"All right, Sonny. I'm afraid I can't help you. In the first place, after our earlier experience together, and this should come as no surprise, I don't like you. And unlike the police, I am under no obligation to help you with anything because I am not a public servant. In the second place, I don't know where your wife is. And lastly, and this is the most important reason. I wouldn't tell you where she was if I did know, because, frankly, sir, I think you are a bad person, and you don't deserve a good woman in your life."

He appeared to think about that for a moment.

I waited. He cleared his throat.

"Mister Gamble, it's a terrible thing for a man have to think that he might lose the woman he loves. I don't know how you formed your impression of what goes on between me and Maddie, but I can assure you, I care very deeply about her. Also, it might make a difference to you that I also know you have a good woman in your life. I know her name. I know where she works and where she lives. And it would be a terrible thing if something were to happen to her. I can guarantee, the pain you'd feel would be just about unbearable."

It took me a second or two to realize what he was telling me, and when the light bulb finally lit up, I had to use all the self-control I could muster to keep from coming across the desk to throttle the life out of him.

"Mister Miles—Sonny—whatever the hell you call yourself. I don't usually make threats, but in this instance, I will make an exception. We are done here, but not before I say just one more thing, and that is this. If anything untoward happens to my lady friend, anything at all—if I find out strange people are hanging around outside her apartment building or her place of employment, or if she starts getting threatening phone calls or emails, or weird shit turns up on social media, know that I will blame you, and I will find you, and I will kill you. I will not have a conversation with you. I will not look for alternative explanations for what might have happened. I will kill you, and I will make sure your remains will never be found. Do I make myself clear?"

* * *

Maggie and I got to the restaurant a little after eight o'clock and asked the hostess to seat us in Rosemary's area. "She's an old friend," Maggie lied. "We promised we'd stop in. She says the food here is great."

The hostess, a fortyish East Indian woman named, from her nametag, Priya, gave us a wide smile. "It is. I'm sure you'll love it."

It wasn't a busy night, so we were seated right away. After a busboy brought water and a basket of warm bread, a waitress drifted over with menus, and, of course, she recognized Maggie right away.

"Miz Totten, I wasn't expecting you so soon. But welcome, just the same." She turned in my direction. "Is this your detective friend? Miz Totten says you wanted to talk to me. You had some questions about Annie Harris?"

"I do," I said. "But it can wait until you have a free moment. Meanwhile, what do you recommend?"

Rosemary went over the list of tonight's specials, all of which sounded good. I ended up ordering *Bife Com Alho*, a prime cut with a garlic rub, together with seasoned rice and a bottle of *Itaipava Pilsen*, a Brazilian beer that reminded me of the Stella I usually order. Maggie went for *Frango com Bacon*, a chicken breast wrapped in bacon. She also went with the seasoned rice and her go-to cocktail when we dine out, an appletini.

After we finished eating, we split a dessert and then enjoyed another round of cocktails. Finally, Rosemary came over to our table with our check. "If you have questions about Annie, I just have a minute, and then I have to get back to work. Management don't like it if we spend too much time visitin' with the customers."

"I understand," I said. "I promise this won't take long."

"Okay. What do you want to know?"

"Like you said, about Annie Harris. I don't know how aware you are about what's going on, but it seems she disappeared a number of years ago. You may also know that her father is in prison, and I'm sorry to say, he has an incurable cancer. He's dying. He wants to see his daughter once more before, well, before his time runs out. He's hired me to find her."

Her mouth turned down just a bit at the corners. "I'm sorry, but I don't see how I can help you with that."

"Let's find out. I'm wondering, after the two of you graduated high school, did you stay in touch at all? I read the inscription you wrote in her yearbook, and it sounded like you were pretty close, at least back then."

"You saw that?"

"I did. I visited with Annie's mother at her home. She let me borrow the yearbook."

"Well, we were close, that's right. We did a lot of things together. You know, we went shopping, we double-dated, we even shared an apartment for a while. But then things changed when she met that Jason fella and got to singin' with that band they put together. It wasn't long after that, she said she wanted to move in with him, and, of course, I couldn't afford the apartment all by myself, so I moved back home for a while. We didn't really keep in touch so much after that."

"Because of the band?"

"Yeah, well, that I guess. Plus, she had big ideas. You know, Annie and Jason, they had plans. They thought they were going to make a whole string of hit records, get rich, live in a big house, and drive nice cars. Then the band sort of fizzled out, and not long after that, I heard she and Jason broke up. I called her up and suggested maybe we could get another apartment together, but she said she was planning on making a singing career and she thought she'd be leaving town for a while."

"Do you know whether she ever did?"

"No, and anyway, I think all she ever really wanted was to find some rich guy who'd take care of her. She didn't have time for people like me anymore."

"How do you mean?"

"I never had no big plans. I just wanted a regular life. You know, get married, have kids. But that wasn't for Annie. I remember, it was a few years later, I thought I seen her at the mall. I was havin' lunch with my boyfriend, and I waved to her, but she just passed on by, you know, like I wasn't even there. But then, after I thought about it, I thought, well, maybe that wasn't her. I mean, she looked, I don't know, different, like."

"Different in what way?"

"I can't describe it exactly, but if it was Annie, she looked really classy. Nice clothes, her hair was different. It even seemed like she walked different. For sure, she was thinner. You know, all she used to talk about was how much she wanted to be rich, but I know that her singing career never went nowhere, so maybe that was somebody else that just looked like Annie." She shook her head sadly.

"People change, you know. Anyway, I haven't talked to her for years and years. She's probably livin' someplace else now. Someplace nicer than before. Anyway, I hope she is. I'd like to think maybe one of us made it."

Maggie and I finished our drinks, and then I dropped her at her apartment and headed for home. But not before leaving Rosemary a two-hundred-dollar tip—in cash. Later, I added it to my expense report as "payment to an informant."

Chapter Twenty-Two

The next morning, I was up and out early. I wanted to get a head start on traffic because I was hoping to catch Detective Lorraine Proctor at her desk. There was something I needed to talk to her about, something that had been bothering me about the Annie Harris case from the get-go. I caught a break and found Proctor right where I hoped she'd be, looking through a stack of paperwork. It reminded me all over again what it was about police work that I don't miss.

"Mister Gamble," she said when she spotted me approaching. "You won't believe this, but you're just the person we wanted to see. In fact, you saved us the trouble of having a couple of unis scoop you up and bring you in for, well, what shall we call it? A follow-up interview."

Before I even had a chance to ask, "Follow up to what?" she said, "Why don't we go down the hall where we can all be more comfortable?" And with that, Proctor and Spillner, who had just come around the corner with a cup of coffee in his hand, ushered me into a windowless interview room and closed the door. I sat down on one side of a long table. The two detectives took seats on the other side, facing me.

Spillner said, "Just so you know, we're recording here. And in case you're wondering whether you should ask for an attorney, we're not treating you as a suspect. As far as we're concerned, you're a witness, so we won't be reading you your rights. Of course, if you've forgotten, we'll be happy to remind you."

"No, I remember. What I don't remember is what is it I'm supposed to have witnessed?"

"Just a minute, and we'll get to that." Proctor placed her phone on the table equidistantly placed between me and the two detectives.

"Just so you understand, Mr. Gamble, I'm using my phone instead of our regular recording equipment to get all this down. As I said, this is just a conversation. You are not a suspect in our investigation. We're just looking for information. The recording is so I don't have to take a lot of notes." She looked across the table at me. "Is that okay with you?"

"Go ahead."

"Okay," she said. "Here goes. We're recording.

"Mister Gamble, you arrived at a crime scene shortly after the police were notified that there had been a suspicious death. The victim turned out to be an individual named Jason Mackey. Can you tell us briefly how you came to be at the crime scene, and what was your connection to Mr. Mackey?"

And so, I took it from the top, explaining that I had been retained by an attorney acting on behalf of a man named Harvey Harris to locate his daughter, Annamaria, or Annie as she took to calling herself later on. Harvey lost touch with her more than a decade earlier. He was currently incarcerated at the Hardeman County Correctional Center in Whiteville. He was there because, although he had been sentenced to death for the murder of two people and an unborn child, he was suffering from pancreatic cancer and had only a short time to live.

Spillner said, "I remember Harvey Harris. He was sent up, what, ten years ago?"

"Something like that, yeah. I met with him at Whiteville. I'd say he hasn't got much longer to go."

"Okay. What's any of this got to do with Jason Mackey?"

"Mackey and Annamaria Harris were bandmates in a group called Midnite Oil. They didn't have much success, and the band broke up. During that time, and maybe afterward for a bit, Mackey and Harris were also living together. I was hoping that they might have stayed in touch, and that he would be able to tell me where I could find Annamaria."

"And did he?"

"I never got the chance to ask. It took me a couple of days to run him down. When I finally did, and I went to interview him, he was already dead. That's pretty much the end of it."

"And you still haven't found the girl?"

"Well, she's a woman now, in her mid-thirties, but no. I'm no closer to finding her than I was the day I started looking."

Spillner and Proctor looked at each other, and it seemed to me that some kind of a signal passed between them.

Proctor said, "Right. Couple more questions, and then we'll be done here. And as long as we're still recording, I want to say thanks for coming in and being straight with us. We always appreciate the help."

"You're welcome. What else do you want to know?"

"Okay, first, do you have any reason to think that Annie Harris had anything to do with Jason Mackey getting killed? Is it possible that, for whatever reason, she doesn't want to be found, and figured getting rid of her former boyfriend would be a good way to stay out of sight?"

I thought about that. "It's possible, I guess, but that assumes she knows I'm looking for her, and that somebody told her I'm looking. So far, I haven't run across anybody who's stayed in touch with her."

Proctor picked up her phone and switched off the "record" function. "This is off the record, and just for our information. We'd like to know who's paying your fees for this investigation. I mean, we know you don't work cheap, and it's highly unlikely that Harvey Harris has any money, since he's been in stir for the last ten years. We also checked up on his wife, and it doesn't look like she's got much money, so who's paying you? And before you start spouting off about confidentiality, let me remind you, this is a murder investigation."

I said, "Harvey has an attorney named Tate. I send a bill every week, and he pays it, although I don't know if he's using his own money or somebody else's. I also don't know why he's even involved. And that's the best I can tell you. You could always ask him, but he'll likely claim attorney-client privilege. He's got a lot more juice than I do, so you won't end up knowing any more than you do now unless you get a court order."

The two detectives sat quietly for a moment. Then Spillner said, "Okay,

Jackson, thanks. I guess we're done here for now," and got up to leave.

I said, "Before you go, Detective Proctor, could I have a word?"

After Spillner left the room and closed the door behind him, she said, "What?"

"I need a favor. I'm hoping you can help me."

"With?"

"Couple things. First, I need whatever you can dig up on a guy named James Figgins." I did my best to spell it the way I'd heard it.

"You don't need to spell it. I know who this guy is."

"You do?"

"Yep. I busted him a few times when I was working vice. Back in the day, he'd hire out as a male prostitute. Mostly, he'd hang around in hotel bars, wait until some business type, usually some guy from out of town, would chat him up. Then they'd go up to the mark's room, start to do whatever it is they were going to do. Then, there'd be a knock on the door, and his partner would show up pretending to be a cop. In the end, the mark would end up paying Figgins and his partner to go away."

"Sounds like a solid plan. What went wrong?"

"His act started wearing thin, and we began to get complaints from the various hotel staffs. So, we sent one of our guys in, you know, to let Figgins pick him up. Then, when the partner showed up pretending to be a cop, our guy busted them both. They took a plea, then spent a year and a day at county. Last I heard, the partner, I forget his name, hooked on at some halfway house, helping ex-offenders to get their lives straightened out. Figgins, I know, got a job working for some music company. Far as I know, he's been clean since then."

"Well, then, let me bring you up to date," I said. "These days, James Figgins works for, or rather used to work for, a guy named Sonny Miles. Miles is an artists' agent. Figgins was his muscle. He tried to lean on me a while back, to make a point his boss thought needed making."

"You mean he assaulted you. For what reason, or is that a private matter?"

"No. Sonny Miles's wife—her name is Madelaine—hired me to find out if somebody was following her around. Turned out, somebody was. It was Figgins, apparently at the direction of Sonny. So, for a couple nights, I shadowed Mrs. Miles. But what I didn't know was that Figgins was shadowing me. He was good, too, because I never spotted him. The next day, Miles and Figgins showed up at my office to tell me to drop the case. I said it didn't work that way, that she was my client. So, when Sonny couldn't bring me to my knees with money, he asked James to find another means of persuasion."

"So, he attacked you. And did you report it?"

"And spoil my tough-as-nails persona?"

"Right. So, is that it? Are we done here?"

"As far as James Figgins is concerned, yes. But I also have a question about Harvey Harris."

"This is the guy whose daughter has gone off the radar. I told you already. I don't know anything about him."

"I know that. But what I need is to get a look at all the arrest reports for Harvey going back to the first time he was busted. This will be quite a while ago, maybe forty years. And it may involve some digging, but I think it might help clear up the cases we're both working on."

"You're talking now about the Mackey killing."

"And the Annie Harris disappearance. I'm not quite sure how they're connected just yet, but I think Harvey is the missing piece."

"You don't want much, do you?" She sounded more than a little dubious. "Okay, look, I'll see what I can find, but no promises. I'm not even sure where to start looking. But if I turn something up, I'm going to want a better explanation, and I mean everything. Understood?"

"Yes."

"Then, is that it? Now, are we done here? Or do you need me to pick up your car and take it in for an oil change?"

"Just one more thing. Can you ask your partner, what's her name?"

"ADA Rosslyn. Why?"

"I'd appreciate it if you'd ask her to check back through all of Harvey's court appearances."

"Looking for?"

"I want to know how many times he was represented by Geoffrey Tate."

"The guy who's paying your fees? Mister Gamble, I think you'd better tell me what's going on here."

"I'm not sure yet, but I think it'll be worthwhile for you and ADA Rosslyn if you can do this for me."

"It had better be," she said. "And you're going to owe both of us big time. Understood?"

Chapter Twenty-Three

On my way to the office following my conversation with Spillner and Proctor, I had an idea. I stopped at a McDonald's on the way and ordered my go-to lunch, a ten-pack of McNuggets, fries, and a large Diet Coke, probably none of which would bring a nod of approval from my cardiologist. I took a seat at an inside booth and, while I ate, placed a call to a lawyer I sometimes did work for named Robert Starnes. Starnes was a partner in a two-person firm that handled a lot of divorce cases, as well as civil suits and the occasional criminal case. He was also on the call list as a public defender.

For the second time that morning, luck was with me, and I caught him at his desk. Unfortunately, he was in a hurry, so no time for small talk.

"I was just about to head out to take a deposition, so if you can make this quick, I'd appreciate it."

"Then I'll get right to it. What can you tell me about a lawyer named Geoffrey Tate?"

"Like what?"

"Well, is he any good? What kinds of clients does he normally take on? That kind of thing."

"I should probably ask you, is this something personal? Are you being sued?"

"Why would anybody sue me? I haven't got any money."

"Yep. And you never color outside the lines, either." He paused and took a deep breath. "Okay, well, then, Geoffrey Tate is what you would call a white-shoe attorney. He mostly represents high-profile clients, usually corporate cases, usually where there's lots of money involved. Med mal, breach of contract, that kind of thing. I can tell you this for certain. You don't want to be on the opposite side of the courtroom from him, or, for that matter, anybody else who works at that firm. They're very good, very well connected, and they almost always win. You haven't said what this is about, but my advice, don't poke the bear."

"How about criminal cases? Does he handle a lot of those?"

"Rarely, and when he does, it's most often white-collar crime. You know, tax evasion, securities fraud, embezzlement. His record isn't quite so good there. I'd say he's batting above five-hundred, but juries can be unpredictable."

"Does he ever do *pro bono*?"

"Where are we going with this?"

I couldn't see any harm in telling him. "It's like this. Tate is representing a man named Harvey Harris. Maybe you've heard of him. He's a career screwup who was convicted of a triple homicide about ten years ago. No surprise, he got the death penalty, but his sentence was commuted to life without parole because he's dying of pancreatic cancer."

"And?"

"And Harvey Harris wants to see his daughter before he dies, but she's gone missing. Geoffrey Tate hired me to find her. He's paying my fees to conduct the search."

"How are the checks drawn?"

"Check. I've only gotten one so far. It was drawn on Tate's law firm account."

"I see. Do you know, did Tate represent Harris at trial? I mean, maybe Tate feels like he should have gotten this guy off, and he's feeling guilty about it."

"I don't know. I was hoping you could find that out. I'd also like to know whether Tate served as Harvey's defense counsel for any of his other trials. There's a Metro detective I know who's partnered with an ADA named Rosslyn. I've got a request in to see what she can dig up, but I'm not sure she'll want to help me, since this is outside official channels."

"Well, I can take a look for you. It'll mean a trip to the courthouse, since

Tennessee is behind states like Kentucky and Missouri when it comes to having a centralized database, so it might take a little time. Also…."

"What?"

"Going by what you've told me so far, there's something very wrong here. Lawyers like Geoffrey Tate don't handle *pro bono* work for what sounds like a real lowlife. Also, I'm at a complete loss trying to understand why he would be paying you. I'll see what I can find out, but you should be very careful dealing with this guy. He's smart, and he's tough, and he's connected. If you try to be cute with him, you might wind up wishing you hadn't."

I hung up the phone, wondering if I'd made a mistake getting the cops involved in what had started out as a fairly straightforward missing persons investigation. After all, the only thing I was being paid to do was track down a young woman that neither of her parents had seen for more than a decade. She had, after all, been pursuing a career in music, and that could have taken her almost anywhere there was a record label, including out of the country altogether. And the fact that I had so far not been able to turn up any meaningful leads suggested strongly that, in fact, she was no longer in the area.

Of course, she could also be dead, and just like if she were still alive, she could be dead almost anywhere in the world. So why, then, was I wasting my time and the client's money trying to dig into Harvey Harris's past? And at the end of the day, what difference did it make? I looked at my watch. Not even three o'clock, and I was ready to call it a day. I certainly wasn't doing anything useful, and, to be honest, I was having trouble thinking of anything I could be doing that could be described as such.

Frustrated, I turned on my computer to read the headlines. The first thing that caught my eye was a story about three separate mass shootings which had taken place over the previous weekend, one in a mall in Iowa, one at a neighborhood block party in Pennsylvania, and one following a church service outside Washington D.C. Once again, local and state officials were quick to offer their thoughts and prayers to the victims and their families, including nine dead and thirteen wounded. But no one was able to determine the motive for any of the three events. One shooter was killed by an armed member of the public, another killed himself, and a third was at large, with no suspect identified.

Further down, the upcoming weekend promised to be hot, with temperatures reaching into the upper nineties and no prospect of rain. Residents were asked to refrain from watering their lawns and washing their cars in order to conserve water. That, at least, was something I could do to demonstrate my community concern.

And then I had an idea. Since it was close to the time when people started getting off work, and the weather was good, it occurred to me that maybe this would be a good opportunity to wander around on Lower Broadway to see whether I could find Lucas Pratt. Since it was a Friday night, I knew the street-corner musician business was apt to be pretty good. Locals might decide to stay downtown for a couple of drinks, and tourists are always hanging around, hoping to catch a glimpse of somebody famous to pose with them for a selfie, and maybe, while they're feeling the vibe, drop a buck or two into a street-corner musician's open guitar case. So, I locked up the office, and since it was a nice day, decided to walk the few blocks to where I planned to begin my search.

Twenty minutes later, I was standing at the corner of North Fifth Avenue, now also known as Rep. John Lewis Way, and Broadway, a block away from Ryman Auditorium. Ryman, as practically anybody with a working brain is aware, is best known as the Home of the Grand Ole Opry, which it was until 1974. That year, the Opry relocated to a new, 4,000-seat auditorium in a venue that also includes the Opryland hotel and, between 1972 and 1997, when it closed for good, the Opryland amusement park. These days, the amusement park site is home to a high-end mall, and the old Ryman hosts a wide variety of concert events, including performances by artists such as Donny Osmond, Vince Gill, Ellen DeGeneres, Joan Jett and the Blackhearts and the Happy Together Tour, which features such '60s headliners as The Turtles, and a collection of other groups that varies from year to year. But I wasn't interested in purchasing concert tickets. I was more interested in the half-dozen or so street performers I could see who had staked out the corners from Fifth all the way down to Second.

The first guy I spoke to was just getting set up, with a Styrofoam cooler, a saxophone, and a paper KFC bucket that he had primed with a handful of silver coins and a few one- and five-dollar bills. He was about twenty-five, dressed for the part in the world of street-corner musicians, including jeans, a long-sleeved denim shirt, and a leather vest. A wide-brimmed hat and a pair of aviator sunglasses completed the look.

He looked up when I approached, then looked away again. "Sorry, I'll just be a few minutes. Then I can play whatever you like."

I dropped a twenty into Colonel Sanders's bucket. "Play whatever makes you feel good. I'm looking for a little information."

Now I had his attention. "Information about what? You aren't a cop, are you? Because I have a union card and a license to be on this corner playing music, if that's what this is about."

"Nothing like that. I'm looking for one of your fellow musicians, or one of your competitors, if you prefer. His name is Lucas Pratt. As I understand it, he plays guitar."

"Is he in trouble? You didn't say whether you were a cop."

"I'm a private investigator." I took out my license and showed it to him. "I need to ask him about a person I've been hired to find." When he didn't say anything right away, I said, "There might be a little do-re-mi in it for him, and maybe for you, too, if you can steer me in his direction."

He took off his hat and propped his sunglasses on top of his head. His eyes got suddenly narrow. "Is there a reward? I mean, maybe I could help you, you know, if there's a reward."

"The person I'm looking for is older. I don't think you'd know her." I took out another twenty and dangled it over his bucket. "But this double sawbuck I've got here is starting to slip through my fingers. If you can point me in Lucas's direction, I might get excited and drop it." And I thought, *it's fun spending other people's money. Especially Geoffrey Tate's.*

He thought about that for maybe five seconds. "Okay. Luke. That's what he likes to be called. Luke usually works the corner down at Third. But most of the time, he doesn't show up until around five. 'Course, there's lots of places up and down Broad where you can kill some time until then."

"Okay, thanks. And, by the way, what's your name? You know, in case Luke wants to know how I was able to find him. I might need a reference."

"Randolph," he told me. "Boots Randolph."

Colonel Sanders and Boots Randolph, in one day. I wondered, in real life, whether the two had ever actually met.

"Interesting. For a guy who's been dead nearly twenty years, you look remarkably good."

I dropped the bill into his bucket, wished him a good day, and drifted down the street to a place called the Rhinestone Cowgirl. The name was a riff on the old Larry Weiss song, "Rhinestone Cowboy," that Glen Campbell turned into a mega-hit way back in 1975. After dark, the Cowgirl was a tuck-a-buck joint with strippers and champagne cocktails that cost more than a steak dinner at a top-notch restaurant. Days, it was just a bar with a jukebox playing country music and television sets tuned to Fox News and ESPN with the sound turned down and the closed captions turned on.

Years ago, I dated a woman named Carly Barrett, who, after our breakup, worked for a time at the Cowgirl. She wasn't a stripper, however, but a waitress, dressed in a *faux* Dallas Cowboys cheerleader outfit, serving overpriced drinks to tourists. Carly helped me find a witness in a case I was working on at the time. Our reunion wasn't a particularly a warm one, and not long after I learned she had married an over-the-road truck driver she said she loved. The last I heard, they had moved to a new home somewhere in Mississippi. I hoped she was happy and that they were doing well.

Two hours and twice as many bottles of Stella later, I was ready to head out and find Luke Pratt, as he preferred to be called, when I felt my phone vibrating in my pocket. Maggie. I thought about letting the call go to voicemail, then decided to go ahead and pick up. At the same moment, somebody dropped a few coins into the jukebox, and a Morgan Wallen song, "Wasted on You," began blaring loud enough to raise Old Hank from the grave.

The first thing Maggie said after I answered was, "Gamble, where are you?"

"Actually, I'm in a strip club. But I was just leaving."

I must have slurred my words just a little, because she said, "Are you drunk?"

"I don't know. Maybe a little. I've been sitting here for two hours. I'm waiting for a street corner musician to show up and start strumming his guitar so I can ask him a couple of questions."

"You mean you're actually working?"

"I am."

"And are you driving?"

"I am not."

"Okay, don't. Call me back after you get your questions answered, and I'll come and get you."

Chapter Twenty-Four

When I got to the corner where Lucas Pratt was supposed to be, he wasn't there. So, I walked around the block, thinking it would kill some time and also work some of the alcohol out of my system. It did, but still no Lucas, and since it was getting on toward six-thirty, I decided tonight wasn't going to be the night, so I gave it up as a bad job and called Maggie. Her apartment is only a couple of blocks from where I was standing, at the corner of Third and Broadway. And so, fifteen minutes later, I was in the passenger seat of her car, buckled up, and ready for whatever the rest of the evening might have in store. Which turned out to be dinner at her favorite restaurant. An expensive one. On me, of course.

After we were seated—there was a wait, since it was Friday night—and had ordered drinks, a Diet Coke for me and a raspberry iced tea for her, Maggie got around to asking some questions. No alcohol, just soft drinks. She was in a mood. Not good.

"So, this strip club deal. Was this work, or just sowing a few wild oats?"

"Work. Absolutely." I tried to explain about finally tracking down Lucas Pratt, only to find that I was too early to catch him at his usual post, so I ducked into the Rhinestone Cowgirl to kill a couple hours until the time he was supposed to show up. Only he didn't, so I pretty much accomplished nothing, except to spend twenty-four bucks on four bottles of overpriced beer and to spiff some street corner saxophone guy another forty for what turned out to be nothing.

"And this has to do with this missing daughter you're still looking for?"

"It does. Lucas Pratt was a member of the band that Annie Harris was in for a while. I thought maybe he'd stayed in touch with her, or at least might have had some idea of what she was doing now. Or who she was doing it with."

"Well, if you're listening to yourself, you know that makes her sound a little like a porn star, right?"

Speaking of porn stars, I started to say. I'd like your professional opinion about a video my client gave me. I was thinking of the one I'd copied from Madelaine Miles's flash drive. Then I realized I'd never told Maggie about Madelaine Miles and the troubles she was having with her husband.

"I doubt that's what she's doing. More likely, she's married to some insurance salesman and living in Atlanta in a tract house with a couple kids and a dog."

"Then I'd say good for her, if she is." She took a sip of her iced tea. "Gamble, can I ask you something?"

Before she could get to it, the waiter returned with our appetizer course, fried calamari with remoulade dipping sauce, and asked if we'd like another beverage.

"I'll have a vodka and cranberry juice. My friend will have a Stella."

"Change of pace?" I asked. "Do you have something planned for later?"

Her tone got serious. "Maybe. But first, my question."

I waited.

"I need to know. What you told the nurse at the hospital, that I was your partner in life. Did you really mean that?"

"Yes, absolutely. Have you ever had reason to doubt it?"

"Does that mean you love me?"

"I'm sorry, what? Where is this coming from?" *Shit! Have I really never said so? And why is she asking me this now?*

"It's a simple question. We've been together five years now, and you've never said. Do you love me, or are we just, I don't know, friends with benefits?"

I wanted to be careful. I wanted her to tell me where this was coming from. But more than either of those, I wanted to get it right.

I said, "Yes, without question, I love you. Do you really need to hear me say it?"

"Then why have you never said so? I allowed you—no, that's not right. That's not how I want to say it. I welcomed you into my life, and I welcomed you into my body. So, yes, I needed to hear you say it, and I'd like to know why up until this moment, you haven't."

"This is going to be a long answer, and I am going to try my best to get it right." I took a deep breath.

"Do you remember when we first connected, when I was looking for that Gabrielle Hawkins girl? There was a Dusty Springfield song that we talked about. It was called 'You Don't Have to Say You Love Me.' You asked me whether I thought I could be close at hand—that's the other part of the lyric. And I said to you that I could be as close as you want, and as far away as you need me to be."

"I remember."

"You were coming off a bad break-up, a divorce. And, yes, I wanted to be close at hand. I did then, and I do now, but I didn't want to crowd you, and I certainly didn't want to pressure you by talking about love. What I was saying was that I was willing to let our relationship develop at whatever pace was comfortable for you, and that I'd let you have as much space as you needed. I guess that's how I would define love."

She gave me the barest of a smile. "Okay."

I said, "I'm going to need a little context here. Did something happen today? Something at work? Is that what this is about?"

"One of my clients." Our drinks arrived, and she gulped down half of it in one swallow. "She wanted to know if she should leave her husband. She said he was good to her, didn't beat her up, wasn't a drunk. He earned a good living. As far as she knew, he didn't have another woman on the side. He told her he was staying with her because he believed in keeping his marriage vows. A promise is a promise, he told her. But he didn't love her. Never had, never would. She wanted to know what I thought she should do."

"And what did you tell her?"

"Well, she doesn't have any kids, so I asked her if she thought she could support herself on her own. If she could, then maybe it was time to call it a day and move on, because life is too short to just go on living in a loveless marriage. If not, then I suggested she should see if she could persuade her husband to go with her to get counseling." She waited while the waiter returned to take our food orders.

"Other than that, what could I tell her?"

I knew I needed to be careful here, talking about failed marriages. Maggie Totten is by far the best thing that ever happened to me, but sometimes, I knew, bad memories can creep back. From all accounts, during most of the time she was married to him, Maggie's ex-husband, Michael Pomeroy, was a decent enough guy, right up until the time he went off the rails and broke into her condo, with fatal results.

I said, "You know, you and I are pretty much in the same business. People come to us with their troubles, and we do what we can to help them. Sometimes, it works out, and we do them some good, and other times, it doesn't. But the thing I try to remember is at the end of the day, all you can do is all you can do. And it doesn't do anything for anybody if we internalize other people's problems. It isn't easy, and it doesn't always work, but besides each other, it's about all we've got. And I guess until one of us wins the lottery, and we can spend the rest of our lives sitting on a beach somewhere warm, we're just going to have to keep on doing it." And even as I was saying it, I realized it was no kind of answer at all.

* * *

After dinner, Maggie dropped me off near where I had left my car earlier in the day. She said she was tired, and after her last client meeting, not feeling much like company. And so, she went back to her apartment by herself, leaving me with a promise that we could get together the next night, and that she would try to be better company. Since it was still early, and I had nothing better to do, I took the elevator back upstairs to my office. The message light on my phone was blinking. Three messages. The first one was from four o'clock this afternoon.

"Mister Gamble, this is Geoffrey Tate. I wanted to let you know that in the next several days, they'll be transferring Harvey Harris from Hardeman County Correctional to a secure ward at West Tennessee Healthcare Hospital in Jackson. I'm afraid his condition has deteriorated significantly, and it's doubtful he'll last out the month. That means you need to turn up the wick searching for his daughter. I need you to call me back as soon as you can to give me a status report on your progress." Then he left a number and hung up.

The second was from Lorraine Proctor, who said she had some information for me. I called her number right back, but it went straight to voicemail. Then I tried her office number, but was informed by the officer who answered she had already left for the day. Was this an emergency, and did I wish to speak to another officer? He'd be glad to transfer my call. I said thanks, but no. I was returning her call, and I'd try back in the morning.

The third message, which was left at around five-thirty, was from Sonny Miles. "Mr. Gamble, we need to talk. As you already know, my wife has not come home, and I have a pretty good idea you know where she is. In fact, I'm sure you do, so I'll give you until tomorrow to bring her on back, or at least tell me where she is so I can go and fetch her. And just so we're clear, unless you're lookin' for a peck of trouble, I suggest you get a move on."

Chapter Twenty-Five

The next day, Saturday, I started making telephone calls from home, beginning with Lorraine Proctor. The callback number on my phone wasn't police headquarters, which I would have recognized right away, so I assumed she had called me on her personal cell. Smart, since if things got complicated, she might have a hard time explaining why she was calling a private investigator's number from her department-issued phone. She picked up on the second ring.

"Mister Gamble. How are we this fine morning?"

"Good, thanks. I got your message from yesterday. I tried catching you at work, but I guess you'd already left for the day. Have you got something for me?"

"First, remind me why I'm doing this for you."

"Because I think it'll help us—help you—find the killer of Jason Mackey."

There was a beat. "Well, yeah, okay, maybe I've got something. I don't know. You wanted me to look into the first arrest record we have for this guy, Harvey Harris. Fortunately for both of us, we actually digitized those old records a few years ago, and I was able to bring it up on the computer. The long and short of it is, he got busted back in 1979 for trying to knock over an all-night gas station."

"So, off to a flying start."

"Funny thing was, and it really is funny. According to the attendant, Harvey and another guy rolled up in an old Ford sedan. Of course, it was dark, and this was before there were things like security cameras at the pump islands. So, the attendant couldn't tell the investigating officers much other than it was a Ford, and it was a dark color. He couldn't tell just what.

"Anyhow, Harvey, damn fool that he apparently is, went and bought a bag of chips and a couple tallboy cans of beer from the cooler, and then started waving a gun around and demanding money. Well, about that time, the guy driving the car must have gotten cold feet. Either that, or else Harvey was just hitching a ride, and the guy wasn't expecting to be a wheelman for a stickup artist. Either way, he took off, leaving Harvey there by himself with no good way to make a clean getaway. So, Harvey panics, drops the chips and the beer, and takes off running out the door. The attendant calls the police, and they pick him up about a half a mile away, walking down the side of the road with the gun stuck in his pocket. They never found the driver, or the car, and Harvey denied there was anyone else involved."

"Interesting," I said. "Think he was covering for a pal?"

"Don't know. Could have been, I guess. But since he was a juvenile, he got off with six months in juvie and a year's probation."

"Okay. Anything else?"

"Not with that case. Juvenile records are sealed, so you'd need a court order to find out anything more. I asked Amanda to look into his trial history as an adult offender, but she hasn't gotten back to me yet. And before you ask, I don't expect to hear much of anything until sometime next week. I mean, it's not like she has nothing better to do than run down old cases for you. Meantime, you said you had something for me about the Mackey killing. What is it?"

"I'm working on it. I'm pretty much convinced what I mentioned to you and Spillner about this Annamaria Harris is right. Somebody doesn't want her found, and I think that same somebody clipped Jason Mackey because the killer thought Mackey knew where she is, or at least where to start looking. I have one more of Annie's old band mates, a guy named Lucas Pratt, that I need to track down, and after that, I think I'll be able to give you something definite."

And then, I thanked her for her time and hung up, but not before promising to follow up with what I hoped to learn from Lucas Pratt. Which, at that precise moment, I suspected was going to turn out to be absolutely nothing.

My next call was to Geoffrey Tate. The callback number he left turned out not to be his office, and, since it was the weekend, instead of reaching his PA, I got a voicemail recording that reminded me of the firm's regular office hours and asked that I call back during that time. In the meantime, I could leave a short message if I wished, so I left my cell number and said he could call me back at his convenience.

After that, I thought about calling Sonny Miles, but then I decided that since I had no intention of telling him where his wife was, there really wasn't any reason for me to bother. So, instead, I put in a call to Wanda Beaudry at Haven. I had no reason to think Sonny knew Madelaine had taken refuge with Wanda, but I was thinking it might be a good idea for both of them to be extra careful to make sure she stayed out of sight. Residents at Haven are free to come and go as they please. They are not prisoners or inmates, by any means. But the worst thing Madelaine Miles could do right now would be to decide she could take an afternoon to go shopping, or call up one of her friends for lunch, and then have Sonny find out about it.

As always, I went through the standard procedure of leaving my name and number and then waiting for callback. This time, it came almost immediately.

Wanda seemed to have read my mind. "Are you calling about your friend Madelaine? Because if you are, I can tell you, she's already talking about leaving."

"What? Leaving to go where?"

"Who knows? Back to her husband. To an island in the South Pacific. Maybe back to her mother and father, if they're still alive. All I know is that she's not like the other women we have staying with us. She's used to a different life, where there's no such thing as poverty, or wondering where the money is going to come from to buy food for your kids, or having to take the bus because your crap car broke down for the last time."

"What about the physical violence? Did she say anything about wanting to go to the police?"

"No. But right after you dropped her off, we did have our doctor look her over just in case she needed to be hospitalized. I mean, we're not really equipped here to handle a medical crisis, and we certainly don't need the liability in case her life is in danger."

"And?"

"And, the doctor said, yes, she'd taken a pretty good beating, but she wasn't likely to die on us. So, she prescribed some pain relievers and said she was okay to stay here."

"But she didn't want to go to the police."

"Again, no. But then, you were a cop. How many times did you go out on a domestic disturbance call, and then have the injured party decline to press charges?"

I didn't say anything to that, because the answer is, almost always. Women in these situations, for a variety of reasons, have nowhere else to go, no real way to escape from an abusive spouse or boyfriend. And I supposed, when you came right down to it, neither did Madelaine Miles.

"You're right. But I think she's in real danger if she goes back. Think about why I brought her to you in the first place. If she goes back, what's to say Sonny won't start in on her all over again?"

"Well, I can't keep her here if she doesn't want to stay. But I did get a look at some of those videos. I couldn't get through all of them, but Gamble, this guy is a beast. Somebody needs to take him off the board. Meantime, I can talk to her, but that's about all I can do."

"Then do your best," I said. "I know you can be very persuasive."

* * *

That afternoon, I talked Maggie into an early dinner downtown, and then maybe an evening of bar-hopping. In truth, apart from spending an enjoyable Saturday evening listening to live music and knocking back a few drinks before heading home to bed, I also had an ulterior motive. I was hoping I could track down Lucas Pratt, strumming his guitar and taking requests for tips and handouts at the corner of Third and Broad.

One dinner, two cocktail lounges, four beers, and three appletinis later, I dropped Maggie at her apartment with a promise to be back in half an hour.

Then, about the time it was getting dark, I wandered over to the corner of Third and Broad where a musician was strumming an electric guitar. He was very tall, very slender, and dressed in what seemed to be standard-issue busker attire, including faded jeans, brown boots, a long-sleeved denim shirt, and a tan leather vest. Somewhat surprisingly, given the fashion of the times, he was clean-shaven, with medium-length brown hair and brown eyes. An extension cord attached to his portable amplifier was plugged into an outlet outside the door to the bar where he was strumming what sounded like a Jim Croce composition, "Time in a Bottle." I waited until he finished the last few chords, and then dropped a twenty into his guitar case.

"Lucas Pratt?"

"That's me." He looked at the bill and then at me. "For that, you get two requests."

"Not music, just some information."

He eyed me suspiciously. "You with the union? 'Cause my dues are all paid up, and I got a license to be a street performer."

That again. "Not the union." I flashed my identification. "I'm looking for some information about somebody you used to know. Her name is Annie Harris."

"Annie?" He looked genuinely perplexed. "I haven't seen Annie in years. What do you want with her?"

"Me personally, nothing. But her father wants to see her. He has a cancer, and he's dying."

"Last I heard, he was in prison someplace for shooting a store clerk."

"He still is, and he hasn't got long to go. He wants to see his daughter before he gets to the end of the trail, and I was hired to find her. So, anything you can tell me could be useful. And there might be a little something in it for you."

The flow of locals and tourists on foot and in cars out for a Saturday night of merrymaking on Lower Broad was beginning to pick up, and along with it the general noise level in the street.

"Look, I don't know what I can tell you. After the band broke up…. Wait, you do know we were in a band together, right?"

"Midnite Oil," I said.

"Midnite Oil, yeah. Well, anyway, after the band broke up, we all went in different directions. I guess Annie decided she wanted to go it alone, so she took off to try to make a new start with a studio in Muscle Shoals. A lot of big names cut records down there. You know, Aretha, Percy Sledge, the Allman Brothers. Even the Stones."

"And?"

"And what? What else do you want to know?"

I took out my wallet and dropped another twenty into his case.

"Whatever you've got."

"Well. How I heard it, she got into a little bit of trouble. In Sheffield or Tuscumbia, or someplace like that."

"What kind of trouble? And how long ago was this?"

"Not long after she got there. I'm not exactly sure what happened, but I heard somebody died. I don't know what happened after that, but if I was a betting man, I'd say these days, Annie is probably a thousand miles away from Alabama."

* * *

After that, there wasn't anything else he could tell me, so I thanked him and dropped another twenty bucks into his guitar case. That made sixty in all, much more than I figured he'd have taken in working his regular gig during the ten minutes or so we'd spent talking. First thing Monday, I'd have to get back in touch with Lorraine Proctor to see if she could find out from the cops in Lauderdale or Colbert County who died, and if there were any wants or warrants for Annie Harris, or whatever she was calling herself during her audition. The way Lucas Pratt told the story, it didn't sound as though it was Annie who was the victim. He also hadn't said if it had been a death from natural causes or a murder, so I had no way of knowing if she was a suspect in a killing or if she was being sought as a material witness.

I walked around Lower Broad for a while, thinking, and not really coming up with any useful ideas how to proceed with the case. I stopped in for a nightcap at Nudies Honky Tonk, and then another at Justin Timberlake's 12/30 Club rooftop bar before deciding it was time to call it a night. By the time I got back to Maggie's apartment, it was nearly ten-thirty, long past the half-hour I'd promised.

"Hey, there, sailor," she said when she opened the door. "Where did you get off to? You get a better offer, or did you go back to that strip joint?"

"Neither one. After I talked to the guy I wanted to see, I just needed some time to think about this case, and whether I ought to just drop it right now and give that lawyer his money back."

"Well, you can always think about that tomorrow. And besides, I went out today and bought a new nightie. I'd love you to give me your opinion. That is, if you think your heart can stand it."

Chapter Twenty-Six

I spent Sunday morning working on an expense report and a billing statement to send to Geoffrey Tate, including the various cash inducements I'd made to the several informants I'd spoken with. I decided to prorate my daily fee based on the number of hours I'd actually worked on the Harris case. I was pretty sure I could have just charged the full daily rate, but somehow, that didn't seem like the right thing to do, so I broke it down to an hourly charge, which was still a significant amount of money. Satisfied that I was nothing if not an honest man, I used Maggie's laptop to type the whole thing up and sent it to Tate as an email attachment. Tomorrow, I knew, I would need to call him to let him know what I had learned from Lucas Pratt about Annie's troubles in Alabama. I thought since Lucas knew nothing of the details, maybe Tate would have the right connections to find out what that was all about.

* * *

Monday, I was back in the office, having spent the rest of Sunday with Maggie, first at a movie she wanted to see, and then dinner back at her apartment—something she found a recipe for online, which she informed me was "heart healthy," and which involved a lot of vegetables. I had a bad feeling this was inevitably going to take us to a place where fried food, cold beer, and McDonald's breakfasts would become increasingly hard to come by. I had just gotten settled in behind my desk when my phone rang. I was expecting to hear from Geoffrey Tate, but instead the call was from the office of the Davidson County district attorney's office.

"Mister Gamble," she said. "This is Davidson County Deputy District Attorney Amanda Rosslyn. I'm calling you at the request of Detective Proctor at Nashville Metro Police."

"DDA Rosslyn. Thank you for calling. Do you have some information for me?"

"Well, yes, and no. Detective Proctor—Oh, what the hell, Lorraine. Lorraine said you were looking for case histories for an attorney named Geoffrey Tate."

"Yes."

"Okay. I don't have time to run all that down for you, so. I'm going to give you a web address and a one-time password you can use to dig that information up for yourself. But I want to emphasize, get everything you need the first time, because if you don't, there's no going back, understood?"

"Got it."

"Okay. Go to…" and she read off a website address, followed by a backslash, followed by what I guessed was the secret word.

"Read it back to me." When I did, she said, "Okay, you're in business. You should know, what you're looking for is all in the public record, and you could have dug it all out on your own if you knew what you were doing. This is just a faster way to get it done."

"Okay, thanks. And, before you go, can I ask you a question?"

"Go ahead."

"Back maybe a dozen years ago, you were the prosecutor in a homicide case against a woman named Wanda Beaudry. She was accused of killing her boyfriend after he beat her up and sent her to the hospital."

"I remember. Why are you interested in that?"

"Because she's a friend. And from what I know, you let her skate on that charge."

"I have never tanked a case," she said, "even when I thought the victim was a no-good son of a bitch who got exactly what was coming to him." There was a pause. "And I will never do it again."

And that was that. I said thanks, and she hung up.

I spent the rest of the morning navigating the website that Amanda Rosslyn had said would help me find what I was looking for. When I first opened it, I was asked for a password, which I typed into the space provided. It worked as advertised, and I found myself staring at a screen that allowed me to search using the name of an attorney, a defendant, a plaintiff, a judge, or a date. Choosing the most obvious, I typed "Harvey Harris," and then clicked on a tab labeled "Criminal Trial." Four entries, not including his 1979 juvie jolt, appeared in 1983, 1988, 1999, and 2015. The last, I already knew, was his trial for the convenience store killing that wound him up on death row, so I saved that one for last.

The 1983 rap was a simple shoplifting charge. Harvey was caught trying to get out the door of a Service Merchandise store, a retail and catalog chain that featured jewelry, sporting goods, and electronics that shut down in the early 2000s. Harvey grabbed a moderately expensive wristwatch when the clerk's back was momentarily distracted. Since nobody got hurt, the stolen watch was recovered, and it was Harvey's first offense as an adult, he got off with a year's probation. Interestingly, the attorney who plea-bargained the light sentence was one Geoffrey Tate, at the time working *pro bono* as a public defender.

The 1988 trial was the result of Harvey being arrested for grand theft auto, or GTA, as it appears in police shorthand. The car was a nearly-new, ivy-green 1987 Ford Mustang GT, one of the hot-ticket muscle cars of the mid-1980s. According to the trial transcript, the owner had stopped to fill up at a Shell station, and when he went inside to pay for the gas and use the restroom, he left his keys in the ignition. Harvey, who was working as an attendant, noticed the keys and, for whatever reason, decided to take an impromptu joyride, which resulted in a call to the police. What followed was a high-speed pursuit that ended up with Harvey running the car into a ditch and destroying the entire undercarriage.

The insurance company totaled the car, which had a MSRP north of fourteen thousand dollars. Serious money for a car in that period, and this time, Harvey took a five-to-ten-year bounce. His attorney, once again, Geoffrey Tate, now in private practice, had argued for a three-to-five-year sentence. But the judge wasn't in a generous mood, and Harvey was off to the Morgan County Correctional Center in Wartburg. A little more digging revealed that, instead of doing a nickel or a dime, Harvey served only three years and three months before being paroled in 1991. The parole board cited his record of good behavior, his contrition and willingness to accept responsibility for his crime, and his self-proclaimed newfound love for Jesus as reasons for granting early release.

Fast-forward to 1999, and this time, Harvey was pinched for armed robbery of yet another convenience store. On this occasion, he got out the door with three-hundred and twenty-seven dollars in cash, and—no surprise—a twelve-pack of Coors Light and a party-sized bag of Fritos corn chips. Unfortunately for Harvey, the Kangaroo Express store he robbed was equipped with CCTV, and the cops had no trouble identifying him as the perp. He was arrested before he was able to spend any of the money, but not before he had knocked back five of the beers and half the bag of Fritos. Once again, Geoffrey Tate appeared on behalf of the defendant, and once again, he lost. Harvey was handed fifteen years, this time at Northeast Correctional Complex, in Mountain City. I had to give him this much: at the rate he was going, Harvey was getting an up-close, all-expense-paid personal tour of the state's penal institutions. And if not for the fact that Whiteville was going to be his last stop, he might well have gotten to visit them all.

Finally, I turned my attention to the most recent case, the 2015 train wreck that landed Harvey on death row at Riverbend Max. I didn't really need to see the transcript, but I wanted to know if Geoffrey Tate was again Harvey's mouthpiece for this one. Somewhat surprisingly, in this instance, he was not. Instead, the case was handled by a public defender named Rahan Vivek. At trial, Vivek pleaded his client guilty and asked the court for leniency, given that Harvey was under the influence of crack at the time of the incident. Another mitigating factor, Vivek claimed, was that, when tested, Harvey's IQ scored on the low side of average. No doubt, he was relying on the fact that, in most cases, a guilty plea will result in a life sentence rather than a death, since it spares the state the cost of a protracted and expensive trial. This time, though, the judge wasn't one bit interested in a plea bargain, and

CHAPTER TWENTY-SIX

Harvey got a date with the needle.

For lack of anything better to do, I dialed the number of the Davidson County Public Defender's Office. When the receptionist picked up, I identified myself and asked to speak to Rahan Vivek in regard to a case in which he had been involved ten years earlier. I was informed Attorney Vivek was now in private practice in Cookeville. The receptionist was kind enough to give me the name of his new practice and telephone number.

When I got him on the phone, after a little more than ten minutes of waiting on hold, listening to the smooth instrumental stylings of what might have been Kenny G, or maybe Boney Jones or Euge Groove, Vivek had a question.

"Why do you want to know about that case? You said you're a private investigator, so you should know criminal trial results are a matter of public record." He spoke with a soft, lilting accent, like someone who had come by his English in India, or perhaps Pakistan.

"Mr. Vivek, I'm aware of the result of the trial. You may not know that Harvey Harris is a dying man. He's been moved from Riverbend to Hardeman County because the governor was persuaded it would be simpler and cheaper to just let him die from his cancer rather than continue to spend government resources fighting his appeals."

"Then what is it you want to know?"

"Just this. I've been retained by Mr. Harris's attorney, a man named Geoffrey Tate, to find Harvey's daughter before he dies. When I was researching Harvey's prior convictions, I noticed that this same Tate had represented him in…" And here I paused to refer to my notes, "…1983, 1988, and again in 1999. What I'm wondering is, why was his last case turned over to the public defender's office when Geoffrey Tate has been representing him right along, up to and including the present day?"

"Mister…Gamble, is it?"

"Yes."

"Can I ask, Mr. Gamble, what is your interest in this? And what has it got to do with finding Mr. Harris's daughter?"

I switched the phone from one ear to the other. "Probably nothing. Call it professional curiosity."

"Well, then, as best I can remember, I spoke to Geoffrey Tate after Harvey Harris was arrested. I don't know what he is doing these days, but in 2015, Mr. Tate's practice was primarily corporate law, not criminal. And based on that, plus the nature of the charges filed against Mr. Harris, we agreed that there wasn't an attorney in the entire history of American jurisprudence who was going to be able to do much about getting an acquittal.

"I don't remember all the particulars, but I do recall that the state's case was rock solid. Plus, Mr. Harris was what you would call a three-time loser—a predicate offender. So, the best we could hope for was life without parole, and that was if he pleaded guilty. But he didn't want to do that, so we went to trial. But as I said, unfortunately for him, the state's case was bulletproof, and, once the reality of the situation finally sunk in, we changed the plea to guilty. At that point, the only thing left to do was for Mr. Harris to throw himself on the mercy of the court at the sentencing hearing. Which he did."

"Right. But the judge didn't go for it."

"Of course not. We did the best we could, but after all, Mr. Harris killed an innocent bystander and a pregnant woman."

Chapter Twenty-Seven

After I hung up the phone with Attorney Vivek, I walked down to the end of the hallway to buy a Diet Coke and a package of peanut butter crackers from the vending machines located there. On the way, I passed a maintenance man, scraping the painted-on letters off the door of what had been a secretarial service office.

"They move out?" I asked.

"Thrown out is how I heard it. Couldn't keep up with the rent. Which I hear is going up come the first of the year."

Terrific, I thought. Next, the guy would be scraping my name off my door.

I no sooner got settled back behind my desk when I heard the door to my outer office open and then close again. Thinking it might be Sonny Miles dropping in to try to persuade me to give up the location of his wife, I opened the bottom drawer of my desk so I could reach the .32 Smith & Wesson in case I needed it. As it turned out, however, the firepower wasn't necessary, as my visitor was none other than Geoffrey Tate.

"Mister Gamble," Tate said, taking a seat in my visitor's chair, "we need to talk." Today, Tate was dressed in a gray pinstriped suit with a pale blue dress shirt and a maroon patterned necktie.

"Okay. Before we start, can I offer you a bottle of water? I seem to remember your PA telling me you're a strong believer in staying hydrated."

He waved that aside with a flick of his wrist. "I need to ask you. How much longer do you think you're going to need to complete your assignment? It's been three weeks now, and from the reports you've been sending—which, by the way, are not at all satisfactory—it doesn't appear you've been making much progress. If, in fact, you're making any at all. From what I can tell, you're running around talking to all kinds of people, none of whom seem to be able to provide any useful information. And before you start telling me how you need more time, I hope I don't have to remind you. Time is a luxury I'm afraid Mr. Harris does not have."

I thought about that. "You know, Mr. Tate, much as I hate to admit it, I believe you're exactly right. I'm not getting anywhere with this case. One of the people I thought might be able to help was murdered in his own apartment, and the police don't have any idea who might have killed him."

"I hope that doesn't mean you think there's a connection."

"Probably not. But it does seem like a bit of a coincidence, wouldn't you say?"

"Don't know. But then, solving a murder is not your problem, is it?"

"No. The police are perfectly capable of that."

"Have you got anything else?"

"Well, I spoke with Annie's mother, and she says she hasn't heard from her daughter in years. I've spoken with a couple of the people who used to be in her band, and they can't tell me anything, except that after the band broke up, she went to Alabama to try to build a career as a solo artist. Obviously, nothing came of it, because if she'd made it big, we wouldn't be sitting here wondering where she is now. After all that, I'm thinking maybe we should just call it a day, and tell Harvey we aren't going to be able to help him."

"And I'm thinking maybe you should get yourself down to Alabama and start looking there." And when I raised my eyebrows, he said, "Whatever it costs." And with that, he got up and walked out, leaving me with no other option except to hit the road.

* * *

From Nashville, Muscle Shoals, Alabama, is a little under a three-hour drive down Interstate 65 and then west on U. S. Highway 72 from Huntsville. Today, Muscle Shoals is a community of approximately 15,000 souls located on the west bank of the Tennessee River. The immediate area also includes the towns of Tuscumbia, Florence, and Sheffield.

Muscle Shoals—the name supposedly came from a corruption of the word "mussel," a freshwater mollusk that could be found in abundance in a shallow part of the river—was originally a Cherokee Indian settlement that came under U. S. control during the War of 1812. For reasons that are not entirely clear, early settlers in the area chose to use the more familiar spelling, "muscle," and the name stuck. Following the completion of the Wilson Dam in 1924, the shallows became deep water, making the mussels, if not the spelling, an historical footnote.

The area gained serious renown as a recording mecca in the early 1960s, when songwriter Rick Hall partnered with a local musician named Billy Sherrill to open the FAME (Florence Alabama Music Enterprises) studio, in its namesake city. Following a falling out with Sherrill, Rick Hall relocated from Florence to Muscle Shoals and, in 1969, opened the Muscle Shoals Sound Studio, located in a nondescript gray stone structure located at 3614 Jackson Highway. It was in this studio that the "Muscle Shoals Sound" that featured a house band known as The Swampers—immortalized by a shout-out in Lynyrd Skynyrd's hit song, "Sweet Home Alabama"—attracted a pantheon of recording greats, including the Allman Brothers, Bob Dylan, Paul Simon, Rod Stewart, the Rolling Stones, Aretha Franklin, Wilson Pickett, and, a decade or so back, a hopeful young vocalist named Annie Harris.

I left home at 7:30 the next morning with the overnight kit I keep packed and ready, and since I was heading away from the city, did not encounter much traffic on Interstate 65 until I got close to Huntsville. The night before, I called Maggie and asked whether she'd like to come along and, as I put it to try and make it sound exciting, "immerse herself in the Muscle Shoals scene." Not surprisingly, she declined, asking, "What scene is that?" and then adding that she had a "real job," and that she was expected to show up every day to do it. She did, however, remind me to bring along my meds and to make at least a token effort to come back in one piece. Her parting words were, "I'll make it worth your while."

I stopped in Huntsville for gas and a Diet Coke, then turned west on Highway 72 toward Muscle Shoals. My hope was that I could get there and get my mission accomplished without having to stay over for another day.

There were actually eight studios in the area, only two of which, Redd Boxx and FAME, were in Muscle Shoals proper. The other six were in Sheffield, a short distance away. That meant, unless I got lucky, this was going to be a multi-day trip. I tried to think like somebody just starting out in the music business in a serious way. Would I start at the top, or at the bottom, and try to work my way up? I decided, if it were me, I'd go for broke. And that meant the FAME studio.

As I found out, FAME was as much a tourist destination as it was a working recording studio. For forty bucks, the curious could wander through the studios, as well as enjoy a "Backstage Experience," which took visitors "behind the velvet rope" for a look at founder Rick Hall's office, which featured selected musical instruments, gold records, and song of the year awards. All very interesting, but not what I was looking for. Indeed, as I arrived at a time when a tour was underway, I had a difficult time finding someone I could ask about Annie Harris. When I finally did track somebody down, a docent named Jeremy, he informed me that he doubted whether any documentation might exist for someone who was not actually under contract. He did, however, check on his computer, but was unable to locate any record of someone named Annie Harris. So, having not accomplished anything, I thanked him and set out for the next stop on my list.

It took three more stops and two more hours before I found a place in Florence called Sound Stage, where a large black woman named Buttercup DuBois—she pronounced it "Doo-Boys"—wearing a yellow pullover that read "e-racism" greeted me like I was some long-lost relative, and then told me she thought she remembered somebody named Annie who had auditioned as a vocalist sometime back in the mid-teens.

"If it's who I'm thinking it is, she was from Nashville, right?"

"She was. And if you don't mind me asking, how can you remember somebody from that far back?"

She waved me into an uncomfortable metal folding chair that faced her desk in an incredibly cramped and cluttered office. Framed photos of musicians and vocalists, including Bobbie Gentry, Mavis and Pop Staples,

Joe Cocker, and many others, hung on the walls next to three battered filing cabinets and a table that held a coffee maker, a stack of paper cups, and a half-empty bottle of Wild Turkey. A grimy window behind her desk looked out into an alleyway. Craning my neck to one side, I could spot the open lid of a blue dumpster.

"Honey, I recollect most everybody what comes through that door. Don't matter when, 'cause when they show up here, they all have dreams, and they're hopin' we just might be the ones makes 'em come true."

I unfolded the Midnite Oil poster I'd gotten from Harvey Harris.

"Just to be sure, this is the young woman here," I said, pointing. "Her real name is Annamaria Harris, although when you met her, she was calling herself Annie, or maybe Annie May." Without explaining the actual circumstances, I told Buttercup that Annie's family had lost contact with her about the time she showed up in Alabama, and that, due to her father's terminal illness, they desperately wanted to reconnect while there was still time. Not a hundred percent true, but close enough, I thought, to head off any probing questions.

Buttercup studied the photo for a moment. "Not much of a picture, but yep, I b'lieve that's her. I remember, she had this Mama Cass kind of thing goin' on. But something's not right here. I mean, you know, she had on this caftan that was about a half-dozen sizes too big. Too bad, 'cause it was really colorful, all blue and silver. Plus, her hair was down to her waist, and she had some kind of a blue stripe on one side. I guess she thought it went good with her outfit."

"The caftan was too big for this girl?" I pointed at the image on the poster. "She looks pretty big in this picture."

"Well, she must've lost a lot of weight, on account of, yeah, this is the same girl. I can tell 'cause she was a pretty girl, and she still had that long-ass hair with the skunk stripe, like in this poster here. But she was definitely not heavy like this when I saw her. Matter of fact, I think we have a photo in the file someplace." She got up from her desk and walked over to the file cabinet."

"You have a photo?"

"Of everybody who comes in. You never know when they might end up bein' somebody big. Here, let me just take a look."

She eased her not inconsiderable bulk around the edge of her desk and began rooting around in the middle file cabinet. "Lemme see...Haines, Hammond...here it is, Harris." She pulled out a green Pendaflex file folder, carried it back to her desk, and opened it. There was a sheet with contact information, listing an Annamaria Harris with a post office box address in Florence. Clipped to that was a black-and-white five-by-seven headshot and a compact recording disc. I picked up the photo and studied it.

Buttercup was right. The girl in the photo was clearly Annie Harris, but her face was much thinner, as if she had spent her time since leaving Midnite Oil, as Jerry Garcia once sang, "living on reds, Vitamin C and cocaine." The skunk stripe in her hair was clearly visible, but, for her audition, at least, she had evidently decided to forego any attempt to apply makeup, so that she looked not only thinner than she was before she left Nashville, but also a good deal less healthy, as if her time in Alabama had been hard on her.

"Got her demo right here. And I think there might be some other stuff on it also. You want to hear her sing?"

"You have a recording?"

"Honey, we record everybody who auditions or pays for studio time. Now, understand, we don't have a label. We just produce a demo, so's the person can use it to try and get a recording contract with a real record company. So, even though we can't sign nobody to a record deal, we try to make them sound as good as we can. Plus, you never know when some other artist or a band don't need a backup voice or two that sounds just so. Saves us and them having to hunt somebody down for a couple hours of session work. We can play their demo, and if they sound like what the next artist is looking for, then we can get 'em in here quick."

I had to admit, it made sense. While I waited, Buttercup fiddled with a CD player for a moment. Then there were a few moments of Annie, I supposed, and an accompanist, talking back and forth about tempo and key, and then Annie began singing "Amazing Grace." As almost everyone knows, it is one of the most recognized songs in Christianity, written in the mid-1700s by John Newton, a slave owner turned minister, and who at one time also served on the crew of a slave ship.

From what I could tell, Annie had a sweet, pure voice, and hit all the notes—which, in the case of "Amazing Grace," there are only five—and after three verses, she was finished.

Buttercup pressed pause. "So?"

I said, "I thought she sounded pretty good. But then, as far as I know, she didn't get a recording contract with a label, so I'm guessing there's something I'm missing."

"'Amazin' Grace' is an easy song, 'cause there's only a few notes, so almost anybody can sing it. People used to believe them notes was what was called the slave scale, I guess because it was simple. For a long time, they also thought that you could only play it just with the black keys on the piano, but that wasn't true, either." She shifted in her chair, causing the springs to creak in protest.

"Anyhow, we tried her on a couple other songs, but she just didn't have a lot of range, and not a very strong voice, either. We could maybe use her as a backup voice once in a while, but at least as far as we were concerned, she didn't have what it takes to be a star."

"And did you tell her that?"

"Best I can remember. We always try to be gentle, but yes, we did. Or rather, I did, 'cause my boss at the time, he never liked handing out bad news."

"And how did she take it?"

"Okay, I guess. I mean, she didn't fall apart and start wailin' or anything like that. But she was sure enough disappointed. But there was something else."

"Such as?"

"Well, musicians come in all shapes and sizes, and all kinds of tempera-ments. You know, some of them are dead serious about what they call their art, others just like to make music and are full of joy. But this little girl, there was something off. I mean, you can't really hear it in her voice, but I'd say she wasn't a happy child. It's like, she was lookin' for something, and I guess maybe she thought it was having a career as a singer, but…Oh, I don't know. It was just like there was something in her life that wasn't quite right."

"Okay. Any idea what happened to her after that? Has she stayed in touch at all?"

She shook her head, no. "Haven't heard a thing after those first few visits. A shame, too, on account of she seemed like a nice little gal, and I wish her voice had been just a bit stronger. We just didn't have anything going on right then where we could use her."

"Do you think maybe she tried another studio?"

"No idea. But I 'spect if she did, she'd have got told the same thing we told her. Nice voice, we can use you as a backup, but you need to think about if a career in music is really what you want to do. Because, and like I said, we were tryin' to be gentle. This is a tough business, and making a recording is expensive. So, you don't want to spend a lot of time with folks who can't hit the notes they need to hit.

It was the same thing Todd Neely at Mix Masters had told me, only he was talking about instrumental backing rather than voices. But in the end, the story was the same. There is playing in the lounge at a convention hotel for a few hundred bucks a night, and then there is playing to a sold-out auditorium in Chicago or Los Angeles or Houston. Or to put it another way, in the music business, nine out of ten just won't cut it.

Before I left, Buttercup offered to burn me a copy of the CD, "Case you want to give it to her folks. It might be a comfort to them."

I thanked her and accepted her offer. And I wondered, if I gave it to Harvey, would it bring him comfort, or break his heart a little more than it was already broken.

Chapter Twenty-Eight

The sun was still high in the sky when I left Sound Stage, and the temperature, which had been fairly pleasant earlier in the day, now was climbing toward ninety degrees, with humidity to match. It had been a long day, and I wasn't feeling much like trying to drive another three hours back to Nashville, particularly since I had one more stop to make, and I needed to make it before five o'clock.

The Sheffield Police Department is located on Seminary Street, across the road from a place called the Audio Hi-Fi House. It is a brown and gray building that did not appear to owe allegiance to any particular architectural style, unless functionality counted. I pulled into the parking lot and left my car next to a black Sheffield Police SUV. Then I went in, but not before securing my weapon in the trunk of my own car. I didn't want any misunderstandings in case I had to pass through a metal detector on my way in.

No metal detector. I showed my ID to a uniformed desk sergeant and asked if there was a detective I could speak with. I told him I was working on a missing person case, and that my investigation had led me to the Muscle Shoals area.

He looked me over for a second or two and then decided, I supposed, that I was on the level. "Wait here." He got up from his perch and disappeared through a doorway behind the front desk, taking my identification with him. It took a few minutes before he reappeared, this time with an older cop, also in uniform. I guessed he was the shift commander.

He glanced at my ID and then looked up at me. "Mister Gamble, is it?"

I said I was.

He handed me back my ID. "You can come on back."

I followed him through the doorway and down a hall into a spacious office that held a small conference table, a wall lined with filing cabinets, a map of the city and surrounding area on the opposite wall, and a government-style metal desk with three facing visitors' chairs. I took a seat in the middle one.

The captain's name was Dawkins. I guessed him to be in his mid-forties. He had blue eyes, light brown hair that was receding a bit at the temples, a ruddy complexion, and an expression that suggested something like mild amusement. He was dressed in dark pants and long-sleeved shirt with a black necktie. He had gold captain's bars on his shoulder epaulets, a gold-and-red enameled nameplate, and "SPD" in gold letters on his shirt collar. A pair of half-moon reading glasses was perched on top of his head. When he spoke, it was with a soft drawl, but I sensed that it could take on a hard edge when it needed to.

"Mister Gamble. My officer tells me you're here on some kinda PI business. Says you're wanting to find somebody who's gone missing. This person got a name?"

"She does. She's from Nashville. Her name is Annamaria Harris, although she sometimes goes by Annie or Annie May."

"If she's from Nashville, how come you're looking for her down here? Don't you have enough places to be looking around back home?"

"You'd think so. But the information I got was that she came down here trying to get a recording career started. Apparently, she didn't have much luck back home, and I guess she figured she'd try someplace else. I don't know, maybe studio time is less expensive here."

"So then, did she go missing in Nashville, or here in Alabama?"

"Last anybody knows, she was here. Where she went missing is anybody's guess. Before I checked in with you, I talked to a woman named Buttercup over at Sound Stage. They made a recording for Annie shortly after she got here, but none of the other studios I visited remembered her."

"And that was how long ago?"

"About ten years."

"That long? Back then, I was working grand theft auto in Montgomery. Let's see if we've got anything here." He pulled his reading glasses down and started fiddling around with his computer. "Annamaria, you say?"

I spelled it for him. "I'm wondering if anyone here ever filed a missing person report."

"Annamaria." He tapped on the keyboard for a moment, then sat back in his chair. "No missing person report that I can find. Do you have a recent photograph of this woman, Mr. Gamble?"

"She was in a band a dozen or so years back. I have a promotional poster for a gig they had scheduled, but the pictures aren't very clear."

"And can I ask, who's your client?"

I couldn't see any harm in telling him. "His name is Harvey Harris. He's the woman's father. Why? Is there a problem?"

Captain Dawkins tapped on his keyboard again. It took a little longer this time, and I had a hunch what he was working on now. A few more minutes, and then he looked up at me.

"Mister Gamble, for some reason, I think you already know all of this, or you wouldn't be talking to me now. But I have a serious concern here. This young woman—well, not so young anymore, I guess—this woman is a person of interest in a suspicious death that took place here in Alabama while she was living here. And her father, well, he's on death row in Tennessee for killing a couple of people in a convenience store holdup."

"Actually, your information is a little out of date. He's not on death row. He's in a medium-security prison in Whiteville, serving life without. And it will be fairly short, because he's got terminal cancer and the state decided to just let him die on his own."

"Interesting. I also ran a check on you."

"Imagine my surprise."

"Yeah, well, you did just sort of show up unexpectedly, so why not take a peek?" He gave me a look over the top of his glasses. "Wonderful thing, the Internet. When it's not trying to sell you something you don't need, or worm its way into your financials, it can give you some useful information. Like in your case, for example." He spun the monitor around so I could see.

"So, I checked, you know, just to make sure you're who you say you are and that your license is still valid."

"And?"

"You seem to be on the level, although I'm disappointed you don't have a website. Might bring a little more business your way, but then, maybe you're already busy enough." I couldn't think of anything to say to that, so I waited.

"Anyway, since there don't seem to be any problems on your end, can I ask, is this this guy Harvey Harris the kind of clientele you usually take on?"

"You mean death-row inmates and lifers? Not generally, no. In fact, I've never had a client like this one. Most of the time, I get bail skips, or runaway spouses, plus stuff like insurance fraud, and tracking down witnesses for defense attorneys. And in this particular instance, I wasn't hired by Harvey Harris. I was retained by his attorney, and that's where I've been sending the bills."

"What's his name?"

"Geoffrey Tate, spelled with a 'G'. But he's absolutely on the level, so you can look him up any time. He mostly handles corporate and civil cases, so I don't know what's his connection with Harvey Harris." I leaned back in my chair. "Look, Captain, I've enjoyed meeting you, but I don't want to waste a whole lot of your time here. So, unless you have some more questions, let me just ask you what I came to find out about, and then you can get back to whatever you were doing."

"Go ahead." He gave a small shrug. "It's not like I'm real busy here."

"Okay, two things, then. First, you said Annie Harris is a person of interest. A suspicious death, I think you called it. Does that mean you think she's good for a murder, or just that she might have some information?"

"She's not a suspect, but we want to talk to her. Or, at least we did at the time. There's still an active material witness warrant. She was the roommate of a woman who died under suspicious circumstances. Which is to say, a fentanyl overdose."

"So, it could have been accidental."

"Could have been, sure. However, when we investigated, your Miss Harris had already cleared out and was nowhere to be found. Complicating matters, the woman who died was a known user, which means there are unanswered questions."

"Such as?"

"Such as, who was her supplier, which is why the case is still open. Also," he tapped the keyboard on his computer again, "I see here both women were arrested a couple of times for solicitation."

"Solicitation. They were hookers?"

"Looks that way, although, interestingly, the incident I'm looking at here seems to have involved both women. It says here charges were dropped for lack of evidence. According to this, their 'date' for the evening—guess he was looking for a two-fer—a guy from Wichita, Kansas, got his wallet stolen, or at least that's what he claimed at first. Then, later, the story changed, and he said he'd just misplaced it, although it didn't miraculously reappear until he was informed that we'd need to call him back to testify when the case came to trial." He raised his eyebrows a fraction of an inch. "I'm guessing that means he was in town for some kind of a church event."

"As I understand it, there's a lot of Gospel music recorded here. And I imagine his congregation wouldn't take kindly to him consorting with prostitutes."

"Probably not. In any case, not long after, the roommate, who it says here was part of the threesome, turned up dead, and your little songbird disappeared. I guess I can understand that, since who the hell wants to hang around if there's a dead body in your apartment and you've already got a rap sheet? But again, no charges were filed, and frankly, after all this time, I don't expect we're likely to solve it. So, at this point, the case is still open, but inactive. That is, unless there's something you can tell me that we don't already know."

But there wasn't, and I admitted as much. In that case, Captain Dawkins said he had to go, that there was a function at his daughter's school that evening, and he promised to be there. I thanked him for his time, assured him I'd stay in touch in case Annie Harris turned up back in Nashville, and headed out to find a hotel for the night. After all, I was traveling on Geoffrey Tate's expense account.

Chapter Twenty-Nine

After leaving Sheffield, I headed west along Highway 72 until I got to Corinth, Mississippi, which seemed like a suitable place to find a hotel and someplace to eat besides a McDonald's. I found a spot on U.S 45, just north of 72 called Cheap Sleep, which turned out to be a lot better than the name would suggest. It was a two-story motel with inside entrances to the rooms, as well as a microwave, a mini-fridge, and both cable and streaming television. Plus, on a hot and muggy night in northern Mississippi, the air conditioning worked just fine.

When I asked the young lady working the check-in desk where she thought would be a good place to grab a quick supper, she asked me whether I'd ever had something called a "slugburger," which, she informed me, was a signature menu item that traced its origins to the area around in northern Mississippi.

"There's a place just about half a mile down the road that turns out the best ones. Just make a right turn out of the parking lot, and you can't miss it."

Intrigued, I decided to give it a try, figuring it had to be better than its name suggested. The place she recommended was called Cal's Slugburger, and, if the full parking lot was any indication, then maybe the young desk clerk had put me onto something worthwhile.

Since the tables and booths were filled, I took a seat at the counter, and when the waitress came to take my order, I asked for a slugburger with a side of onion rings and a Diet Coke. Reading the back of the menu, I learned that the original name of the supposed delicacy was the Weeks Burger, and that it was created by a Chicago native named John Weeks, who arrived in Corinth in 1917. I also learned that, since 1988, Corinth has hosted an annual Slugburger Festival, which includes an eating contest once won by an individual who gobbled down forty-three of the concoctions in ten minutes. The basic ingredients included a mixture of ground beef, ground pork, and an extender, which, in the present day, is soy grits. The whole shebang is then shaped into a patty and—what else—deep-fried in oil until it's crispy. I had to admit, when it showed up, it was pretty good, and I ordered a second one to take back to the motel.

When I got back to my room, I called Maggie to let her know where I was and that I wouldn't be back to Nashville until the next afternoon. I didn't mention the slugburger, since I figured that once I got to the part about deep-fried, the result would be another pep talk about watching what I ate.

"What are you doing in Mississippi? I thought you were coming home."

"I was. But then, I thought maybe it would be a good time to confer with my client before he shuffles this mortal coil."

"You're talking about Harvey Harris?"

"Yes. So far, the only communication he's had from me, if, in fact, he's had any at all, is through Geoffrey Tate. I want to find out whether he's been told anything since the first time we met."

"You mean you want to know if he's aware your investigation seems to be going nowhere." It wasn't a question.

"Hey, you know, sometimes these cases don't work out the way we'd all like. Plus, there're a couple of questions I need to ask him."

"And you'll tell me all about it when you get back. Which will be when?"

"Tomorrow afternoon, probably late. You want to have dinner? I'm still on expenses."

"Then I'll pick someplace special. Call me when you're close, and I'll tell you where to meet me. And Gamble? I know you, and I know you'll probably eat something enormously destructive health-wise as soon as we hang up here."

"But?"

"But I wish you'd try to take better care of yourself. Besides my father, you're the only decent man I've ever had in my life."

I promised I'd try to be careful, and then we said goodnight. And I was glad all over again that I hadn't mentioned the slugburgers.

* * *

The next morning, early, I was on the phone to the Hardeman County Correctional Facility to inquire about making an unscheduled visit to see Harvey Harris. The officer I spoke with wasn't inclined to approve my visit, but I explained that I had obtained a visitor's pass a few weeks earlier and that I was working for Harris's attorney, Geoffrey Tate. That got me a ten-minute wait on hold while the officer checked with his supervisor, I supposed. When he came back on the line, he said it was against policy, but since I was working for an attorney, it would be all right. I was to check in at the reception center, and then I would be cleared to enter the facility, to, as he put it, "confer with my client." I thanked him and said I'd try to be there before lunchtime.

With that taken care of, I grabbed a quick shower and a shave. I put on a clean shirt, microwaved and ate the slugburger I had brought back from the restaurant the previous evening—it tasted better the first time—bought a tank of gas and a 20-ounce Diet Coke at a nearby filling station, and was on my way to Whiteville by eight-fifteen. Without pushing, I was able to cover the 72 miles in a little under an hour and a half. By ten o'clock, I was standing in the reception area, going back through the same drill I had experienced a few weeks before. I was patted down for weapons and given a form to sign indicating I had been advised of the penalties for bringing contraband into the prison. I asked the CO if I could take my phone with me because I needed to ask Harvey a couple of questions, and I wanted to record his answers in the hope that they might help me with my investigation. I could tell he wasn't happy about it, but when I hinted around about attorney-client privilege, he grudgingly agreed.

"Also, I have a CD of Harvey's daughter singing, as part of an audition some years ago. It's just one song, but it might do him good to hear her voice."

"Leave it here with me. We'll see he gets a chance to listen to it."

After that, I was escorted back to the same room where Harvey and I had met the first time. This time it was me who had to wait.

Forty minutes later, Harvey finally showed up, this time seated in a wheelchair pushed by a uniformed corrections officer.

"Sorry about the wait. We had to get Mr. Harris ready for your visit, and we didn't want to disturb him until we were sure you were actually here."

If it is possible to be dead and still be breathing, I would say Harvey Harris qualified as Exhibit A. He had gone downhill considerably since the last time I saw him. His color was grayish-yellow, and his breathing was labored. His head lolled to one side, as if his neck were made out of rubber, and he seemed to be having trouble keeping his eyes focused.

"Harvey," I said. "Thanks for seeing me. I can see you're having a hard time, so I'll try to keep this short. I only have a couple things I need to talk to you about."

He managed to lift his head a little, and when he spoke, it was in a low, hoarse whisper. At that, it was quite an effort. "Have you found my Annamaria? Is she coming to see me?"

"I'm afraid not yet. I spoke with her mother and with a couple of the people who were part of her band back when they were still together. I also talked to one of her high school girlfriends, but they're all telling me pretty much the same story, which is, they haven't had any contact with her in close to ten years."

When he didn't say anything, I said, "What are your doctors telling you?"

"Doctors? This ain't the Mayo Clinic here, Mr. Gamble. There's just this one doc who should've lost his license years ago that drives down from Jackson every Tuesday to look in on things. Other than that, we got a couple medics. But to answer your question, he's tellin' me the end is comin' up fast, now." He paused, confused. "What day is today?"

"Thursday."

"Okay, Friday, that's tomorrow, right? Friday, they're movin' me to the hospital in Jackson, they say, to a secure wing." A cough. "That's a joke, don't you think? A secure wing, like what? Like they think I'm gonna bust out? Shit. They could leave me in the lobby all by myself with a getaway car parked at the curb, and I couldn't make it to the front door if I had all day, shape I'm in now."

"Harvey, I'm doing my best, and I'm not giving up. So, let me ask you. Did you know your daughter left Nashville shortly after her band split up and went down to Muscle Shoals? What I was told, she wanted to try to carve out a singing career on her own. So, two days ago, I drove down there. I thought she might still be there, or if not, maybe somebody might know where she went next.

"I stopped by several recording studios, and finally one of them remembered her. It was like you said. She had a nice voice and could sing a little. They thought they could use her as a backup for some of their headliners. But in the end, she just didn't have a strong enough voice, or the range, to be a success as a standalone act." I paused, trying to think of a good way to tell him the rest.

"There's more. Before I left Nashville, one of the people I spoke with said they had heard that Annie was involved in some kind of an unexplained death while she was in Alabama. So, the last thing I did before coming here was to talk to the police in Sheffield—that's the next town over from Muscle Shoals. What I got was that she was a person of interest. The police there said it was a drug overdose, and Annie wasn't a suspect, but they did still want to talk to her. Of course, it's been ten years now. The case hasn't been closed, but it's no longer active, so I doubt anything is going to come of it.

"But the thing is, one of the other members of Annie's band, a guy named Jason Mackey, who supposedly was close to getting married to Annie way back when, was found dead in his apartment a couple weeks ago, with a bullet in the back of his head. Now, you can read into that whatever you want, and I'm just telling you what I've found out. But that's two deaths that are at least circumstantially linked to your daughter. And maybe there's nothing to it, but you have to admit, it looks more than a little fishy."

When he spoke, it was with great effort. "My daughter went to Alabama? And you're sayin' she's a killer?"

"I didn't say that, and I'm not trying to make a case for it. You asked me to find her, and I'm working very hard to do that. I'm not a cop, and I don't work homicide cases, if that's even what this is. I'm just letting you know what I've found so far. And from your reaction, it sounds like your lawyer hasn't been keeping you up to date."

A cough. "I ain't spoke to him but a couple times."

"Has he been to see you?"

He shook his head, no.

"Okay, I'm just about done here, but I have one more question for you. It's something that's been bothering me since the first time we talked, and if you don't mind, I'd appreciate an honest answer."

"Go ahead."

I took out my phone, pressed "record," and placed it on the table between us. "This is just for the record. You know, in case there's a problem later. Do you mind?"

"What the hell do I care? You think somebody'll want to sue me? I'm not gonna be around long enough for any of this to make any difference, no matter what you do with it."

"Okay, then answer me this. A few days ago, I was able to get a look at your arrest records, going back to 1979, where you tried to hold up a convenience store. It was a juvie bust, so the records are sealed, but I was able to find out from the police there was a witness who swore that there were two guys in the car when you rolled up."

He started to shake his head, no, but I said, "Bear with me. This witness—the store clerk—said there were two guys in the car, but when you went inside and started to wave your gun around, the other guy took off. When the case went to court, you claimed you were acting alone, which seems kind of funny to me, since, if you were alone, how did you plan to make your getaway?

"Then I dug into your other cases, and these are all public record, so I wasn't violating any confidences. What I found out was that, in 1983, 1988, and 1999, you were represented *pro bono* by an angel named Geoffrey Tate, the same guy who's paying my fees right now to find Annie. So, I'm wondering, Harvey. Is it just possible that the other guy involved with you in that 1979 caper was your angel, Geoffrey Tate? Because, if he was, and if he'd gotten caught along with you, there was no way in hell he'd have gotten into a top-notch law school with a criminal record. Not back then, anyway. And what I'm thinking is that you guys were somehow friends, and for whatever reason, you took the fall all by yourself to protect him. And because of that, he's been paying you back ever since."

Again, no answer, but this time, the look on his face told me, without a doubt, that I'd nailed it.

"So, what happened in 2015? Looks like that time your friend Tate punted, and handed you off to another public defender, a guy named Vivek."

For a moment, he was silent, and I thought maybe he hadn't understood the question. When he spoke, it was with obvious effort.

"Wasn't really no choice. They had me dead to rights. The whole thing was on CCTV, plus there was a witness who saw me drive off." There was resignation in his voice.

"Geoff said he didn't really handle criminal cases anymore. He said I'd have a better chance with a public defender, and that he knew a good one. He told me, considering what I done, the best I could hope for was life without parole, and that this other guy, he knew better how to do that."

"Only he wasn't able to get it done for you."

"No, and I got no complaint. I got what I deserved, and what the hell? It wasn't like I was gonna turn my life around and become an upstanding citizen. But Geoff, he felt bad just the same, and that's why he's picking up your tab now. I know he comes across sometimes like a stuck-up prick, but down deep, he's an okay guy, and he's paid me back a hundred times over for leavin' me holdin' the bag at that gas station." He started coughing violently, coughed, and I thought for a second he'd come to the end of the trail right there and then.

"So, now that you know, tell me. Are you going to make trouble for him?"

"Why should I? That juvie bounce was forty-six years ago. Nobody is going to be interested in pursuing it, except for maybe the tabloids, and even if they did, nobody could prove anything. It was just something that was bothering me, that's all."

"Then you'll keep looking for Annie?"

"I will do my best, Harvey. If she's out there, I'll find her. You have my word." But I didn't tell him then, or ever, that his daughter was very probably also living a life that she wasn't likely to turn around.

Chapter Thirty

That evening over dinner, Maggie asked me about my trip to Alabama. So, I filled her in on my visit to half a dozen recording studios and then Sheffield police.

"And she never got a recording contract. How sad for her."

"It's a tough business. The best she was able to do was at a place where they told her they didn't think she could succeed as a standalone artist. But they did say they could use her on occasion as a backup singer."

"That must have been a comedown."

"I can't even imagine. And it gets worse."

I told her about my conversation with the police. "She's apparently not a suspect. They just want to talk to her, or at least, that's what they told me. Also, it turns out both Annie and her roommate had a side hustle turning tricks. Of course, after almost ten years, the case is yesterday's cold potatoes. At this point, I doubt they'd even know what questions to ask if she walked in the front door and announced her presence."

"But you're no closer to finding her."

"No. And that's what I told Harvey this morning. I wanted to bring him up to date, because I haven't spoken with him since I started working on this case. Also, I wasn't sure what his lawyer was telling him. If, in fact, he was telling him anything." I waited, but no questions.

"He looked like road kill, in case you're wondering. He's being moved to a secure wing in the hospital in Jackson. I doubt he'll last another two weeks."

"Then that means he probably won't see his daughter again before he goes. What do you think happened to her?"

"Who the hell knows? I'd say she's probably married, got a couple of kids, and living who-knows-where. Either that, or she's moved on to someplace like New Orleans, where she's trying to scratch out a living singing for tips in bars, or maybe turning tricks. If she made it in the music business, I'm pretty sure we'd know."

Maggie reached across the table with her fork and speared one of the grilled scallops off my plate. "These are very good. I should order this next time." She always does that.

"Would you like to try one of my beef medallions?"

"No, thanks. I'm trying to watch my cholesterol."

"I'm proud of you. How well did you watch it when you were in Mississippi?"

I was going to tell her I filled up on salads and grilled fish, then thought, who's kidding who, and admitted to having a couple of slugburgers.

When I described what they were, she said, "It sounds like deep-fried meat loaf. It's no wonder your arteries are a mess."

After we finished eating, we wandered around downtown for a while, stopping in at a couple of bars to listen to music and enjoy drinks, mojitos—something different for Maggie—and Stella for me. Afterward, I let drop a few not-too-subtle hints about staying the night at her apartment, but she begged off, saying she had an early meeting the next morning, and that we could make it up over the weekend. So, I dropped her at her front door, waited until she was safely inside, and then headed for home.

* * *

My house is situated in the middle of the block on a side street off Nolensville Road, about a twenty-five-minute drive from downtown at nine o'clock at night. It was already dark when I pulled into my driveway and shut off the ignition. Maybe it was the too-many beers I'd had during my dinner and then later with Maggie, or maybe I was just tired from my whirlwind tour of northern Alabama and Mississippi, and southwestern Tennessee, but when I removed the keys from the ignition, the ring slipped out of my hand

and fell to the floor mat between my feet. As I reached down to pick them up, the rear backlight in the Ford exploded into tiny fragments as a bullet tore through the glass on the passenger side, passing by the spot where my head had been a second earlier, and exiting through the left corner of the windshield before lodging in the garage door.

The first shot was followed in rapid succession by a second, again through the opening where the rear window had been. That one penetrated the head restraint on the front seat before hitting the windshield a second time, about a foot to the left of the rear-view mirror. By that time, I was crouched on the floor, and the shot passed harmlessly over me.

There is a widely held, and wildly wrong, belief, propagated by both television and motion pictures, that a person can take cover behind a car door during a shootout, and that the door will somehow stop a bullet. Unless the bullet is a small caliber round, the sheet metal on a car door will do little or nothing to protect the person hidden behind it, or even deflect the bullet, unless it strikes the side-impact collision barrier inside the door.

I didn't take time to think about that. Instead, I reached for the door on the driver's side, crawfished backward out of the car, and squeezed underneath, scorching my backside on the hot exhaust pipe, and, at the same time, drawing my .380 from my shoulder rig. My hope was, since the courtesy lamp inside the car was broken and did not light up, the shooter had no way of knowing whether he'd hit his target—meaning me. Then I waited.

After a minute that felt like a lifetime had passed, I heard footsteps approaching from the street. My would-be killer, I assumed, coming to verify whether I was alive or dead, and to finish the job, if it turned out I was still breathing.

Another few seconds went by. Then, in the illumination cast by the street across the way, I was able to make out a pair of legs walking slowly toward the car from the passenger side, moving cautiously, like a hunter approaching a downed, but potentially still-dangerous animal. In retrospect, I thought, it was an apropos comparison. And then, I recognized the Cody James boots, about ten feet behind the car.

James Figgins. Back for round two.

"Gamble? Are you there, Gamble, or are you already dead?" He hadn't seen me bail out of the car. He took another step.

"I'm thinking, since you aren't talking, I must have at least hit you, so, if you can still hear me, what's about to happen is called payback. You made me lose my job, so now you're going to lose yours. For good."

Another step.

"C'mon, Gamble. Aren't you even gonna put up a fight?"

Figgins took another step closer, and when I had a clear line of fire, I cocked back the hammer on the .380 and fired a round into his leg, just above the ankle. There was a scream, then, "Fuck!", then four shots fired wildly into the air as he tumbled onto his back near the edge of the driveway, less than an arm's length from where I was still hunkered down under the car. I could see just enough of his AR-style rifle to know that it had fallen onto the front lawn, out of his reach, about four feet away. When he realized where it was, he started to move toward it, although with a shattered ankle, he had to use his shoulder muscles to edge his way forward.

That left me with choices, but no good options. Since James was on the ground in front of me, the only way I could get out from under the car was to crawl backward. But I knew if I did that, he would almost certainly be able to get his hands on the rifle before I could either get to my feet and run around the car stop him, or find another place to take cover. And in any event, the last thing I wanted was to engage him in a shootout in the middle of a residential block. That meant either I was going to have to convince him to give up the fight right now, or else I was going to have to shoot him again and put him down for good.

Although my heart was pounding from a massive adrenaline surge, I tried to keep my voice under control. "James, this doesn't have to go any further than it already has. I think we both know that I don't have time to crawl back out of here before you can get to your gun. I need you to give me your word that you will stop moving right now and stay where you are. If you do, I will call an ambulance for you, and you can figure on getting through the rest of the night still breathing. If you don't, if you keep going for your weapon, I have seven more rounds in my gun, and I will put every one of them into you."

When he didn't say anything, I said, "I am not fucking around here. Are you going to stay put, or am I going to have to kill you?"

He turned his head so he was facing me. Even in dim light, I could see there was pure hatred in his eyes. "Do what you have to do."

But as it turned out, I didn't have to do anything, because in that same moment, I heard the unmistakable noise a pump-action shotgun makes when a round is being racked into the chamber. And then I heard a voice say, "Move just one more inch, and I will blow your fucking head into the pavement." It was my across-the-street neighbor and sometime fishing buddy, Kline, coming to the rescue.

I crawled out from under the car and walked around to where James was lying on his back in the driveway. Kline had his shotgun, which I recognized as a 20-gauge Remington 870, aimed squarely at my would-be killer. Sensibly, he was standing far enough back that Figgins, even though he was more or less immobilized, couldn't make any move to grab hold of the end of the barrel. Up and down the block, porch lights were coming on, and a few folks had stepped outside to see what was the ruckus. In another moment, I knew, there would be a crowd milling around in my front yard.

Kline gave me a look fueled by a pure adrenaline surge. "You want me to finish him?"

I shook my head. "Be more trouble than it's worth. For both of us."

I walked out onto the lawn and picked the rifle up by the end of the barrel, in order not to leave any fingerprints on any part of the stock.

I said to James Figgins, "You are a dumb son of a bitch." And then I went inside to phone the police.

Chapter Thirty-One

It wasn't necessary for me to call the cops because Kline, who just happened to be in his front yard moving his lawn sprinkler, got on the phone the second he spotted James Figgins prowling around my property with a weapon tucked under his arm. By the time the shooting started, a couple MPD radio prowlers had already been dispatched. I had no sooner gotten the key into the lock on my front door when I heard sirens blaring in the distance. I shouted to Kline to put his Remington on the lawn and step away from it.

In another moment, the MPD cruisers converged on my driveway, each coming from opposite directions. I knew from experience, in situations like this, the best way to get through first contact without any more shots being fired was to stand in plain sight with my arms away from my sides, my .380 on the ground in front of me. Sure enough, four uniformed officers popped out of the cars with their weapons drawn, pointed squarely at me and Kline. I couldn't blame them. At first glance, it appeared that the shooter was either me or Kline, and since he was flat on his back on the driveway and not moving, the victim was Figgins.

It took a few minutes and a conversation between Kline and the cops to get everything settled down. After that, along with a small clutch of neighbors who had gathered at the curb, we waited outside until a couple of night watch detectives showed up to interview me, and an ambulance arrived to remove a barely conscious James Figgins to a hospital. While that was going on, one of the uniforms kept a close eye on me, as the other three began interviewing the neighbors to find out if there were any more witnesses, and if there were, to take statements. The detectives, however, were first interested in visiting with Kline, who, from what I could tell, was reveling in the attention he was getting from the cops and from the local Eyewitness News crew that showed up a few minutes later.

After they finished with Kline, the dicks got around to talking with me. The lead detective was a short, stocky guy named Ramos, whose first name was Detective—or at least, that was all I got. He was in his mid-forties, dressed in gray slacks, an olive-green sport coat, and a mint-green dress shirt, no tie. His partner was a younger guy, Black, tall and thin, wearing a gray pinstriped suit, a blue dress shirt with a button-down collar, and a red and blue necktie. Dressed to impress, or at least for the possibility of promotion.

Ramos spoke first. "Mister Gamble. Seems to me I've heard your name once or twice. You seem to be something of a known quantity around police headquarters."

There was nothing in that for me, so I waited.

"Can you tell us what happened here?"

The younger detective spoke up. "Shouldn't we read him his rights first?"

"Good question." Ramos turned to me. "What do you think, Mr. Gamble. Do we need to advise you of your rights? Not that you don't already know them backward and forward."

I shrugged. "Up to you, Detective. If you do, I'm going to ask for an attorney, and then you can arrest me on suspicion of trying not to get shot, and then we can spend the rest of the night downtown hashing this out."

"You're not a suspect, Mr. Gamble. You're somewhere between a witness and a victim, so again, how about you just tell us what happened here."

"Well. I was out. I was having dinner with a friend. I dropped her at her apartment downtown, and then I came home. When I was getting out of my car, my keys fell out of my hand, and when I bent over to pick them up, two shots came through the back window of my car." I pointed to the damage. "One of the slugs is embedded in the garage door. It's there in case you need to make a ballistics match.

"After the second shot, I bailed out on the driver's side and crawled under the car. I didn't know how many shooters there were, or where they were located, so I figured the safest place to be was down low."

"And this guy that just went to the hospital, he was the only shooter?"

"Far as I could tell, yes."

"So, the old guy didn't do any shooting?

"You mean *Mister* Kline? No. But he probably saved my life."

"Well, good for him. We'll put him up for a medal." There was a pause. "And why do you think this other guy was shooting at you

"Well, during the time he was here, he didn't tell me, but if I had to guess, I'd say he was upset with me because he thinks I cost him his job."

The other detective spoke up. "His job. Did he work for you?"

"No. His name is James Figgins. He was working for a guy in the music business, a guy named Wilton Miles, although he mostly goes by the name Sonny." I noticed the younger cop was writing down what I was saying in a small notebook.

"You might want to start with a clean page, Detective. This is about to get complicated."

"Thanks. I think I can manage."

So, I told them about my brief encounter with Madelaine Miles and the subsequent visit to my office by Sonny Miles and James Figgins to convince me to drop the investigation. "And when I refused, Miles had Figgins try to rough me up to make his point."

"And did he?"

"A little. He sucker-punched me, but that was as far as he got. There was, what shall we call it, a brief altercation, and then I sent him back to his boss with his tail between his legs."

Ramos made a noise that could have been a laugh. "Tough guy."

"Tough enough. Anyway, I guess since Figgins fumbled his assignment, Sonny fired him, and Figgins blames me. Tonight was his way of settling the score."

"So, he took a couple of shots at you and missed, and you took cover under your car. Then what?"

"Then he must have thought he'd hit me, and he walked over to the car to check whether I was dead or alive. When he got close enough, I shot him in his leg, and when he fell, he landed right next to me and dropped his gun. When he tried to go for it, I had a choice. I could either shoot him, or I could let him shoot me, or try to stop him some other way. But before I had to do anything, my neighbor—the old guy, as you referred to him—stepped in. Two seconds later, your guys showed up. And here we are."

After that, there wasn't much more to tell. Since I had fired my weapon, Detective Ramos had me hand over my .380 and informed me that I would need to come down to police headquarters to make a statement. He also told me that he'd be getting a statement from James Figgins. My story seemed to square with what Kline had told them, so he didn't expect I would have any criminal charges arising from the incident. Also, there would be a copy of the police report made available to me to provide to my insurance company so I could get my car windows fixed.

* * *

After the cops left, I went into the house and sat down on the couch. I was way too keyed up to even think about trying to get some sleep, so I turned on the television and found a black-and-white movie on TCM called, appropriately enough, *Nobody Lives Forever*, with John Garfield, Walter Brennan, and Geraldine Fitzgerald. Somewhere around the halfway point, when I was on my third bottle of Stella, and Garfield's hoodlum character decides he wants to clean up his act and go straight, I heard a car door slam. Then somebody was leaning on my doorbell.

Maggie. Not good. I opened the door.

"They said on TV you were shot."

"Did you want to come in, or are you going to just stand on the porch?"

I waited until she was inside. "I wasn't shot. Somebody tried to shoot me. That guy got shot instead. By me. But it wasn't bad. I wounded him in the leg. They'll patch him up at the hospital, and then the cops will take him to jail."

She glanced around my living room, taking a quick inventory. From the expression on her face, she was clearly not liking what she was seeing. "And now, you're doing what? Sitting here drinking beer and watching some old movie?"

"Maggie, what should I be doing?"

She spun around on her heel and punched me, hard, in the stomach. It was enough to knock the breath out of me. I have to say, for a small woman, she packed a lot more wallop than I would have thought.

"What was that for?"

"That was for…I don't know what for. Do you have any idea how frightened I was?"

I said, "Maggie, if you thought I'd been shot, why did you come here? Why didn't you call the police to find out if I was dead, or if I'd been taken to a hospital?"

The fight, if that's what it was, seemed to go out of her. "Because…because, I don't know why. I hate it when you're logical with me."

I took her in my arms and pulled her close. "Maggie, I'm fine. A guy took a couple of shots at me from across the street because he was mad at me. He lost his job working for some bigfoot in the music business, and he blamed me for getting him fired. He wanted to get even."

"By killing you?"

"I guess it was a really good job."

I thought for a moment she was going to sock me again. Instead, she pushed herself away from me and walked toward the bedroom. "I told you before. I have an early meeting tomorrow morning. You can sleep in the other bedroom."

Chapter Thirty-Two

I didn't sleep in the spare bedroom, mostly because, as I explained to Madelaine Miles in what seemed like a lifetime ago, there isn't a bed in there. I keep it as a home office, crammed with a bookcase, my old LPs, and a stereo system I bought several years ago at a time when I was feeling flush. There is also a desk and a chair, my laptop computer, and some assorted old crap that I should probably haul out to the trash, but keep thinking that someday, I might find a need for it.

So instead of sleeping on the floor, or trying to sweet-talk my way into bed with Maggie, I finished the movie I was watching, tossed back a couple more Stellas, and then conked out on the living room couch. I was still there the next morning when I heard her rattling around in the bathroom. Which was a problem, since, after blasting through an entire six-pack of beer, I needed to do a little rattling of my own. And so, having no other alternative to intruding on whatever she was doing at the moment, I went outside to the back yard for a bit of fresh air, and to do what was immediately necessary. Then, when I was breathing more comfortably, I walked around to the front to survey the damage to my car in the bright light of day.

It could have been worse. The back window had completely shattered, leaving tiny bits of tempered glass strewn across the package shelf, the back seat, and the floor. Up front, there was a single large hole where it appeared the trajectories of the two rounds had more or less converged, not coincidentally, almost perfectly in line with where my head would have been had I not leaned over to retrieve my keys from the floor mat. I knew when Maggie saw that, she was likely to get upset all over again—if, in fact, she had calmed down from the night before.

When I went back inside, she was in the kitchen, dressed for the office, hair and makeup in place, brewing a cup of coffee from the Keurig I keep just for her. I waited until she had her coffee ready before I took a Diet Coke out of the refrigerator and popped an English muffin in the toaster. She shot me a disapproving look.

"That's what you eat in the morning?"

"Every day, unless I stop at McDonald's."

She shook her head slowly. "Gamble, we have to talk."

"About?"

"About us. About you. I mean, look at how you live your life. You eat badly. You already have trouble with your heart. And you're in a line of work with unpredictable hours, and that's nearly gotten you killed more than once in the time we've been together, including, in case I need to remind you, less than twelve hours ago."

No argument there. "So, what is it you're telling me?"

"I'm telling you that you're a good man. You're a decent man, and I care so much for you it hurts sometimes. And when I think that I might lose you because of the way you live your life and because of this stupid, horrible job you have, well…I don't know what I think, except that I know it would destroy me."

I didn't have the haziest idea what to say to that. We sat in silence while she finished her coffee and I spread peanut butter on my English muffin. Then she got up to leave.

"I'll call you when I get home from work." She gave me a small smile. "Maybe we can do something special."

* * *

After Maggie left, I got on the phone to one of those auto glass repair outfits that come to your location to replace broken windows. While I waited, I showered, shaved, and put on a fresh dress shirt—light blue with a button-down collar—gray slacks and Topsider moccasins. It took about two hours after I called before a guy named Adnan showed up in a snappy red-and-white Ford transit van, and another two hours to replace the shattered windshield and missing backlight. So, except for the hole in the driver's side head restraint, the Ford was as good as new. Seven-hundred dollars later, I was handed a receipt, and Adnan went on his way. I spent another twenty minutes vacuuming stray shards of safety glass off the front and rear seats and floors. Then I grabbed my brown corduroy sport coat and headed downtown.

My first stop was police headquarters. After a wait that seemed longer than necessary, I was escorted up to the third floor, where Detective Ramos was waiting. We exchanged pleasantries for just long enough to reassure one another that we were both fine, that we both had a busy day ahead of us, and so why don't we just get to it? And then, it took another hour or so to swear out a formal statement regarding the incident from the previous evening, which nearly got me killed. Of course, it also wound James Figgins up in the secure wing at Nashville General Hospital with what I was told was a shattered right tibia and fibula that would probably leave him with a noticeable limp once the wound healed.

No surprise, we went back through the same questions I'd answered the night before, plus some additional ones. How did you know the shooter? Do you have a history with him? Why do you think he was shooting at you to begin with? You said he had previously attacked you in your office. What was the reason for that? Why didn't you shoot to kill when you fired your weapon at him from underneath your vehicle? Are you willing to appear in court when this comes to trial? Is there anything more you've thought of since last night that we should know?

When we finished up, and I signed and dated the statement, Ramos said, "You can pick up your gun in a couple days, after we run ballistics. Also, from what you've told us, I'd say you're lucky to still be alive."

Good thing Maggie wasn't along to hear that.

Chapter Thirty-Three

I had no sooner gotten back to my office and settled behind my desk when the telephone rang.

"Gamble, this is Wanda. I wanted to let you know." Her voice sounded hoarse and weak. Knowing about her illness as I did, I was immediately concerned she was calling to tell me her time had just about run out.

"Know what?"

"Your friend, Madelaine. She checked out early last night."

Shit. "Did she say where she was going?"

"No, but I got the impression she was going back home to her husband. She did say something to one of the staff about the surroundings here. As you know, this isn't a five-star hotel. I think maybe she found our little house of refuge a trifle *déclassé.*"

"Well, her call, I guess." I took a deep breath, then, "How are you feeling?"

"Some days okay. Other days, not. On the 'not' days, the pain is getting worse. Today, in case you were about to ask, is a 'not' day."

"The oxy isn't helping?"

"Oh, sure, but I try to keep that to a minimum. You know, a lot of the women here aren't just on the run from bad situations. They're also recovering alcoholics, or addicts, and it wouldn't be right for me to be floating around here in an opioid-induced fog. I mean, what kind of an example is that? I'm supposed to be helping them straighten out their lives, not flaunting the positive effects of loading up on painkillers."

"Not really the same thing, Wanda. You're not an addict. You're a patient being treated for a disease."

"I'm an addict now, Gamble, and I hate that fact even more than I hate the pain."

"I'm sorry, Wanda. I wish there was something I could do."

"Well, there isn't. And, anyway, I didn't call you to talk about my troubles. I just wanted to let you know about Madelaine Miles."

"Okay, got it. She went back to her husband. Unless she changes her mind and asks for help, there isn't much either one of us can do about it. And since we're going down that road, you're sure there's nothing I can do for you?"

"Gamble, we've known each other a very long time, and right now, the last thing I need from you is sympathy, so don't even start."

There was a pause, and then I heard her coughing, but less distinctly, as if she had put her hand over the phone.

"Okay, if you want to do something, there is one other thing. And I hate to bring it up, but you know my situation."

"What?"

"Just this. Haven is going to need somebody to step in and run the place after I'm gone. I seem to remember your lady friend has a graduate degree in social work. It doesn't pay much, but you might want to mention to her that there will be a job opening very soon."

* * *

My conversation with Wanda left me feeling indescribably sad and also angry. Sad, that my friend, with whom I had been through a lot, both good and bad, was incurably ill and did not have much longer to live. I wanted to do something to help her. But then, what can anyone do for a dying friend except continue to be a friend and be there when the time came? Wanda was a tough woman. Always had been, and I knew the last thing she would want was for me to start smothering her with sympathy, and somehow making her last days about me. If what she wanted was to die with dignity, then I would do my best to respect her wishes.

And then I was angry, that after all the trouble I had gone through to help

Madelaine Miles make a break from her abusive husband, she had apparently chosen to return home, to face what? More abuse? And then I remembered a conversation I'd had with Maggie on the day we'd first met, when we were talking about essentially the same problem faced by so many women. She had wondered, why did so many women choose to live in circumstances that an ordinary person would recognize as intolerable? And the answer, of course, was that they had no choice. I had no idea what Madelaine's background might be, or whether she had an education, or a marketable skill set. Maybe latching onto Sonny Miles had seemed like a dream come true, promising as it did, a life of moneyed ease for a woman who may not have had any other realistic options. Part of me wanted to drive out to Brentwood and haul her out of that big house and take her—where? But the other half of my brain said, rightly, that it was none of my business, and that all of us make choices we have to live—or die—with.

After I hung up the phone, I was feeling restless, like I should be doing something useful, except that I wasn't sure what. Finally, since I couldn't think of anything else, I decided to drive out to Jason Mackey's apartment to see whether there was anything the cops might have overlooked that could point me in the direction of Annie Harris. On the way, I tuned the car radio to our all-news station, thinking that, since it was an election year, I ought to make an effort to get caught up on whatever were the burning issues of the day.

Instead, I got a news flash about an A-list rock musician who talked a would-be suicide off the Siegenthaler Pedestrian Bridge over the Cumberland River before she jumped to her death. According to the story, the singer was in town recording a music video for a new album he would soon be releasing, and the spot they were filming was near where the incident took place. Well, good for him, I thought. At least he saved one despondent soul from being tomorrow's headline. And then, somewhat puckishly, I wondered. Would the jumper have a cameo in the music video?

When I entered Mackey's apartment building, no surprise, the crime scene tape had been removed. Evidently, whatever the cops might have been looking for, they either found and removed, or else they found nothing of any use and decided to turn their attention to other aspects of the victim's life. Which reminded me, I should probably get back in touch with Detective Proctor to find out whether she and her partner had made any progress with their investigation.

One problem: How was I going to get into the apartment? That trick on television where somebody opens a locked door using a credit card only works if the door is secured with a spring lock and not a deadbolt. I have a set of lock-picking tools, which are, of course, illegal. But even with the tool set, it takes a deft touch and quite a little bit of time to manipulate the tumblers. I supposed I could have just kicked the door and hoped nobody up and down Mackey's hallway was home to hear it, but that seemed like a long shot.

While I stood there staring at Mackey's door, thinking about how to proceed, a door behind me opened, and I found myself face-to-face with a neighbor who was most definitely home. It was a guy, about twenty years younger, and half a head taller than me, with a shock of red hair and a medium-length beard the same color. He was dressed in jeans, no shoes, and a red t-shirt with "Rock Will Never Die" printed in white, block letters.

"You looking for Jason? 'Cause, if you are, in case you haven't heard, he got killed a couple weeks ago. Somebody shot him."

"I did know that," I said, unsure of how to proceed. Since it was during normal workday hours, I hadn't expected to run into any of Jason's neighbors. So, I did what I often do in situations like this. I made up a lie.

"I'm with the Nashville *Times*. I'm working on a follow-up story about Jason. I've already talked to the police, but they haven't been able to tell me anything I don't already know. So, now I'm stuck, and I thought maybe I could get a little bit of background about his life before he was killed." I gave him a look that I hoped projected sincerity. "Did you work together?"

"No."

"Friends?"

"Friends, yeah, but not close. I mean, we didn't have a lot in common. I'm a programmer, so I pretty much work from home. I guess you already know Jason was a musician, so he was out of town a lot, and he worked a lot of nights. Sometimes, when he was back after a road trip or a tour, he'd come over, and we'd kick back and have a few beers. He'd tell me stories about playing with this group or that singer, or whatever. I don't know. Long bus trips, late-night suppers, not much sleep. It didn't sound like much of a life to me."

"Maybe not, but there must have been some compensations. Otherwise, why do it?"

He scratched his head, as if giving the question some thought. "I know those guys, those session musicians get paid pretty well, so there was the money. I mean, after all, why else does anybody do anything?"

I could think of all kinds of reasons, but I kept them to myself. I wanted to see where he was going with this line of thinking.

"I'm not a musician," I said. "I know you figure they get paid well, and from what I understand, I guess the good ones do. But it seems to me that being on the road constantly, or being on call from a studio at unpredictable times, or, hell, I don't know. Working a gig until all hours of the morning seems like a recipe for getting old quickly. I have to think there's more to it than that."

"Well, I can't speak for all of 'em, but in Jason's case, I guess if I had to pick one other thing, I'd say it was the women."

He had my attention now. "What women?"

"I don't know their names. I just know there were lots of 'em. I guess back in the day, they called 'em groupies. These days, I don't know. It just seemed like Jason had a knack for attracting pretty women. All hours of the day and night, too. Once in a while, there'd be a party, and Jason would invite me over." He paused, as if remembering some of the good times. "I guess now that I think about it, I'd have to say, Jason was a good neighbor. I'm gonna miss him."

I had a thought. I took out my phone and scrolled through the photos I had stored until I found the headshot I'd snapped of Madelaine Miles when she turned up in my office. I showed it to my new acquaintance.

"How about this woman here? You ever see her coming around to visit Jason?"

He looked. "You gotta understand. It's not like just because I work from home, I camp out in the hallway all day long to keep track of who comes and goes. But this woman here, I believe I have seen her, yeah. I used to see her every now and then. I think she even had a key to Jason's apartment. I got the impression they knew one another pretty well."

And there it was. It had been staring me in the face all along. I just wasn't able to see it.

Chapter Thirty-Four

After I left Jason Mackey's apartment building, I thought about driving back downtown to check in at the office before deciding I wasn't interested in fighting the traffic. Then I had another thought. So, instead of heading into the city, I pointed myself toward the university and parked on the street half a block down from the offices of Geoffrey Tate, Attorney-at-Law.

It was near the end of the working day, as the receptionist I'd met during my previous visit was clearing off the top of her desk and exchanging her high-heeled shoes for Sketchers. She looked up when she heard the door open.

"I'm sorry, but we're just finishing up for the day. And since this is Friday, perhaps you could come back Monday morning." She gave me a smile that didn't quite reach her eyes. "But if you need to see Mr. Tate, he doesn't usually see anyone without an appointment, so please be sure to call first. Mondays are usually pretty busy, and he'll need to clear a spot on his calendar."

"You probably don't remember me. I was here about three weeks ago at the behest of Mr. Tate. He retained me to look into the disappearance of a young woman named Annamaria Harris. I just wanted to give him a progress report if he's available."

"I remember. It's Mr. Gamble, isn't it? I open all of Mr. Tate's mail, including the expense and activity reports you've been sending. If you'll pardon me for saying so, you seem to be doing a lot of running around with not much to show for the effort."

"Right." Another critic. I said, "Ms. Adkins, is your boss here or not? If he is, could you please tell him I've been down to Whiteville and spoken to his client, and there is something I'd like to discuss with him. If he's not, please leave a message for him to call me at his earliest convenience. My own calendar is pretty crowded, and I'm going to need to find time to squeeze him in."

Cheap shot, I knew, and patently false. But it made me feel better.

She gave me a look like you'd give to a raccoon snuffling around your trash cans after dark. "One moment." She got up from her desk and went into Geoffrey Tate's office. Two minutes later, she emerged and held the door open for me to go in.

"Mister Tate will see you now."

Unlike the last time I'd been in his office, Geoffrey Tate did not stand, or extend his hand, or offer me a bottle of water. He wasn't smiling, either. He was, however, dressed to the nines as before, with a charcoal suit, white shirt, and a maroon necktie.

'Mister Gamble," he began. "What is it that's so important that you couldn't have telephoned first?"

He didn't invite me to take a seat. I sat down anyway.

"Well, first, as you asked, I drove down to Muscle Shoals. I visited several recording companies before I found one that remembered Annie Harris. What I was told was that she auditioned, but, although she had a nice voice, they didn't think she was headline material. They did, however, suggest they could use her from time to time as a backup singer. Apparently, that didn't sit too well, because she left and never came back. They also made a recording of her audition. They gave me a copy.

That seemed to get his interest. "Do you have it with you?"

"In a minute. I don't remember whether I mentioned this to you in one of my reports, but one of Annie's former bandmates I spoke with told me he'd heard that she had gotten into some trouble during the time she was in Alabama. So, as long as I was there, I checked in with the police in Sheffield. I found out Annie had been identified as a person of interest in the death of a young woman she was sharing an apartment with. Miss Harris wasn't charged with anything, so no worries there. And the case is still open, although after more than ten years, I'm guessing not much is ever going to come of it. But the prospect of being charged might have been enough to send Annie heading for tall timber, because she disappeared about the same time as her roommate turned up dead."

"Then she's not a suspect."

"No. I already said that."

"In that case, I suggest we leave the matter alone. If, as you say, the police aren't interested in pursuing the matter, I don't see any reason to spend any more time talking about it." He paused to open his mini-fridge and take out a bottle of water. He didn't offer me one.

"You mentioned a recording."

"Yes. But I don't have it. I left that with the prison officials when I stopped at Whiteville to pay a visit to Harvey Harris."

"You did what? I specifically instructed you not to contact my client!"

"You did, yes, but you also asked me to do a job, which, regardless of what you might think, I am very good at. That means sometimes, I need to follow my own instincts. In this instance, I felt Harvey deserved a chance to at least hear his daughter's voice, even if he might never see her again." I could see from the color of his complexion he was getting angry. Well, good. Maybe if he got upset enough, I might get some straight answers.

"Also, I had a question for him. Something I asked you about earlier, but which you, what shall we say? Tap-danced around?"

"You wanted to know why I'm paying your fees to search for Harvey's daughter. And did he tell you?"

"He did." I took my phone out and placed it on his desk. "And before we go any further, you should know that I recorded our conversation." When he didn't say anything to that, I went on. "Harvey told me you were supposed to be the wheelman for his first stickup. The one that got him half a year in juvenile detention and a year of probation. Only thing was, after Harvey went in to stick the place up, you took off and left him holding, well, nothing at all, except a juvenile jacket. Or are you going to deny it?"

He glanced at the phone, then shook his head.

"What would be the point? It happened nearly fifty years ago, and the statute has long since run out. And that's assuming what happened that night was even a crime, at least where I was concerned."

"Harvey also told me he believed down deep, you are a good man. And in this instance, I have to agree, because ever since that night you drove off and left him, you've been making amends up to him by representing him *pro bono* whenever the need arose."

"I did what I could."

"I'm sure you did, but didn't it ever occur to you there might be some other way to help him? I don't know, find him a job, maybe? Or get him into some kind of a training program so he could do something with his life besides do drugs and commit petty crimes?"

He sat quietly for a moment, thinking. "How much?"

"How much what?"

"How much to keep this to yourself? I'm aware I can't be prosecuted for what I did, if, in fact, I did anything at all. But if this gets out, I'm sure you can imagine what it would do to my reputation, to say nothing of my law practice."

I had to shake my head at that. "Mister Tate, I don't want anything from you, and I certainly don't have any interest in tearing you or your law practice down. What would be in that for me? I just wanted an answer to the question I asked you, and you dodged, the first time we talked. Like you, I have a business to run and a reputation to look after. I make it a practice find out about my clients before I agree to take them on, because I don't like nasty surprises to pop up later.

"As far as I'm concerned, this is as far as it goes. But I do have one thing I'm going to ask, and that is this. When Annamaria Harris turns up, if she needs an attorney for any reason, I'm going to expect you to go to bat for her just like you did for her old man. No argument, no fees, no fobbing it off to a public defender. Just make sure you take care of her the best way you know how. Understand?"

"Does that mean you think she's in some kind of trouble?

"I think she's about to be, yes."

"Then you know where she is?"

"Yes, sir. I think I do."

Chapter Thirty-Five

Over dinner, I filled Maggie in on what had not been one of my better days, beginning with my call from Wanda. Maggie, as she always does, had a lot of questions.

"Your friend. Wanda. She's dying?"

"Ovarian cancer. It's metastasized. And frankly, I think she's given up."

She reached across the table and covered my hand with her own. "I'm really sorry, Gamble. I know she means a lot to you."

"She was my partner. When you're a cop, it means everything. Your partner is somebody you trust with your life."

That said, I never told Maggie about any of the extracurricular activities I helped Wanda carry out when she decided she needed to settle a score with an abusive husband or boyfriend. Maggie and Wanda are in related professions, but their approaches to conflict resolution are quite different. As far as I know, Maggie has never tracked down an abuser to clip the tip off his penis, as Wanda once did, to punish him for his abusive behavior.

I ate a bite of my entrée, gulf grouper with shrimp and crab sauce. "There's something else Wanda told me. That woman, the one I met at the Red Dot function? Her name is Madelaine Miles."

"I remember. For a while there, I thought she had her eye on you."

"Yeah, never happened. I guess I wasn't her type. Anyway, the reason she needed to talk to me was that she thought somebody was following her whenever she went out by herself, and she wanted me to look into it. So, I tailed her one night when she went to her Bible study, but I never noticed anyone following her. Two days later, her husband showed up in my office to warn me off. I told him I wasn't working for him, and that his wife could fire me if she wanted, but he couldn't. So, that evening, Mrs. Miles did call and whistle me off."

She took a sip of her cocktail. "And you think her husband forced her to do that?"

"I thought so at the time, but I never followed up. I was busy with my other case, and if Madelaine Miles was having trouble with her husband, that's more your department than it is mine, and I sort of forgot about it."

"Why do I hear a 'but' coming?"

"Because there is. A week or so ago, she showed up in my office. Her husband beat the hell out of her. She showed me what he did, and it looked bad. The way I got it, he was angry because she had approached me, and decided she needed to be punished. His words, not mine." And then I told her about the game room. And about the videos her husband had made.

"Why does she stay with him?"

"You already know the answer to that. Short of going to the police and then hiring a divorce attorney, what can she do? That's why she came to me, looking for help."

"To do what?"

"Just the usual. She wanted me to kill her husband."

"And you jumped right on that. Just out of curiosity, how much was she offering?"

"I didn't ask. I took her to Haven. I knew she'd be safe with Wanda until she could work out some other kind of arrangement. But then, when I talked to Wanda, she told me that Mrs. Miles had left, and was probably going back home to her husband."

"Well, if it makes you feel any better, you're right about having nowhere else to go. In my line of work, a story like that is almost a daily occurrence. These women don't have jobs, or if they do, they don't pay enough to let them move out and live on their own, especially if they have kids. Plus, a lot of the time, they end up blaming themselves. You know, 'I shouldn't have talked back to him,' or 'He had a bad day at work, and I should have just let him go ahead and do whatever he wanted.' So, these bastards get drunk, screw other women, smack their wives around. And there's nothing anyone can do about it."

"Thanks, but somehow, none of that makes me feel better. I just—I have a bad feeling somebody's going to get hurt."

"In these situations, somebody always gets hurt, Gamble. Somebody always does."

She was right, of course. Somebody always ends up getting hurt, and sometimes killed. While I thought about that, the server came and cleared our plates and asked if we'd like to see the dessert menu. I knew Maggie would go for that. It took her about five seconds to spot and order something called Death by Chocolate. I settled for another Stella.

"You said there was something else."

"There was." I waited while the server brought the dessert concoction Maggie ordered, and then while she sampled it.

"Want some?"

"Thanks. Chocolate and beer don't go together. Anyhow, I also talked to that lawyer, Geoffrey Tate. I told him on my way back from Muscle Shoals, I paid a visit to Harvey Harris. I'd been looking into some of Harvey's previous arrests because I was curious about why Tate is paying my fees to try to find Harvey's daughter. I also wondered why Tate represented Harvey three other times when he got pinched for some petty beef."

"What did he tell you?"

"At first, he didn't tell me anything. Not until I mentioned that Harvey had told me Tate was supposed to be the wheel man on Harvey's first caper. But Tate got scared at the last minute and took off, leaving Harvey holding the bag. That meant Tate had a clean record when he applied to law school. Tate's been trying to make it up to him ever since."

"How did he take it when you told him you'd found out his deep, dark secret?"

"Well, he got a little nervous, because he thought I was going to use the information to torpedo his reputation, and maybe his law practice as well. But that wasn't what I wanted. The first time I talked to Tate, I asked why he was so interested in helping Harvey find his daughter, and he told me in so many words, it was none of my business. I just wanted to let him know I'd discovered the truth, and that if Annamaria ever turned up and needed legal assistance, I expected him to do whatever he could to help her."

Maggie gave me a smile. "Always ready to help a lady in distress. Is there anything about you that isn't perfect?"

Later that night, when I was lying in bed next to Maggie, unable to sleep—she was snoring like a chainsaw, and my brain was spinning in high gear—I thought of something I failed to do when I was in Alabama. In the morning, I would take care of it first thing.

* * *

The call to Alabama ended up having to wait. Maggie and I were camped out on her narrow balcony overlooking downtown Nashville and enjoying our morning breakfast when my phone began vibrating. Not good. In my business, nobody calls late at night or on a weekend unless either they're in some kind of trouble, or else I am. I went inside to take the call.

"Mister Gamble, this is Monica Hart, at Haven. I don't think we've met, but I work with Wanda Beaudry."

"Yes." I felt the floor starting to drop out from under me. "Has something happened?"

"Mister Gamble, I'm sorry to be the one telling you this, but Wanda passed away late last night. Sometimes, she sleeps over here at the shelter, and one of the staff found her this morning." Monica's voice started to break. "There was a bottle of pills on the night table next to her bed, along with an envelope with your name on it."

My head was spinning. "Where is she now?"

"She's here, and so are the police, and some other people also. They said they were from the coroner's office."

"Okay. And where is the envelope she left for me?"

"I have it. I didn't show it to the police because I thought, whatever it is, you should see it first."

"Thank you for letting me know, Monica. I'll be there as soon as I can."

I ended the call and told Maggie I had to leave. She must have read the look on my face, because she said, "I'm going with you. And don't even think about arguing."

* * *

Twenty minutes later, Maggie and I arrived at Haven. As Monica Hart had indicated, there were already a Metro police cruiser and a medical examiner's van parked in the lot. Since we were expected, we had no difficulty entering the building, which, under normal circumstances, would have remained secured without me calling ahead to let somebody know we were coming. When we went inside, the first person we encountered was a uniformed officer, who asked who we were and to show identification. While he scrutinized my PI license, a young woman, Monica, I assumed, stepped out of the office.

"They're all right, officer. I called Mr. Gamble and asked him to come." The cop took another look at my license, shrugged, and then handed it back. I got the impression this was not the first DB he'd had to deal with, and couldn't have cared less who else showed up to take a look.

We followed Monica down the hall and into the office, adjacent to which was a moderately-sized bedroom, sparsely furnished with a small desk, a reclining lounge chair, a small, flat-screen television, and a single bed, where Wanda slept nights when she didn't go home to her apartment. Like last night, where she lay down, swallowed a handful of oxy, and went to sleep for the last time on this earth. The ME's guys, who were standing by, had already rolled in a gurney with a heavy black plastic body bag. They were preparing to remove Wanda's body, which lay cold and still on the bed. Interestingly, if that is the right word, there was an expression of peace, and maybe relief, on her face.

I stood for a long moment looking at the woman who had been my partner and my friend for more years than I cared to think about. Maggie waited quietly at my side before lightly touching my arm.

"Gamble, there's nothing we can do here. We need to go. These men have work they need to do."

"I know."

On the way out, Monica handed me an envelope with my name scrawled across the front.

"I didn't show this to the police, because I'm sure they would have taken it. I don't know what she wrote, but I know she thought of you as her closest friend, and I wanted to make sure you at least got to see it first.

It wasn't until we got back to Maggie's apartment that I opened the letter. What Wanda had written was short and indescribably sad.

Gamble,

After our conversation, you probably think now that I'm taking the easy way out, don't want to fight the fight, whatever. But know two things.

One, that the pain is simply too great to continue down this path, the one that will inevitably lead me to where I already am, by the time you read this.

Two, that you are the best friend I have ever had, and if I ever truly loved a man, it was you. If you can find it in your heart, because I'm sure right now, you're angry with me, try to remember me fondly.

Also, I've emailed you the ID and the password to get into NCIC, just in case you ever need it.

PS: Talk to your friend Maggie about taking over at Haven. What I know, she'd be a good fit.

Your friend, always,

Wanda

Chapter Thirty-Six

The hours on Sunday rolled past on square wheels as I tried to come to terms with the death of my friend. It wasn't as though we spent a lot of time together, or that we were drinking buddies, or even physically close, except during the times we shared the front seat of a police car when we were partnered as fledgling detectives with the Metro cops. And, in fact, about the only time we ever got together in our post-police days was either when she needed my help to track down some boyfriend, or husband, who had treated his woman badly, or else when she was running a fund-raiser for Haven, and asked me to help out.

Maggie did her best to ease me out of my funk. She suggested brunch at one of the upscale hotels, a movie and dinner, a walk in Centennial Park, or just stay home and watch a baseball game on television. I wasn't in the mood.

Finally, she said, "Gamble, do you know there are statistics that indicate more couples than you might think go home and have sex after attending a funeral? It's believed that the act of love-making is a reaffirmation of life in the presence of death."

I thought about that and decided it was an idea that had merit.

* * *

Monday morning, having spent a good part of Sunday reaffirming life in the face of death, I was back in the office and on the telephone to Captain Dawkins, of the Florence, Alabama, police department.

"Mister Gamble. I thought we'd heard the last from you. You got another case you need some help with?"

"No, sir, I'm still working on the last one. But I do have a couple more questions for you."

I heard a sound like paper rattling on the other end of the line. "Go ahead."

"Okay. When we met earlier, you told me that Annie Harris was a person of interest in the suspicious death of the young woman who was her roommate."

"Yes."

"So, first of all, what was the roommate's name, and how did the police know that there had even been a death? Or to ask it another way, how long was the young woman dead before the body was discovered? And what was it that made your department think it was anything other than natural causes? I mean, there wasn't a bullet in her brain, or a kitchen knife sticking out of her chest, was there?"

"Off the top of my head, I don't recollect. It was a long time ago, and we've had a few other suspicious deaths since then, though not as many as I figure you all have up there. So, before I send somebody chasin' after the file, let me ask you. Have you found this little old Harris gal?"

"Not yet. But I think maybe I'm close."

"Then maybe I'll have somebody give you a call back."

It took the rest of the morning and on past lunchtime, which I killed paying bills, playing games on my computer, and scanning Internet headlines for something interesting to read. One item I ran across was about a man in a small town in Idaho who killed his mother-in-law by cutting her head off with a chainsaw. That was a new one on me.

Another was about a 100-year-old man, a veteran of World War II, who married his 96-year-old love on Omaha Beach, near Normandy. The groom served in France during World War II as a radio technician assigned to a P47 Thunderbolt fighter unit. The pair lost track of each other during the war and somehow reunited 80 years later. It was a nice story, one that I forwarded to Maggie, although I had serious doubts whether she'd still want to put up with me in the unlikely event I lived to be a hundred. Finally, about the time I was ready to call it quits, I got a return call from a Florence police officer named Jenrette. I glanced at my watch. It was two-thirty.

"Mister Gamble, Cap'n Dawkins asked me to get back to you with the information you's lookin' for, 'bout this gal." Officer Jenrette spoke with a soft accent that made him sound like he was from the Acadian region of Louisiana.

I said, "Thanks for getting back to me."

"No problem. Here's what we got. The dead woman's name was Madison Loftus. She was twenty-five years old, and according to the coroner's report, she died on or about August 27, 2015. She was living with a roommate in an apartment building downtown. It was the apartment manager that found the body 'cause them two tenants, Madison and Annamaria, was late with the rent, so after a day or so, she went in to see if maybe they'd skipped out. You know, it's a shame, but sometimes, people do that."

"Okay."

"Anyhow, she knocked on the door, and when nobody answered, she let herself in with the passkey, and there was the body. Not lookin' too good, either, from the report here. Blue lips, plus dried foam and vomit around her mouth. And the way her body was sort of contorted, it looked like she had some kind of seizure. My experience, pretty standard stuff for an overdose."

"But the manager was able to identify her?"

"Well, yeah, she knew who she was lookin' at. I guess it took a little work to make it official, though, on account of when our men showed up, they couldn't find any identification. Her purse and her billfold were both gone, so I guess the other gal must've taken it with her when she left."

"But they were sure who it was?"

"Identified her as Madison Loftus. They matched her prints with her previous arrest record. You knew about that, right?"

"I did. And was the overdose accidental, or did somebody give her a hotshot?"

"No way to tell. When we started askin' around, it turned out she was a steady user, so, I guess maybe she just got into a bad batch."

And that was all he was able to give me. I thanked Officer Jenrette and asked him to pass along my appreciation to Captain Dawkins. Then I hung up.

Chapter Thirty-Seven

I spent the next half-hour sitting at my desk, thinking. By this time, I pretty well knew how the investigation I had taken on to reunite Harvey Harris with his daughter was likely to turn out. I also knew, again with almost complete certainty, what needed to be done about Sonny and Madelaine Miles, and, just to round things out, who had killed Jason Mackey. The only question left was, should I take action myself, or leave it to the legal system to sort things out. In the end, however, I decided there was really only one course of action left to me.

It was late afternoon when I retrieved my car from the parking lot near my office building. From there, my first stop was police headquarters, where I was able to retrieve my .380. After that, I threaded my way through downtown traffic, inched past a short construction zone slowdown, and finally reached the Brentwood exit off Interstate 65. After that, it was another fifteen minutes before I reached the home of Sonny and Madelaine Miles. It was a pleasant afternoon, not as hot as it had been over the weekend, and, except for the sound of lawn sprinklers making soft, slapping sounds up and down the block, very quiet.

I pulled into the driveway and made my way along the front walk to the front door of a two-story, plantation-style home made of white-painted brick accented with black shutters and trim, a style that lately seemed to be all the rage in Nashville's tonier suburbs. I wondered, if tastes ever changed, how difficult—and expensive—it would be to remove the paint and restore the natural brick finish.

I pressed the doorbell and waited. No answer, so I knocked hard. Still nothing, except that a neighbor who was walking his dog noticed me. I gave him a casual wave, as if I had every right to be standing on the front porch of a two-million-dollar home pounding on the door like some process server intent on handing over a summons to appear in court.

When after another minute, I still got no response, I stepped off the porch and peered into the house through the front windows. By now, the dog-walker had stopped, and was staring at me, probably deciding whether he should say something, sic the dog on me, or maybe call the cops. Instead, he did none of those things. He took out his phone and snapped my photo, and a photo of my license plate. So much for a stealthy investigation

It took a moment for my eyes to adjust to the light level inside the house, and when they finally did, I was able to see Sonny Miles, seated in a chair facing the window. There was blood on the side of his face and on the left shoulder of his white shirt. He wasn't moving. I turned to the dog-walker and yelled, "Call the police. Tell them there's a body!"

Then I got back in my car and got the hell out of Brentwood as fast as I could, watching my rear-view mirror the entire way to see whether there were flashing blue lights closing in behind me. When I got close to downtown, I called Lorraine Proctor on my cell.

"Mister Gamble," she said when she picked up. "What is it this time?"

"Just a quick question."

"It'd better be. I'm busy."

"When a woman is in trouble, and I mean real trouble, who is she most likely to run to?"

"What, are you watching *Jeopardy*?" When I didn't answer, she said, "Well, her husband, I guess. Or her best friend. Or maybe her mother."

I said, "Detective, this is your lucky day." I gave her an address. "Meet me there in an hour, and I think I'll be able to give you the person who killed Jason Mackey, and maybe a couple more. And bring the Brentwood cops with you while you're at it. They're going to want in on this."

She started to ask me something else, but I hung up before she got the chance.

Chapter Thirty-Eight

When I pulled up to the house where Emmy Lou Harris lived, there were lights on in the front room, and the Mercedes-Benz ragtop belonging to Madelaine Miles was parked in the driveway. As I did when I visited Mrs. Harris the first time, I parked on the street and walked around to the back of the house. I could see two women, Mrs. Harris and Mrs. Miles, seated at the kitchen table. A small, chrome-plated revolver with pearl grips was lying on the table next to Madelaine's purse.

Instead of knocking, I just opened the door to the kitchen and went inside. As I entered, I reached inside my jacket and took hold of my .380, just in case one of the women decided to grab the revolver and start shooting. Neither of them did, so I pulled up a chair and sat down between them.

"Mrs. Harris." I nodded to the older woman. "And Mrs. Miles. Should I call you Annamaria, or Annie May?"

She looked at me. "You know?"

"I had an idea. I'm not sure when it first came to me. But then I talked to a police captain in Alabama, and he mentioned that Annie May Harris had shared an apartment with a woman named Madison, and I began to wonder. I mean, Madison, Madelaine. They do sound a little bit alike."

"But how did you know for sure?"

"Up until just now, I didn't. Not for sure, anyway. But thinking back through the chain of events that got me here, there just isn't a better explanation."

Emmy Lou started to reach across the table. I thought she might be going for the gun, so I picked up a paper napkin from the table and pulled it away, leaving it resting directly in front of me. Mrs. Harris wasn't reaching for the gun, though. Instead, she took her daughter's hand in her own.

"I never told him nothing, Annie. Nothing. I swear I never."

"No, you didn't. You were protecting your daughter. But you lied when you told me you hadn't heard from Annie in ten years. I think you two have stayed in touch right along, and Annie looked after you the best way she could. So, I'm guessing after I visited with you, as soon as I left, you called to tell her that her father had hired me to find her. I didn't realize it at the time, but I did wonder about all the nice appliances and the expensive television you have here in the kitchen. I mean, look around. This isn't an upscale neighborhood, or even a particularly nice house. Pardon me for saying so, Mrs. Harris. We're not in Brentwood or Belle Meade.

"So, having this stuff, the refrigerator, the stove, the TV. Unless you're a lot better off than you look, somebody else must have paid for it. And it certainly wasn't Harvey, since he'd been inside for the past ten years. But even though it seemed out of place, I didn't attach any importance on it at the time. Looking back, I imagine Annie May must have bought it for you. After all, she was married to a rich man. She had plenty of money, and she is your daughter after all.

"And you're right, Mrs. Harris. You didn't tell me much of anything. You did, however, mention that during the time Annie was with Midnite Oil, she had a boyfriend named Jake, or Jacob. I asked, 'Could it have been Jason?' and you allowed as how it might have been. So, I thought, this is a guy I need to talk to, because he might still be in touch with Annie. Worst case, he at least might know where she was living.

"My plan was to talk with him the night Red Dot threw a coming-out party for the Braxton Brothers. But then Jason didn't show up. And I couldn't reach him afterward, either, because, as it turned out, he was dead. Somebody shot him, with a gun that I think is very likely the same one you have sitting here on the table."

Annamaria—I decided in the moment I liked that name better—shot me a stricken look. "You think I killed Jason?"

"I don't know whether you did or not, Mrs. Miles. I guess it's possible James Figgins killed him. For that matter, I suppose it's also possible Mrs. Harris here might have pulled the trigger." I paused to look her way. Her face was an icy mask, and I wondered for a moment whether I had guessed correctly.

"Or maybe it was your husband. That makes sense, since it could be argued Jason was killed because somebody was worried people would find out who you actually are."

"And just who am I that's so terrible, Mr. Gamble?"

"You're the daughter of a convicted murderer. A man who, until recently, was sitting on death row for killing a pregnant woman and her unborn child. Not your fault, obviously. You had nothing to do with that, but all the same, how do you think that little bit of family history would be likely play with the crowd Sonny was used to running with? I think that's why you made up a story about somebody following you. You figured that was the way to get me to drop the case."

"What do you mean?"

"I mean, nobody was following you, were they? Nobody except me. And James Figgins, of course, but that wasn't until you told your husband, I'm guessing, the same story. You were worried, because you knew I was looking for you—for Annie Harris. At the time, I didn't know that was you, but all the same, you needed to get me to drop the investigation. You hoped Figgins would scare me off, which he tried to do, or that your husband would buy me off, which he tried to do, and then I'd stop looking. Or maybe you hoped Harvey would just go ahead and die, and then the whole business about me finding his daughter would come to an end. But none of that worked out the way you hoped."

The three of us sat quietly for a moment, thinking. I said, "Mrs. Miles, was your husband aware of your family history when he married you, or did he think you were somebody else?"

"Somebody else, like who?"

"Like Madelaine Loftus, for one. When I talked to the police in Florence, I was told they found Madison's body, but they never found her purse or any other identification. I know it isn't difficult to create a fake ID. So did Annamaria become Madison become Madelaine when she got back from Alabama?"

When she didn't say anything, I said, "I'll take that as a yes. And as long as we're talking about Madison, what did happen to her?"

"All I know is, she met a guy, a musician. They started dating, they got serious, and he got her to start using. One night, I went out by myself, and when I came back, I found her in her bed, not breathing. I didn't want to get mixed up in what looked like it might turn out to be a murder investigation. So, I took her purse and her ID, and got out of there as fast as I could."

"Okay. And where did you meet Sonny?"

"Here. After I left Alabama, I came back to Nashville and got a new driver's license. I told the man at the license bureau I'd just moved here, and that I'd lost my Alabama license when I got my purse snatched. So, I made up a name, Madelaine Loftus. And I stayed here for a few months, so if somebody checked, this is where they'd find me. Then I started all over again, trying to get a job as a singer.

"Sonny came into a studio one day when I was auditioning." She gave me a small smile. "Never give up, right? Anyway, one day he came into the studio, and he heard me. He didn't think much of my voice, but I'd lost a lot of weight by that time, and I was looking pretty good. He probably thought I was easy, so he asked me out, and pretty soon, we'd gotten together. I knew by then I wasn't going to be a big star as a singer, but Sonny was rich, and I figured, well, maybe that was good enough."

"Right. But somehow, Sonny found out who you really were, and that you were also in some trouble back in Florence. I mean, he gets around, doesn't he? And I'm betting he wandered into some studio, either here or in Alabama, maybe started showing around a picture of his pretty new wife, and he ran across somebody who remembered you. And that's why he treated you the way he did, because he thought when he met you, you were Madelaine Loftus. And then he found out you were Annie May Harris, from the wrong side of the river, and the daughter of a triple murderer.

"That's when the stars fell away from his eyes. After that, you were just eye candy he could treat whatever way he wanted, and there was nothing you could do about it, because, if you went to the cops or tried to leave him, he could just send you back to Alabama and let the cops there put you through the wringer."

"He liked strange sex. I just had to put up with it."

"Or else, it was back to your old life. And then today, what happened? I'll bet he wanted another session in the game room, only this was one time too many. And so, you killed him. And then you came running home to your mother. Because, when all is said and done, you had nowhere else to go."

I started to say something else, but was interrupted by the sound of someone pounding on the front door. "That will be the police." I used the napkin to pick up the gun from the table and drop it into my jacket pocket."

"You two just sit tight. I'll go out and talk to them so there's no misunderstanding, and they don't come through the door with guns blazing. Mrs. Miles, as far as shooting Sonny goes, I think you have a pretty good case for justifiable homicide, and that's what I'm going to tell the detectives. But if the bullets from this gun turn out to be a match for the one they dug out of the back of Jason Mackey's head, then you're going to have a problem. Unless, of course, you can convince them it was Sonny who killed Jason, and not you. What the hell. If I were you, I'd give it a shot."

Chapter Thirty-Nine

I opened the front door and found four police officers standing on the porch, including Metro Detectives Spillner and Proctor, another detective dressed in plainclothes, and a uniformed patrolman, both of whom I assumed were from Brentwood. Nobody had a drawn weapon, and nobody had a battering ram ready to break down the door. I took that as a plus.

Since I already knew Spillner and Proctor, the Brentwood cops identified themselves as Detective Michael O'Malley and Officer Bobby Tomlinson. For their benefit, I identified myself and showed them my ID. I also gave them a heads-up before I raised my hands and waited until Spillner slipped on a latex glove to reach into my jacket pocket and take out the revolver I'd removed from the kitchen table.

"Careful how you handle it. You're going to want prints. You're also going to find it's been fired, and I'm pretty sure this is the gun that killed Sonny Miles. And unless I miss my guess, it's also the gun that was used to kill Jason Mackey."

I explained as succinctly as I could that I had spotted a body at the home of Sonny and Madelaine Miles, but that I hadn't gone inside and I hadn't touched anything. I also told them Madelaine Miles admitted to me she had shot her husband, but would be claiming self-defense. I sweetened the story a bit by telling them he had sexually abused her on numerous other occasions, and, according to her, was getting ready to start in on her again. And so, she shot him and then ran to the home of her mother, since it was unlikely she had anywhere else she could go. I also told them that at least on one other occasion I could testify to, she'd been beaten up by her husband, and had asked me to take her to the Haven women's shelter, where they would have a record of the attack. Plus, I had photos and a video to prove it, and when they searched the house, they'd find videos as well.

"You're probably going to want those."

"Anything else?"

"The rest you can figure out for yourselves. You should know, though, that Mrs. Miles has an attorney. His name is Geoffrey Tate, and I will tell you, you're going to want to be careful dealing with him. He is not some numbnuts public defender you're going to be able to jerk around."

And then, since they didn't have any more questions for me, I walked back to my car and drove home, with instructions to stay close until they could get a formal statement.

* * *

Over the next several days, events began to unfold pretty much the way I thought they would. The Brentwood cops advised Madelaine Miles of her rights and took her into custody. Then she was transported back to the Williamson County lockup, where she was fingerprinted, and a DNA swab was taken. After that, a nurse checked her over to make sure she wasn't addicted to anything that would cause problems while she was being held overnight, pending arraignment the next morning. By that time, Geoffrey Tate had been alerted, and, good as his word, following a brief appearance in arraignment court, he got her released on a five hundred-thousand dollar bail, which, thanks to Tate, she was able to raise on the spot. However, she was ordered to surrender her passport, and she was instructed not to leave the jurisdiction without prior approval.

Two days later, Tate was able to secure permission for Madelaine/Annie May to accompany him and her mother to the West Tennessee Healthcare facility in Jackson, where mother and daughter were able to visit with Harvey Harris for what proved to be the last time. I never found out how the reunion went, whether there was joy, or tears, or forgiveness, or hard feelings all around. But the good-byes they exchanged turned out to be forever, because forty-eight hours later, Harvey drew his last breath and went to whatever reward awaited him in the afterlife. His body was returned to Nashville for a funeral and burial at Mount Olivet Cemetery. I was not invited to attend the ceremony, nor did I wish to.

Unlike the funeral for Harvey Harris, the sendoff for Sonny Miles was exceptionally well-attended, with mourners showing up not only from Tennessee but also from Muscle Shoals, Miami, Austin, Memphis, and Los Angeles. The hymns sung during the church service were performed by several well-known artists, including—who else—the Braxton Brothers, who took time off from their six-state tour to honor their erstwhile agent. And, no surprise, their first recording release shot to the top of the charts inside of two weeks.

Following a coroner's inquest a week after his passing, and after the Brentwood cops got a look at Sonny's videos and the photos I'd taken and forwarded to them, the death of Sonny Miles was ruled justifiable homicide. As a result, the Williamson County charges were vacated, and Mrs. Miles was able to skate on that one, at least. Geoffrey Tate called me at home to give me the news and to let me know that a final check for my services rendered would be forthcoming before the end of the month. It turned out to be a fat one.

Annie May's luck ran out a few weeks later. Nashville PD forensics compared the slugs fired from the little .22 caliber revolver she used to kill her husband with the one dug out of the back of Jason Mackey's head. No surprise, they found a match. They also found her fingerprints on the gun as well as those of her late husband. Nevertheless, Spillner and Proctor took a drive down to Brentwood and re-arrested Mrs. Miles on a charge of murder. Once again, Geoffrey Tate stood by her side in arraignment court as she pleaded not guilty, claiming it was her husband who had actually fired the fatal shot into the back of Jason Mackey's head. The prosecuting attorney, Amanda Rosslyn, as it so happened, argued that the state had sufficient evidence to obtain a conviction. The judge said Mrs. Miles's guilt or innocence was a matter for a jury to decide. No lowball bail this time, her bail was set at two million dollars—which she was able to raise, I was told, with no difficulty whatsoever.

The police in Florence, Alabama, meanwhile, sent one of their investigators north to Nashville to have a chat with Annie regarding the circumstances surrounding the suspicious death of her former roommate, Madison Loftus. The last I heard, there was a reopened investigation underway, but the Alabama cops were willing to hold off pursuing the matter any further until her difficulties back home were resolved. I doubted whether anything would ever come of that. And as it turned out, nothing ever did.

* * *

At the beginning of August, after finding a place to board Stanley for a couple of days, Maggie and I caught a Delta Airlines flight, first-class, to LAX. We were scheduled to meet with the producers of the upcoming film starring the comeback-kid actor I had agreed to babysit during the time filming was to take place in Nashville. The first night, we were taken to an expensive and uber-trendy restaurant on the ocean front in Malibu. There, in the company of one of the associate producers and his heart-stoppingly beautiful female assistant, we ran up a thousand-dollar dinner tab, which included an entrée called a "Seafood Tower" for me, which, since I mentioned I liked fish, our host insisted I try, and which included a whole lobster, Alaskan king crab legs and a half-dozen jumbo shrimp. Maggie, as always, ordered something more sensible—but still in the spirit of wretched excess—and went with Dungeness crab cakes and a side of truffle fries. Our meal was accompanied by a two-hundred-and-seventy-dollar bottle of Henriot Brut Rosé champagne.

The next day, we were picked up at our hotel by a studio limo and driven to meet the star. In the flesh, he seemed like a perfectly okay guy and not at all like his reputation would have suggested. The meeting, which lasted about forty-five minutes, was followed by another over-the-top buffet lunch, during which the director, a tall, fidgety guy who talked faster than the announcer on a late-night television infomercial, mentioned that Maggie seemed just right for a small, walk-on part in the film—if she was available, of course. I wondered if that was just to schmooze me, or if he really thought she had that "something special."

Before we said our good-byes, I was handed a check for five thousand dollars, a down payment for the job I had agreed to do. I was also asked to sign a non-disclosure contract to ensure the privacy of the star while he was in town. I was only too happy to comply.

Back at the hotel, we arranged for a rental car and drove to the beach, where we held hands and walked barefoot in the sand, and then watched the sunset over the Pacific Ocean. After that, we had dinner, a couple of hot dogs on the pier at Newport Beach. Then it was back to the hotel for a night of raucous sex, and a cab ride back to the airport late the next morning. The fare, naturally, was charged to the hotel, which, in turn, forwarded the bill to the studio. On the way to the airport, Maggie allowed as how she could get used to treatment like what we'd had, and wondered whether I should consider relocating my business to Southern California.

"You mean because of the ocean, or the climate, or the lifestyle?"

"All of it. What did you think?"

Our flight arrived back at BNA in the late afternoon. We retrieved Maggie's car from the airport parking lot and headed back downtown to her apartment, where we made a bowl of popcorn and watched a couple of late movies before heading to bed. Stanley, we decided, could wait one more night before coming back home.

That night, after popcorn-and-a-movie, we held each other close in bed until Maggie finally drifted off to sleep. Still keyed up from the goings-on of the last few days, I got up and went out onto the balcony overlooking downtown Nashville. And by the time I felt sleepy enough to go back to bed, I had all but forgotten about Annamaria and Sonny Miles, and Harvey Harris, and Geoffrey Tate. And I slept the sleep of the innocent until it was well past noon.

Ackinowledgments

Goodbye is Forever is the fifth installment in the Jackson Gamble series, and, as with the previous four volumes, my thanks go to Verena Rose, my first primary editor at Level Best Books, who has since moved on to other endeavors, and to Shawn Reilly Simmons, who has taken over in her stead. Without their support and dedication (and a little finger-wagging), PI Gamble would still be buried deep inside the confines of the hard drive of my computer.

Thanks also go to the many "Besties" with whom I have become acquainted through LBB, including Skye Alexander, Wendy Sand Eckel, Kerry Peresta, Lori Duffy Foster, Linda Lovely, William Ade, Cathi Stoler, Mark Levenson, and Gerald Elias. You guys are all pals and amazing writers, and I'm grateful for your support over the years. Special thanks must also go to longtime friend (and one-time collaborator on a screenplay that pancaked off the end of the runway) Bob Moore, who managed to talk me off the ledge more than a few times during the early stages of writing this book when it seemed as though it was never going to get done. Finally, a big shout-out to my wife Carol, who provides valuable proofreading and critical input, and who puts up with my disappearing act and sometimes foul mood while I'm squirreled away struggling to put words on a page. I am beyond blessed!

Sources

Goodbye is Forever is clearly a work of fiction, but even so, I believe it is important to get the details right, especially in areas where some technical knowledge is crucial. Failure to pay attention to the small things can distract the reader from the essence of the story, causing the all-important suspension of disbelief to fall away. To that end, there are numerous references to the history and workings of the music industry, Southern regional cuisine, cardiac disease and care, and forensic science. To help ensure I had my story straight, I relied on the several Internet sources listed below, as well as input and advice from friends, many of whom are accomplished authors in their own right.

- https://en.wikipedia.org/wiki/Whiteville_Correctional_Facility
- https://www.tn.gov/content/tn/correction/sp/visitation.html
- https://en.wikipedia.org/wiki/List_of_awards_and_nominations_received_by_Emmylou_Harris
- https://www.nashvillemusicians.org/
- https://www.medicinenet.com/what_are the stages of rigor mortis/article.htm
- https://en.wikipedia.org/wiki/MC5
- https://www.healthline.com/health/coronary-artery-disease/coronary-artery-occlusion#treatment
- https://www.nhlbi.nih.gov/health/stents/preparing
- https://sci.ccc.nashville.gov/Reporting
- https://www.udiscovermusic.com/in-depth-features/muscle-shoals-studio-history/https://pch.tncourts.gov/

- https://www.tn.gov/commerce/regboards/pi/license/get.html
- https://www.prisonsinfo.com/level-1-level-2-level-3-level-4-prisons-in-the-state-of-tennessee/
- https://www.udiscovermusic.com/in-depth-features/muscle-shoals-studio-history/
- https://en.wikipedia.org/wiki/Muscle_Shoals,_Alabama
- https://blackamericaweb.com/2015/07/01/little-known-history-fact-amazing-grace
- https://www.livescience.com/58682-fentanyl-overdose-characteristics.html
- https://www.policeinterceptor.com/pdf/2011orderguide.pdf

About the Author

Greg Stout is the author of *Gideon's Ghost*, and *Connor's War*, both young adult novels set in small-town America in the mid-1960s, and *Lost Little Girl*, a detective novel set in Nashville, Tennessee, which received the 2022 Shamus Award for best first PI novel. His latest PI novel, *Long Time Gone*, was released in December, 2024. Greg resides with his wife Carol and two cats, Wallace and Gromit, in Cape Girardeau, Missouri, where he is a member of the Heartland Writers Guild, the Southeast Missouri Writers Guild and is a member of the board of directors for the Missouri Writers Guild.

AUTHOR WEBSITE:

https://www.gregorystoutauthor.com

SOCIAL MEDIA HANDLES:

https://www.facebook.com/greg.stout.560
https://x.com/GregStout16

Also by Gregory Stout

Gideon's Ghost (Beacon Publishing Group, 2019)

Connor's War (Beacon Publishing Group, 2022)

Lost Little Girl (Level Best Books, 2022)

The Gone Man (Level Best Books, 2023)

Woman in the Wind (Level Best Books, 2023)

Long Time Gone (Level Best Books, 2024)

Railroad Histories (22 titles, Morning Sun Books and White River Productions, 1995-2021)